# When The Drums Stop

# When The Drums Stop

*D.W. Roach*

*For Grandpa...*

*"The past is dead; let it bury its dead, its hopes and its aspirations; before you lies the future—a future full of golden promise."*

**- Jefferson Davis**

# Contents

# Preface

The Civil War of the United States is one of the darkest times in our history. Family and friends alike fought for and against each other. A nation divided by political, economic, and ethical issues turned to violence to resolve their long-standing dispute. Four years of unfathomable bloodshed left much of the United States in ruin, but with darkness came an overwhelming and undeniable light that shone through the heroic deeds of brave men and women alike who were determined to see this great nation move forward and become a beacon of hope for the world.

My motivations for this book came from my Grandfather, Bill Roach, who discovered a direct ancestor that not only fought through the last two years of the war but who survived it. Anderson Roach was born in Tennessee and just prior to coming of legal age he selflessly joined the Union Army, Eighth Tennessee Volunteer Cavalry assigned to Fox Company. Although this is a work of historical fiction I have done my best to follow Anderson's footsteps through the conflict and attempt to illustrate the many hardships he would have endured. As a former U.S. Marine, I am no stranger to the demands placed upon a military man and the great strain on one's mind, body, and spirit. Anderson himself participated in nearly forty-seven recorded engagements with Confederate forces during his two-year tour; many of which lasted for several days at a time. I am dismayed to say that although I did not cover every engagement I have tried to cover those that were most significant for his unit and the war effort.

So, it is that I hope I have captured some of Anderson's experiences and emotions through the trials of Civil War era combat, the bonds that he undoubtedly forged, and the terrible pain of loss he most certainly would have experienced on a regular basis. We salute you Anderson Roach and thank you from the bottom of our hearts for your great sacrifice. You will not be forgotten.

# One
# Reflections – August 1922

What is it that makes men hate each other with such fervor? What is it that would drive brothers and cousins to murder one another for an ideal and cast away the love that they once had? It is only truth that nature, and the animals within it, can be unforgiving as they strive to endure; but then, then there is man, and man is a whole different creature entirely. Men will murder each other simply for an ideal, and if your ideal differs from theirs they will burn down forests, poison streams, and paint the once serene green fields a bloody crimson until they have what in their mind is just and right.

The thick fog of death is a vile thing, and in those days it happened again, and again, and again, and no matter how many times death visited it never became any easier, it never sat right with me what we done. It only poisoned me further and drove me to do things with my hands I never thought I would do. Even in my worst nightmares I had never dreamed of the things that I witnessed with my own eyes, the terrors that happened right there in front of me and the shadow of the past that I would carry through the rest of my life. War is often a necessary thing and it is only right to serve one's country in the struggle of a good cause; but for those of us who fought that war, who lived through it, the cause become lost somewhere between decaying corpses and bloodied fists.

\* \* \*

"Mr. Roach?" A soft young woman's voice called out to me but I found myself staring blankly at the census paper I had received in the mail just a fortnight ago. Despite her welcoming call I felt no sense of urgency to respond to her and continued to stare vacantly at the page gleaming over its many seemingly innocent questions. *Government of the United States*, it read in bold faced letters. It all seemed so official and reminded me of those papers posted all over dusty little towns during the war. "Mr. Roach?" she called out to me again just a little louder this time. I slowly lifted my head and nodded at the young woman sitting across from me behind a makeshift desk in the primary school gymnasium. Pressing my hand firmly against the chair next to me I forced my aching body upward and straightened out my back pushing the weight of my frame against a worn oak cane I held with a numb hand. Each step I embarked upon was planned and mindful so not to fall over. As I reached the chair across from the young woman I slowly sat down and adjusted my wrinkled shirt as to be presentable in public. The young woman was slender, dark hair and fair skin with chestnut brown eyes that I seemed to fall into like warm quicksand. She reminded me of someone, someone I had known long ago in a place that somehow no longer seemed real or even possible. She pulled loose strands of hair from her forehead and tucked them behind her ear as she quietly cleared her throat. Her clothing was simple, a long grey dress, stockings, and black flat shoes; perhaps the daughter of a businessman in town.

"Good afternoon..." I said with a hoarse voice. Clearing my throat, I repeated myself. "Good afternoon Ms. How are you today?"

"I'm just fine Mr. Roach, thank you for asking and good afternoon to you as well. Mr. Roach my name is Miss Johnson. Thank you kindly for taking the time to meet with us today. I see you received the census the U.S. Government had sent you. Were so happy you decided to come today." There was something about this young woman. I couldn't put my finger on it and I couldn't bring myself to look away from her face either. She seemed put off by this bewilderment of mine but tried hard not to show it. I gazed down at my hands that rested on the top of my cane; pale white and cracked I hardly believed they were my hands at all.

"Well young Miss I am obliged to be here." I pulled my cane in further to the front of me and adjusted both hands on top leaning forward so I could hear her clearly. My hearing just wasn't what it used to be and sometimes they would ring something awful or I would hear things that weren't even there.

"Did you have an opportunity to fill out the form Mr. Roach?" I slowly lifted the paper from the desk and handed it over to the young woman.

"It should all be there. It should all be there Miss." She gently took the form from me with her long slender fingers and quickly looked over my answers. I found myself nodding off to sleep and swiftly sat up straight to wake myself. Old age is a terrible state, one that I hoped I could muster the strength and resolve to get through with some dignity. The young woman placed the form firmly against the thick oak table and straightened out her simple dress before posturing upright behind her type writer. She placed her hands gracefully over the mechanical writing tool extending her fingers straight as a board.

"Mr. Roach, the U.S. Government has asked us to record as much information as possible from the men who had served in the Civil War and I wondered if it would be alright for me to ask you some questions and strike them down for the record on my type writer?" I nodded and smiled politely. Glancing at the bulky grey machine sitting in front of her I rolled my eyes and scoffed at the thought of the typed word. I never did learn how to use a typewriter. Damn things seemed just wrong to me, just wrong. The inventions they created these days were just appalling and appeared aimed at encouraging the very laziest of people to indulge in their sin. How could a typed letter ever convey ones' character or sincerity?

"Of course, of course. It's not often I get a chance to meet new people." I coughed and cleared my throat before looking at her again and smiling. She smiled back with rosy red lips and dimples in her cheeks that just lit up the room like fireflies on a warm summers evening.

"Thank you Mr. Roach. Mr. Roach, can you please state your full name for the record?" I took a deep breath and replied confidently.

"A.J. Jackson or Anderson Jackson Roach if it pleases you Miss." She quickly went down a list she had laid out on a wooden clipboard checking things off as she went with a lead pencil. The paper was worn and it seemed that she had interviewed many other gentlemen before me. I glanced at the names curious to see if I would recognize any of them from service. Some of the names had check marks next to them, others had question marks and some a line through the name and check box entirely, probably deceased long ago. It was a wonder I had lived this long and a miracle by the grace of god that I made it through the war when so many men, young and old, did not. I was spared the bullet, the bayonet, and the cannon but old age showed me little mercy and at times the bullet would have seemed a mercy to the ravages of time.

"And your age Sir? How old are you?" I stopped and thought about it for a moment. I wasn't quite eighty years old yet but things were a little fuzzy these days.

"Old? I'm not old young Miss. I am seventy-five years young Miss, born in the year of our Lord, Eighteen Forty-Seven." The woman laughed under her breath but quickly composed herself pulling a loose strand of hair back behind her ear.

"And what state and county were you born in Sir?" My heart warmed and I proudly replied.

"The great state of Tennessee in the greatest county of Tennessee that there ever was, Grainger County Miss. Grainger County Tennessee."

"And what state and county were you living when you enlisted in the Confederacy or Federal Government?" I found it interesting that she said Confederacy first probably assuming my allegiance to the South since our state had seceded and so many had joined the ranks of Old Johnny Reb.

"I enlisted in the Federal Government in Grainger County Miss. Grew up there all my young life and lived there most of my life after the war."

"And what was your occupation before the war Sir?"

"I worked the land just as most good men did. I was a farmer." She grinned and glanced up at me with a crinkled nose.

"And your father Sir? What was his occupation?"

"My father was a farmer and his father before him. Farmers all around Miss. No better way of life. I'd imagine even our ancestors from the old country were farmers to. Runs in the blood." She placed her hand over her mouth and gently cleared her throat then reached down and took a sip of water from a short glass.

"Did your family own any slaves Mr. Roach?" I quickly shook my head and laughed quietly.

"No Miss, oh goodness no. Do I look like a wealthy man to you? We were a proud family but not a wealthy one. Always enough food and money to get by but certainly not enough to purchase slaves. If we had owned a plantation I most likely would have been on the side of the Confederacy. Though, if we owned a plantation I most likely would not have fought in the war at all." She seemed shocked by my answer but I wasn't sure why. Seemed to be just a matter of fact to me.

"And how much land did your family have before the war? Did your family own land before the war?" It had been so long but I thought back hard to Paw and all the talk he gave me about our great piece of earth. Paw loved that plot of dirt dearly and although it did not bring us much in the way of fortune it sure did bring a lot of great memories. On our land, we were kings, on our land we were free to do as we pleased.

"Thirty-five glorious acres of Tennessee soil, some of it black as oil and some of it as red as blood. The perfect place to grow your crop."

"Do you recall the value of the property owned by your family?" I scratched my scalp through my balding head. What I wouldn't give for a full head of hair again.

"Oh, I suppose it was no more than five hundred dollars at the time. Land was cheap back then but you must understand that was a great deal of money for the time. How my father ever came across that much money in the first place I will never know."

"What sort of home did your family reside in Mr. Roach?"

"Oh, nothing that you would be familiar with. It was a simple home, a single room log house that my father had built with him and his kin. Always smelled like smoke and dirt." A loud bang erupted from behind me and I turned quickly ducking down in my chair. Gazing across the room I could see the janitor had dropped a broom handle and quickly picked it up from the floor. My heart pounded but I felt foolish, quickly sitting up and wiping the sweat from my brow.

"Sorry." The young man apologized aloud for his folly but the damage was done. I felt embarrassed in the presence of Miss Johnson and suddenly felt anxious to leave and escape my humiliation.

"Are you alright Mr. Roach?" I cautiously lifted my hand and nodded my head several times before pulling a handkerchief from my left breast pocket quietly clearing my nose.

"I'm fine young Miss. Old habits die hard don't you know." She nodded and happily returned to her typewriter.

"That's fine Mr. Roach. Shall we continue or would you like to take a break?" I waved my hand from the top of my cane several times urging her onward.

"Yes, please do Miss. My attention is short so you best make the most of it." She smiled and returned her gaze to her paper.

"Mr. Roach, what occupation did your father and mother have?"

"Paw was a farmer and a blacksmith when he had to be but mostly a farmer. He pretty much did anything that required handy work and sometimes assisted with good works in the community, especially the church. Mother did what all mothers do, rearing to little ones, spinning, weaving, cooking, and other general house work. Maw would assist in tending the fields from time to time but Paw wouldn't let her work out in the heat or rain. He was a gentleman in that manner. A true man of Tennessee."

"How was your occupation regarded in your community?" I cocked my head and squinted at her as I did not understand her question.

"I'm sorry Miss but could you clarify your query?" She nodded.

"Yes Mr. Roach. Did people of your community look favorably or unfavorably in regards to your occupation?" Now I understood her meaning clearly.

"Respectable work. It was very respectable work. Most men of Tennessee were farmers or miners."

"Did the white men in your community usually participate in such work?"

"Yes of course. We were proud to work hard and earn our keep. Don't nothing come free you know."

"No, I suppose not." She replied with a smile. "Were any of the white men in your community leading lives of idleness or consumption?" I smiled and chuckled a bit. Clearly she had never lived in a small town and certainly was not appraised to the living conditions of the time.

"Few, but very few. There were of course the town drunks but even they had to work to get back into the bottle and we had a few folks living out in the wood. You had to keep your distance from those folk. They were wild and often an unpredictable sort of people. I did not much enjoy the company of those sorts."

"What about the slave owners? Did they freely mingle with those men that did not own slaves?" I slapped my knee and let out a wheezing laugh that was chased by a cough. I cleared my throat and laughed again shaking my head enthusiastically.

"Heavens no! Oh, goodness! No Miss, slave owning families were those of elevated living status and did not freely engage with the common folk of town. We were in their eyes, beneath them." It was unfortunate but all too true. I remember those men riding down the road in their fancy carriages and fancy clothes and if you didn't get out of the way they'd run you over sure enough. Bunch of mean old cusses they were. I did not care for them much either. In fact, now that I thought about it I preferred the company of the town drunk and the wood folk over the slave owners.

"What about at church, school, or other public gathering places? Did the slave owners freely mingle then?"

"No Miss, they did not. They had their own schools and churches where those privileged enough would attend. Unless you were on their property or attending their functions, it was rare to see people of elevated status."

"Were the slave owners friendly to non-slave owning white men?" I nodded my head.

"In general yes but when a white man was hired under the employ of a slaveholder the treatment was not much better than that of a slave. That's why many of us stuck to farming our own lands. Better to be a king in a dirt home than a peasant in a castle." She giggled again, I don't think she much heard men speak the way that I did.

"Were there good opportunities in your community for poor young men to earn an honest wage, save money and buy a farm or other small business?"

"No mam. Life was hard on the poor and rarely could one elevate themselves beyond what they were born as. That's why most of us joined the Union, so we could get away and start anew. Perhaps find our fortunes in battle and somehow strike it rich. Spoils of war you know."

"Did the slave holders give any opportunity to poor men to earn a better living and perhaps elevate themselves to a higher living status?" I became annoyed as the questions seemed to be the same thing over and over just asked in a different way. I suppose that the lifestyle during that time seemed strange, perhaps even crude to the young and educated of this day.

"Uh, no Miss. The slaveholders only did what was good for slaveholders. They did not care much for the conditions of the poor. We had to fend for ourselves as best we could. Charity was in no way their strong suit."

"Strong suit?" she repeated. "Are you a card player Mr. Roach?" I felt a mischievous smirk crawl up my face.

"Once upon a time, perhaps. It's been ages since I cut cards. What about yourself?" She smiled and shook her head in fast short turns.

"No I don't think so. A game of cards is not something a lady would participate in." She returned to her paper. "What kind of school or schools did you attend Mr. Roach?" School? Huh, I can barely recall that little shack of a building we called school but I could still remember the faces of the children who were there with me as if it were yesterday. Playing outside the schoolhouse and running around the creeks catching tadpoles were some of my fondest memories. Then there was good old Miss Parks, my teacher. She was a gentle soul who cared deeply for her students.

"A public primary school Miss. That's all we had in our town."

"And how long did you attend?"

"No more than ten months." These days it seemed many people were more educated in Tennessee and I was a little embarrassed to admit I had only gone to school for ten months in my life. It was common back in those days but to a young woman like this it must have seemed so strange. "We didn't have much need for school you know. Manual labor was the only kind of labor. If you sought a fancy education at the time you had to travel far east to Washington or New York. Most families did not have that kind of money."

"And how far did you have to walk to school?"

"Oh, about ten fields over yonder, maybe twenty each way." She typed rapidly and I was mesmerized by the graceful movement of her fingers.

"How long did the school run?" I had to think about this for a moment. I was never good at keeping track of the months let alone the days.

"Only about one season for three years. Always just after the harvest and just before winter. Farming was life back then you understand, everything depended on the harvest. We never strayed far from the fields."

"Did the boys and girls in your community attend school regularly?"

"No Miss, most children had to work to support their families. School was a luxury. My paw did not care much for school but my mother insisted. I figured she'd seen some of them fancy men in town and probably thought that if I'd go to school I could be one of them." The young woman pulled her hands away from typewriter and placed them in her lap as she flattened out her skirt. Her hair came loose again with a strand hanging idyllically in front of her left eye. She quickly removed it placing the strand gently behind her ear and looked up batting those chestnut brown eyes at me.

"Thank you so much for your patience Mr. Roach I have just one last question, can you tell me about your experience in the war? The places you went, people you encountered along the way? Perhaps even some of your experience fighting if you wouldn't mind." My mind swirled with thoughts and incoherent images of ghosts that flew passed. Times since long gone to be brought back to the present. I leaned forward and rubbed my forehead coarsely trying to calm my throbbing head. My shoulders became heavy as if a man was standing above me pushing them down to the ground. A sudden thirst took over my throat and my eyes became dry and burned something awful.

"I am unsure if such stories are appropriate for a young lady such as yourself. They are somewhat, colorful if you get my meaning."

"Mr. Roach? Are you alright Sir? Can I get you a glass of water?" I closed my eyes tightly and a familiar smell entered my nostrils, a most potent and intoxicating aroma; gunpowder. My eyes opened quickly and I gazed upward at the young woman unblinking with a fire in my heart and tears in my eyes. "Mr. Roach?" she asked nervously.

"You want to know about the war? I'll tell you about the war…"

# Two
# The Farm – July 1863

"A.J.?" a voice called out gently and then a frigid hand gripped my shoulder like death itself and shook me something fierce. "A.J. git up lazy bones!"

"Huh?" I turned over peering through the slits of my eyes; something blurry standing above me waving a hand back and forth.

"A.J. get up you lazy bones before your paw catches you sleeping in again. There's work to be done in the fields but first you best to git yourself on to school."

"School? Aw, c'mon maw. Today's my birthday!" Mother grinned and turned away.

"Son, you're not gonna skip out on your education. I've got big plans for you boy and you're not going to disappoint your mother; are you?" I rolled my eyes slightly annoyed and shook my head a few times. Maw and Paw ain't never been to school so I don't know why in thunder I had to.

"No maw…" I replied unconvincingly.

"Good. Stop shakin your head at me young man. Now git your clothes on and make yourself proper. I set a pot of clean water. Wash your face and be on your way. I don't want to hear any more sass out of your mouth. Do you understand?" I nodded, wiping the drool from the corners of my mouth.

"Yes maw." I pulled the dark wool cloth off my body and sat up rubbing my eyes to greet the day. It was my birthday of all days and I had just turned seventeen years of age, the age of manhood. The last thing on my mind was school. My brother had been fighting for the mighty Union for nearly two years taking up all the glory. He left when he turned seventeen and I was sure it was my time to go so I could help beat back the Johnny Rebs. Maw was determined to keep me out of the war but I was a man now and it was my choice and I was done with farming this dirt patch. I grabbed my leather boots turning them upside down and shaking them out to make sure there weren't any critters inside. I strapped them on then shook out my white long sleeved shirt; pulled it over my head and buttoned up the two wooden buttons on top. Our log home stank of smoke from the previous evening's fire and the coals from the oak timber still burned hot in the pit. I had hoped to see maw working on breakfast but instead she pushed some five-day old bread towards me that had been sitting on the wood cooking table. I grimaced and slowly retrieved the bread from the counter. I pawed at it for a while breaking up small pieces between my fingers worried I might find a maggot or some mold on the inside but thankfully it was clean. I hesitantly took a bite and ripped a piece off with my teeth. The bread wasn't yet hard but tough to chew making my teeth ache a bit. What I wouldn't give for an egg and a fresh slice of bacon.

"If you're still hungry grab an apple from the orchard on the road and make sure it's from our orchard and not the neighbors. You know how they feel about you swiping their crops. Last thing I need is to have you coming home with a bottom full of shot." School was nearly two miles away, it seemed like five miles, but between home and school was an orchard owned by the Petersons. Maw thought they were a mean bunch but they weren't so bad. They didn't mind much people snatchin' an apple on the road if they were hungry but you best not be caught taking entire baskets away or else they will sick the dogs on you. Mean little bastards those dogs, mutts through and through. They've chased me all my life but never got a piece of me yet. I had fun teasing those mongrels every chance I got. I took the bread with me and pushed open the heavy oak door that creaked something awful. I caught the glint of my musket next to the door and looked back to see maw still had her back to me.

"Have a good day Maw!" Leaning over I snatched the rifle as quickly and quietly as I could.

"Don't you even think about taking that rifle coon hunting. A.J.?" I slammed the door shut on the way out and ran for my life straight through the fields. "A.J.!" I looked out in the pitches for Paw but couldn't spot him, he must've been on the far side somewhere so I decided to get done with coon hunting and then get on to school without seeing him. The stables were quiet even for Digger our donkey who stood silently outside tied to an old hitching post. The chickens were out doing what they do best eating seed and digging for grubs while a couple of our mutts ran in the fields like they owned the place. Up against a tired looking shed our shovels and axes rested waiting for us to pick them up and go to work; but today would not be a day for the tools. The dirt roads were warm already and the sun was coming down hard on my head. I sped up a bit and then ran to the end of our property line until reaching the main road that led to town. The orchard was not far off and I smiled just thinking about getting my teeth around one of the Petersons apples just to get the taste of stale bread out of my mouth. I ran down to a creek where a row of trees lined the bank as far as the eye could see. The coons always stayed close to these trees and they'd come down at night to kill our chickens when the dogs slept. The rifle was always loaded just in case there was trouble so I had one shot to get even with those coon varmints. I heard some scratching against the trees and then ahead about fifty yards I saw a whole family of coons just having a good time up in the branches swinging this way and that. I took a good spot near a smoothed-out rock and leaned against it while I cocked back the hammer. The big one walked right into my sights so I rested my cheek firmly against the walnut buttstock and tucked it tight into my shoulder.

"Breathe…" I said quietly. I took a lungful in and slowly let it out. I placed my finger firmly against the trigger but was careful not to be too firm. Breathe in, breath out; my breath paused naturally and the big one was in my sights. I pulled the trigger, a loud bang and a flash of fire erupted in the dry creek bed as smoke surrounded me. The coon dropped fast out of the bush and the others scattered to the wind leaving their kin behind. I got up and ran straight to him to see him shot good and dead. The round hit him just behind his shoulder and probably went through his heart, couldn't have been any cleaner, no Sir. Picking him up by his long striped tail I ran back home and as I approached the doors I slowed down and hushed my steps lightly placing the coon on the ground and the rifle leaning against the door frame. I knocked hard three times and ran back to the road.

"A.J.!" Maw yelled as she opened the door to see the surprise I had left her. Maw was furious but at least I got her a fresh coon to skin for a hat and meat to cook for super. I hoped she'd thank me later but didn't count on it. Once on the road I heard a clamor come up from behind me and then recognized the sound of horse hooves.

"Yah, yah!" a man yelled in the distance. Around the corner of the orchard came a soldier clad in blue and gold carrying a cobalt flag on a wooden staff. I stepped aside briskly to let the rider pass and then I noticed a wagon pulling up behind him being towed by two beautiful Clydesdales. The wagon was filled with Union soldiers and I could feel the excitement rising in my scrawny bones. Their barely used muskets sat upright shining brightly like swords in the morning sun. The wagon driver slapped the reins loudly and the horses approached passing me quickly. I turned my head following the flash of blue and metal insignias that neatly presented themselves in front of me like a parade.

"Where yall headed?" I asked aloud. A solider in the back turned towards me placing his hands on the rails and leaning out the wagon.

"Were going to town kid. You comin?" I smiled from ear to ear and chased after them running as fast as my legs would carry me but the wagon was just too fast. I could see the soldiers smiling and laughing at me as I tirelessly tried to catch up. Shortly I ran out of breath and after a brisk run I stopped in place putting my hands on my knees to brace myself as I leaned forward panting like a hound. Those were federal soldiers! Maybe they knew something about my brother? Where he was, what he was doing? I stood upright and walked onward reaching a fork in the road that I had passed many times before; but today it just felt different. To the right was school where maw expected me to be and to the left was town where the soldiers had gone. If I didn't go to school maw would have me paddled or take me out in the orchard and beat my bottom with a switch, especially after going coon hunting when I wasn't supposed to. But if I didn't go to town I might not find out about my brother. Maybe if they heard something I could tell maw and paw and then they'd be excited for what I done.

"It won't hurt none if I go to school late." I said aloud and turned to the left making my way to town. Maw didn't like me going to town by myself neither. She said I'd get into trouble and that I needed to stay away from strangers but of course I never listened any good. I snuck away to town every chance I got meeting up with my friends to see who was riding in. Wasn't much in town to look at anyway, just a post office, lumber yard, saloon, and a church. The brush on either side of the road began to clear and the dirt path opened up to the town. I found several soldiers posted up just outside the post office drinking from their canteens and snacking on salted crackers. Without delay I approached them and nodded gleefully when their eyes swiftly met with mine.

"Well hey boy." One of the guards called out to me. "I didn't think you'd make it running after the wagon like that. You here to enlist?"

"Enlist?" I asked curiously. I thought they were just running through town? The soldiers almost never stopped here; the town was too small for them to pay much mind.

"Yeah, Sergeant Hollyfield is just inside getting some other boys signed on. You should go on inside and talk to him." I was ready to jump through that door and sign papers set for the adventure of a lifetime but I stopped myself short thinking about maw and paw and what they might think about it.

"Hey, my brother has been fightin with the Union for the last two years. You might know him, his name is Alfred, Alfred Franklin Roach.

Sometimes he goes by Al." The soldier looked up for a moment and thought about it but then shook his head.

"Can't say I do son but if you join up maybe you'll get a chance to see him. There's plenty of brothers and even fathers and sons fightin side by side." I like the sound of that!

"He's serving with the First Regiment, Tennessee Cavalry. You sure you haven't heard of him?" He shook his head again.

"How old are you son?"

"Seventeen this day Sir." I replied without hesitation. He looked over at the other guard.

"Well I'll be. Seventeen? You hear that Private Nicholas?" He nodded.

"I heard that Private Carter." He leaned forward and placed a hand on my shoulder. "Look son, you look like a healthy young man. We need more spring chickens like yourself to help win this war. If you just go in there and talk to the Sergeant he'll tell you about all the great things you get for joining. What'd ya say?"

"Like what?" I asked curiously.

"Well, first of all you get paid to carry around a rifle and you get three square meals a day. Have you ever had three square meals everyday son?" I shook my head. Best I ever got was one and a half.

"Well if you join up you will and none of that old bread or rotten fruit they probably got you eating out here. No Sir, you'll be eating like a king. Fresh meats, baked beans, and all the clean water you could hope for. Hell, we even drink whiskey in the camp."

"Whiskey?" The solider stared at me perplexed.

"Ain't you ever had whiskey before boy? Some of that good old Tennessee brown?" I shook my head again.

"No? Well, if you join you'll get that to. It'll put fire in your blood so you can run straight at them Johnny Rebs like a real man. They even get you brand new clothes, boots, and no more hand me downs like the rags you're wearing. Only the best for those that serve in the Union, that's what Sergeant Hollyfield says. So, what you think boy? You gonna go talk to the Sergeant? He ain't got all day and when we ride out of here we won't come back for a least a month. Wouldn't want to see you and yours get swept up by them Johnny Rebs." I stood there feeling pulled apart. One side of me wanted to say no and respect the decision of my parents but there was another side that just kept screaming at me ready to head out of town and finally be a man; a real man. If I stayed here I might miss the war entirely and then when my brother got back I'd never hear the end of it; how he was a veteran and how I never lifted a finger to fight against the South. I could feel a crooked smile creep up on my face and I nodded enthusiastically.

"Alight. I'll do it. I'll speak with the Sergeant." Private Carter slapped me on the shoulder gripping it tightly.

"Good for you boy. It'll be the best decision you ever made son. Let me just check with the Sergeant real quick." Private Carter left me outside with Private Nichols who had a mischievous grin on his face for some reason but I paid it no mind. "Hey Sergeant, I got a prospective recruit for you outside. You got time to see him? Looks like a real brawler; you know the type." I heard some deep mumblings and then footsteps back in my direction. "Sergeant Hollyfield said he'd see you now. Make sure you are respectful and address him as Sergeant. You understand son?"

"Yes Sir." Private Carter gently pushed me inside and I walked down a narrow corridor until reaching a room painted white where all the mail was kept before it got to where it was going. In the center of the room was a large desk where a big barrel chested Sergeant sat drinking whiskey straight from the bottle. His piercing blue eyes quickly locked on to mine peering like knives through his beard and he stood tall as an oak to greet me.

"Well welcome son, welcome. I'm Sergeant Hollyfield the regional recruiter for the great state of Tennessee. What's your name son." I swallowed nervously and tried to speak with confidence as a man would speak.

"Anderson Sergeant, Anderson Roach but people around here just call me A.J."

"Roach huh? You mean like the bug? Ah hell, you know almost everyone in the Army gets a nickname but I dare say you already got one." He extended his arm pointing to a chair across from him.

"Have a seat son, make yourself at home." I sat down in a large wooden chair and made myself comfortable. The Sergeant swung around the other side and sat down pulling up a corn cob pipe and striking his match to light his tobacco. I watched as he puffed on the pipe and the embers in the bowl grew bigger and brighter. He peered down at the glow and seemed content with the result pulling the match away and waving it in the air until the flame extinguished leaving behind only smoke. Leaning to the left he reached down into a desk drawer pulling out a small metal cup and a few pieces of paper. "Do you drink son?" I shook my head.

"No Sergeant." He pulled the pipe out of his mouth and looked at me suspiciously. Had I said something wrong?

"You know it's hard to trust a man that doesn't drink. Especially when one is discussing the terms of enlistment. Makes a man seem untrustworthy." He stared at me with a most serious look and so I grabbed the cup and held it out for him to pour. "See, that's better. Glad we could continue our conversation." He lifted the bottle making a healthy drizzle into the cup and then pulled it away. "Take a drink son. Rest your bones a bit." I pulled the cup up to my lips and pretended to drink and then pretended to swallow hoping he would not notice my ruse. I placed the cup down gently while the Sergeant aimlessly fumbled through his papers.

"Thank you Sergeant." He looked up from the papers pulling at his beard and adjusting his collar. It seemed tight against his neck as a vein bulged towards his jaw and sweat gathered at the rim.

"You are most welcome. Now, first things first. Private Carter tells me you are eighteen years of age, is that correct?" Why would Private Carter say that? Did I not just tell him that I was seventeen?

"Uh..." I stuttered but was quickly interrupted.

"Because if you are in fact lying to me I cannot in good conscious allow you to join the Army of these United States. So, you are eighteen, right?" I paused for a moment and then spit out a bold face lie.

"Yes Sergeant. I am eighteen years of age." The Sergeant smiled, not a smile of happiness but one of getting away with something he shouldn't have. I quickly caught on that the Sergeant needed me to do things his way if I wanted things to work out. That was fine by me but I didn't much like lying.

"Excellent. Now, we are recruiting for the Eighth Tennessee Volunteer Cavalry however we do have openings in the Infantry if you would prefer to go that route? That's usually for the boys we conscript and not volunteer." I didn't need to think about it, not in the least. I wanted to fight with my brother and ride like the wind over the battlefields.

"I'll stick to Cavalry Sergeant. If it's good enough for my brother it's good enough for me."

"Good, good. Now, you can run, shoot, ride, no conditions I should be aware of?" I shook my head.

"No conditions Sergeant. I can do all those things. Especially the shootin part." He smiled and slid two pieces of paper towards me.

"Can you read son?"

"I can Sergeant." He nodded with a surprised expression on his face. Something told me he was used to doing this part without anyone reading the papers. If there was one thing maw and paw told me that I would never forget it was not to sign something without reading it first.

"That's good son, not many of your ilk in these parts can. I'll let you go ahead and read these. When you are done just go ahead and place your mark on the bottom of both papers. That is, if you agree to join the Union. Just remember son, once you sign on the line there is no going back. However, if you don't sign, well let's just say that when the war is over you may not be much of a respected man in these parts. Just keep that in mind son." I looked down at the pages and read them word for word. It told me what I was signing up for, how much they would pay me every month, the number of uniforms I would be issued and described the benefits I would receive upon my death. That part about death stuck with me for a moment and for some reason it had never crossed my mind that I might get killed out there. The contract lasted for three years or until the war was over. I lifted the quill and without hesitation put my name to the paper.

"There you are Sergeant." I slid the papers back across the desk. He stood and extended his hand.

"Welcome to the Army Private." I smiled and shook the Sergeants hand firmly but he gripped my hand so hard it popped my knuckles.

"What now Sergeant?" I asked curiously.

"Now? Now you go home, tell your family goodbye and tomorrow you get here first thing in the morning. We're riding out for Camp Nelson at first light."

"Kentucky?" I asked. I'd never been to Kentucky before.

"That's right Private, the state of Kentucky. We'll swear you in to-morrow with the others and then ride out. Bring a few things with you for the road but pack light. It's gonna be a long march."

"Yes Sergeant. Thank you Sergeant!" I released his hand and turned to walk away.

"Oh, and Private." I stopped in my tracks and looked over my shoulder.

"Yes Sergeant?" he pulled at his long beard and then picked up the metal cup finishing the whiskey I had not touched.

"Good luck." He said with a crooked grin. I nodded and smiled.

"Thank you Sergeant. I'll see you first thing in the morning." I ran out of the post office and jumped down off the porch to the dirt road.

"Did you sign?" Private Carter yelled out to me as I ran down yonder toward the road and back to school.

"Yes I did!" I replied with great excitement.

"Yee-hah!" he cried out. "Were gonna lick'em good now!" I was so excited I couldn't hold it back.

"Yee-hah!" I yelled back. I ran and ran and ran as fast as my legs would take me back down the road and onward to school. I wasn't too late so I thought that maybe my teacher wouldn't give me too much of a lickin'. I ran all the way to the steps of the schoolhouse and stopped on the steps of the porch catching my breath. I could already hear my teacher giving her lesson and making the other children read aloud. Slowly I walked inside but the door caught on the rusty hinges and made a loud sound. Miss Parks turned around quickly placing her hands firmly on her hips.

"Anderson Roach. Where have you been? You're late!" she exclaimed.

"I joined the Army!" I couldn't hold it back. The words sat at the tip of my tongue and I just blurted them out.

"What was that?" Miss Parks dropped her arms to her sides. Her anger disappeared and was quickly replaced by concern.

"I joined the Union Cavalry. I'm riding out tomorrow to go fight them Johnny Rebs!" Miss Parks walked towards me quickly turning my body around and pushing me by the small of my back urgently outside.

"Everyone get back to your lessons. I expect five rows when I return." I stepped off the porch down the steps and onto the dirt ground. Miss Parks shut the door firmly behind her and turned around rushing toward me placing a firm hand on both my shoulders. "Anderson, what have you done?" she said with a trembling voice.

"I told you. I joined the Army. I'm gonna go fight with my brother." She shook me and held her face close to mine looking angry as a hornet's nest.

"You're seventeen, how did you join?" I placed my hands behind my back and looked at the ground.

"I just did." I said coyly. She raised her hand and pointed her finger in my face.

"You lied to them, didn't you? Told them you were eighteen! I'm gonna go tell them." She turned to stomp off to town and I grabbed her wrist stopping her in her tracks. She was smaller than me now so it wasn't difficult to hold her back.

"No you can't!" I protested.

"Oh yes I can!"

"If you do they'll throw me in the holding pen for sure!" She stopped fighting me and turned.

"What?"

"If you tell them I lied they could put me in prison. It's a crime."

"Anderson, do you know how many boys don't come back from this? Do you know how many of my students I've had to watch get buried just out back? How could you?"

"It ain't gonna be like that!" I thought back to that part in the contract about death. Who was I kidding, it could happen.

"Why Anderson, tell me why. Cause you're special? So were those boys and they went and got themselves killed just weeks after joining. This isn't a game Anderson!"

"I know it ain't a game but it's done. I joined. I'm leaving tomorrow." She wrapped her arms around me giving me a hug while I kept my arms outstretched to the sides. She never hugged me before, always yelling at me and slapping my wrist with the ruler. She let go and put a hand on each of my cheeks.

"You take care of yourself A.J.; do you understand me? You be good out there and don't go rushing into anything." I nodded.

"I won't." Her eyes filled with tears that began to stream down her face.

"You're a good boy Anderson. Did you tell your parents yet?" I shook my head.

"I was gonna."

"Well alright then, get yourself on home and tell them. This might be the last time you get to see them for a while." She came in for another hug and I returned the gesture. "Go, on. Git." I took a few steps walking backwards seeing tears stream down Ms. Parks face and then turned to run back home. "Be careful Anderson!" she yelled as I ran off.

"I will! I promise!" Running back home my excitement had turned to a sort of grief in my heart. I spent all this time thinking about all the good things to come but Ms. Parks talked had soured my mood. Running down the beaten dirt road I came around a corner and spotted four or five men crouched down by some trees. I couldn't make out who they were hiding in the shade like that. One of them stood turning his head towards me.

"Hey boy." he called out quietly. I stopped and hesitated to reply. He took a swift step towards me and the other men behind him stood up with rifles in hand. "Come here boy." The man called out as the group of men walked cautiously towards me. As they walked forward the light revealed their grey uniforms and insignias, these were no farmers or Union soldiers, these were Confederates! "You deaf son? I said come here." I turned and ran straight into the brush. "Git him!" The branches and leaves cracked loudly under foot; my heart pounded as I rushed out deeper into the woods. I looked back behind to catch a glimpse of the men catching up. Just ahead a tall pine presented a chance to escape. I leapt straight up the trunk and pulled myself upward to the nearest branch. Without looking down I climbed up as high as I could until finally I felt that I could climb no more. "Come on down boy, we just want to talk to ya." I looked down to see four of the five men circling the tree. Looking outward I could see the fifth man in the distance nearer the road keeping watch.

"You can talk to me just fine from down there." I replied. The man lowered his head and then raised it up shaking it from side to side.

"Now you listen here. We just, want to talk at you son. Just come on down and we can settle this all civil like."

"Ain't nothin' to settle. You chased me. Help!" I called out. The men swung their heads about to see if anyone was around to hear my cry for help.

"If I have to climb up that tree and drag your ass down here I will."

"Try me!" I taunted. "Help!"

"Alright, I warned you son." The man removed a large knife from his belt placing the handle in his teeth as he began to climb the tree. I gripped the pine as tightly as I could, hoping the if he did reach me I might be able to kick him down. My palms began to sweat and slip from the branches. I looked up to see if I could get any higher but I worried the thin branches might break under my weight. Looking down

I could see him getting closer, the green of his eyes shined brightly against the bright silver blade. Suddenly the fifth man darted back from the road.

"Yanks comin' boss. We best go!" The man in the tree climb down without hesitation and then jumped back down to the ground once he reached the last branch. I took a deep sigh of relief knowing the impending danger was for now, gone. Looking down the man gazed upward at me and pointed.

"This won't be the last you see of me boy. You can count on it." Without another word the man and his comrades slipped away deeper into the woods and disappeared from sight.

# Three
# 8<sup>th</sup> Cavalry, Camp Nelson
# Kentucky – July 16, 1863

I regretted telling maw and paw the way I did. Maw's heart was broken in a hundred pieces; I could tell by the way she just kept looking away from me. Paw seemed more upset that maw was upset. He was no stranger to the Army and that's why he didn't want me to have anything to do with it. I promised I'd write them just as my brother does but their disappointment in me was apparent. I had disobeyed my parents and joined the Army without their permission. I now hoped that with time their disappointment would fade and perhaps they would one day find pride in what I had done. The next mornin' I reported to the Sergeant in town just like I said I would. The barrel-chested Sergeant's demeanor had changed drastically from the eager eyed recruiter to a hard and cold man. Sure enough, he got us in line real quick and marched us out straight away without much warning into an early morning sunrise. The light of day would not be kind.

\* \* \*

Covered in sweat, dirt, and grime our march was about to come to an end. In the distance faint candlelight, could be seen from lamps that hung like ghosts waving gently back and forth in the midnight air.

We approached tall white picket fences that stood as vigilant sentries in the darkness and a wooden gate with two noticeably tired looking guards standing watch.

"Halt!" Sergeant Hollyfield ordered to the gaggle of boys behind him. We stopped in our tracks and looked about wondering with great curiosity what would happen next. Sergeant Hollyfield hopped down form the wagon at the head of our formation, landing heavy on the dirt trail and approached the guards handing them a small piece of parchment. Muffled words were exchanged along with a few laughs before they nodded and turned away from one another.

"Open the gate." One guard commanded loudly to the other. The rusted iron chain that held the gate in place was unwrapped and the gate pushed open wide as a solider ran behind pushing until it slammed against the back side of the picket fence with a loud crash. The Sergeant stomped back to our side and raised his hand high in the air.

"Forward, march!" we stepped frontward without hesitation following the bleak heavily worn path in front of us. One of the guards left his post smartly carrying a rifle and a lamp to lead the way in the dead of night. We trooped for no more than a few minutes until more lamp lights could be seen coming from a large white building in front of us. The Sergeant marched us straight to it and then stopped us near its doors. Just behind us was a field full of white tents and small camp fires that smoldered with little but coals to lend light in the darkness. All was quiet; it seemed that most of the troops were either asleep or gone. The door of the white building suddenly swung open loudly, two half-dressed men armed with pistols emerged and stepped outside followed by a third dressed in a fine blue uniform with gold lining his jacket and collar. Clearly an important man with something important to say. He briskly buttoned his jacket reaching the final button nearer his neck where he had to turn his head about just to get his finger to the clasp.

"Alright you bunch of pecker woods, listen up and listen good. This is Brigadier General Fry, the Commanding Officer of this here supply depot. You will give him your undivided attention and keep yer mouths shut!" The Sergeant turned around facing Brigadier General Fry and crisply saluting him. The General returned the salute but with a weaker less rigid arm and walked down the three steps of the porch as he did so. One hand he placed in his pants pocket and the other gripped the handle of a bright cavalry sword that shone radiantly against the lamp lights. I couldn't take my eyes off that sword and wanted nothing more than to have my very own to fight off Johnny Reb like one of them fancy knight's maw would tell me story's about.

"Gentlemen, you are in fine company indeed. Welcome to Camp Nelson Kentucky. We are the Union supply depot responsible for offensive actions in the state of Tennessee. Gentlemen, we hold the line, that is what we do, that is what we have always done. We hold the line, no matter the cost. Even now you tread on hallowed ground gentlemen. The camp is so named after our beloved Major General William"Bull" Nelson who died fighting those bastard sons of the South. But victory, Gentlemen, victory is at hand. We are beating the Confederacy in every major battle that we engage in. Perhaps some of you had heard of a little battle called Gettysburg?" Some of the men began to chuckle under their breath and quietly celebrate. "But if we are to have peace, if we are indeed to have a truly unified United States of America we must crush the resistance and their unenlightened ideals. It will not be easy and I will not lie to you, no, I will never do that. Many of you will die in these efforts and it is for that reason and that reason alone that I am honored to have you here.

Let me set down the rules before you begin your training here. First and foremost, anyone caught deserting, murdering, or opening their mouths to strangers about our activities will be treated as a traitor and shot on site or hung at my discretion and let me tell you gentlemen we prefer to hang traitors around here. Secondly, if you are caught stealing, lying, or otherwise not following the orders of your superiors in any fashion you shall be flogged mercilessly. Keep your nose clean, serve your country well and you shall have nothing to fear. We shall clothe you, feed you, and train you well to fight the enemy. God bless

you all. Sergeant, take charge of the men and carry out your duties."
The Sergeant saluted General Fry and only dropped his salute after
the General had dropped his and returned to his sleeping quarters.

Sergeant Hollyfield turned to us and looked up and down our ranks
with steely eyes. "Listen up, your training begins tomorrow. For now,
we go to see the Chief Quartermaster, Captain Hall. There you will be
issued your uniforms, weapons, and other various items. I know you
are tired but there are men out there in the fields fighting at this very
moment. I need you to do as your told and keep your mouth shut. Is
that understood?" Some of us replied yelling.

"Yes Sergeant!" others mumbled saying yes or yup and some said
nothing at all. The Sergeants face turned a bright red, the vein in his
neck bulged in the center and I feared it would burst violently. He
threw his arms in the air and charged forward at our formation flailing
his right arm about pointing his rigid fingers at us.

"When I give you an order you will respond with, yes Sergeant! Is
that fucking understood?"

"Yes, Sergeant!" we replied in unison without hesitation.

"You're in the Army now boys. Time to start acting like it. If you
are unable to conform you will quickly find yourself on the other end
of my boot! Is that understood?"

"Yes Sergeant!" He stepped backward several paces, straightened
out his body, threw his shoulders back and lifted his chin upward.

"Right face!" most of us turned right, some turned left. The other
men fixed themselves quickly fearing an immediate and violent
reprisal from the Sergeant. "Forward march!" We stepped off quickly
and marched further down the path reaching a large unpainted barn
that seemed to have only been recently built by the look of the fresh
timber. "Halt!" we stopped again and the Sergeant left us outside in the
cool summer air while he walked into the barn. I could hear several
voices emanating from the inside but no one came out to greet us. We
waited in the dark for what seemed like an eternity. I felt hesitant and
somewhat fearful to speak to the others but as time passed small talk

broke out in the formation and I too began to feel relaxed with the present circumstances.

"Hey." A quiet voice called out from behind me. "What's your name?"

"A.J." I replied. "A.J. Roach." The young man snickered and slapped his thigh.

"Roach? You mean like the bug?" I shot the young man a weak smile and nodded.

"Yeah, like the bug. What's your name? The young man extended his hand.

"I'm Billie, Billie Jones." I extended my hand and shook his with a tight grip.

"Pleased to meet you Billie." Billie seemed like most of the other boys who had come from Tennessee. His skin was tan probably from working out in the fields for days on end. He had dark colored hair that wrapped carelessly around his ears and bright blue eyes, cold as a Tennessee winter. It seemed that at one point his nose had been broken, no doubt from a fist fight with some other boys of his town leaving his snout leaning slightly to the left.

"You were a farm hand, weren't you?" I wasn't sure what Billie was getting at but I answered.

"Of course." I replied proudly. "Weren't you?"

"Me? Naw, I was a merchant's son. I just reckoned you worked the fields cause you got that strong grip." I guess I was wrong about him working in the fields but a merchant's job was no easier with all the lifting and moving of goods to do.

"If you were a merchant's son what are you doing here? Didn't your family have a job for you?" Billie smirked.

"Yeah but I kept getting into trouble."

"Trouble? What sort of trouble?" Billie seemed hesitant to give up any details so I crossed my arms and leaned a bit closer to him. "You gonna share or you just gonna sit there all quiet?"

"Well you see I got this bad habit of bedding the ladies. One day my father caught me with his boss's wife out in the supply room. He told me I had to go or Mr. McCray was gonna kill me. Said he'd put an ax right through my skull if I didn't leave and string me up from the hanging tree."

"It sounds like your father did you a favor." Billie chuckled.

"Yeah, maybe. What about you? Why are you here? Ain't you got a turnip somewhere that needs to be pulled?" he joked.

"My brother has been fighting for the Union for two years. Maw and paw wanted me to stay behind and be a farmer but I didn't want to do all that. I want to fight and send those Rebs back to where they came from." I was assured of my confidence and could feel hot blood running through my veins despite my exhaustion.

"Pretty brave words for a runt who's never been in a fight." I turned about to find the man who had cast an insult in my direction. Dressed in a faded blue uniform and bearing two broad stripes on each sleeve the tall dark mustached man approached me quickly and stood no more than a hands length away. "Well boy? Ain't you got something to say?"

"I don't understand? What do you want?" I asked confused at the mans unprovoked aggression.

"Are you stupid boy? They really make you back woods hill billie's dumb as they come. Next time you talk to me you address me as Corporal! Do you understand me boy?" I stood up straight and tried not to provoke the Corporal further.

"Yes Corporal." The tall man stepped back half a step and bared down on me with a steely gaze.

"Alright boy. Put up your fists, let's see what you got." Was he trying to trick me? Get me thrown into the holding pen? I knew very little of life in the Union Army but I knew better than to raise a fist to someone who out ranked me. "Are you a chicken shit boy? C'mon put'em up!" The Corporal stepped forward and pushed me hard in the chest. I fell back but stood upright quickly while the other boys taunted from all around.

"I don't want to fight you Corporal." He dropped his fists halfway down from his chest.

"What was that boy? I don't think everyone heard you." He was mocking me and he knew it. The bastard was trying to get me into a fight.

"I said I don't wanna fight you Corporal." The man rolled up his sleeves and wiped his nose with his thumb.

"Well why the hell not? That's what you're here for ain't you? To fight the Rebs? To be a big fucking hero?" He raised his fists again and struck me in the chest once more. "C'mon boy, I won't tell you again. Do you wanna be court martialed for disobeying a direct order from a Non-Commissioned Officer? Now put up your dukes!" He lunged and struck me square on the right cheek. I barely saw it coming. Everything went dark for a second as my head swung around and down near my chest. I opened my eyes and the throbbing pain shot into my neck. I quickly raised my fist and swung but threw it wide and missed by a mile. The Corporal grabbed my arms and pulled them behind my back. I could hear the men all around me yelling in an uproar but could not make out what was going on. Two dark figures suddenly appeared in front of me, both wearing Union uniforms they hit me in the stomach knocking the wind out of me. They hit me repeatedly as the Corporal laughed loudly in my ear.

"Corporal O'Brian!" a loud voice sharply called out silencing the excited crowd. He released his grip of my arms and I fell to the ground coughing, wheezing, and trying desperately to catch my breath. "Just what in the hell do you think you're doing?" Loud footsteps approached as the men around fell dead silent. "Get him up off the ground. Now!" Hands gripped my arms and quickly lifted me upright. Still looking at the ground I noticed black boots shined like a mirror reflecting the light of the moon. Gazing upward I found myself staring at an Officer, a Captain no less standing before me. "Corporal O'Brian I distinctly remember asking you a question and I expect you to answer in kind. What in the hell do you think you are doing?"

"The new recruit spoke out of line Sir. I was just trying to discipline him appropriately." The Captain shook his head in disappointment. He pointed a rigid arm at the Corporal and I with all his fingers extended like a large knife.

"You call this discipline Corporal? This boy hasn't even seen the pickets yet and you're working him over as bad as the Rebs. How do you expect our new men to train to fight if they are injured before they ever arrive to the field of battle?"

"I was just..." The Corporal was quickly interrupted.

"You were just what Corporal? Losing the respect of men you intend to lead into war? I'll be surprised if you don't end up with a bullet in your back by the time this fight is over. Get the hell out of my sight and go see the cooks. I'm sure they have potatoes that need peeling." Corporal O'Brian shot over a mean glance to me and then turned his attention back to the Captain.

"Yes Sir." He replied sharply throwing a salute and quickly made his way into the darkness followed by his two companions. I was relieved to no longer be the scarecrow that he beat on mercilessly but feared the swift and unjust reprisal that may come sooner than I would hope.

"Are you alright son?" The Captain asked placing his hand on my shoulder.

"Yes Sir. I reckon I'm just fine." I replied as I wiped the dirt off from my trousers.

"Good, that's just fine then." He stepped back and towards the center of the formation. "Gentleman I am Captain Hall, the Quartermaster of Camp Nelson. It is my duty and privilege to outfit you with your basic supplies and needs to help get you through this war." The large barn door behind Captain Hall opened being pushed by two large negro men in uniform. "This is Private Smith and Private Johnson. They will be assisting me in issuing you your necessities." A grumble grew amongst our ranks, some of the men didn't fancy the idea of having colored folk touch their belongings. It was a strange thing that the colored folk were here fighting not just to survive but also to free men that most of us cared nothing for. I hadn't quite made up my mind on slavery. Many of the refined folk of our town owned slaves and everything seemed to work out just fine. They worked in the fields, minded their own and never caused any trouble. It had seemed the natural way of things but Mr. Lincoln, our President had other plans. I don't claim to know everything and maybe this Lincoln knew a thing or two about right and wrong. Captain Hall seemed to be a gentle soul with warm eyes and a friendly face. He was a short and stocky man with a neatly trimmed beard. The way in which he carried himself led me to believe that he had been serving in the Union Army for quite some time. The Sergeant suddenly emerged from the light of the barn waving his arm and carrying a lamp.

"Alright, two lines, one to the left and one two the right. Shut your mouths and do as your told. The sooner we get this done the sooner yall can get some food and rest. The Captain ain't got all night to be waitin around on us." We did as we were told and split up into two lines that stretched back a ways. I stood behind Billie who kept looking back to see what I was doing.

"Take one and pass it down." Captain Hall handed Billie a stack of papers.

"Yes Sir." Billie replied. He turned back and handed me the stack. I took one and handed it back.

"Now I know not all of you can read so I'm gonna tell you what you have. This is your supply list; each of you will receive a chit to sign out for your equipment. Keep this form on you, you will be expected to return this equipment at the end of your service. Is that understood?"

"Yes Sir." We replied in unison.

"Very well. I'm going to go down the list and call out the items you will be receiving. Then Private Smith and Johnson will issue the items to you one at a time. Once all items have been handed out I will go down the list one item at a time and ask you to hold it in the air to ensure you have it in your possession. Is that understood?"

"Yes Sir." We replied.

"Very well, the supplies you will be receiving is as follows; dress coat, over coat, pants, shirts, drawers, socks, blanket, knapsack, canteen, haversack, hat, and boots."

"What about our rifles?" a young man excitedly called out. I expected Captain Hall to be angry at this outburst but he smiled and laughed quietly under his breath.

"I know that many of you are eager and even elated that you will be issued your very first rifles but I can promise you this, after you have lugged those heavy barrels around all up and down this country you'll get tired real quick of carrying them. In any case your rifles and weapons will be issued to you at training. Now, when you get your blanket lay it out on the ground and place your supplies on top of it so we can account for each item. Get it done." Private Smith and Johnson moved quickly grabbing items from the stalls of the Quartermasters supply barn. They started by handing out rolled blankets to each of us, then the dress coats, the over coats and so on and so forth. I eagerly took the new items and placed them atop the blanket I had laid before me. It wasn't often that I had been given new shirts or trousers but to receive an entire new wardrobe was a rarity indeed. Gazing across the barn I could see the look of excitement on the other men's faces. It was almost like we won an award just for signing up to fight. After an hour or so had passed it seemed that everything had been issued out to each of us and Captain Hall was eager to get a move on.

"Are they ready?" Captain Hall asked of the two Privates.

"Oh yes Sir. They have everything on the list." Captain Hall nodded and stepped on top of a worn wooden crate for all to see.

"Very well. Gentleman if you will look this way please. I'm going to call out your supplies one at a time. When I do hold them high in the air so I can clearly see that you have them in your possession. Is that understood?"

"Yes Sir." We replied.

"Very good. Dress coat!" I bent down quickly grabbing my dress coat and holding it high in the air. Captain Hall looked around the barn until he could see everyone's arms outstretched with the coat in hand. "Very good, put them down. Over coat!" I dropped the dress coat to the ground and picked up the over coat holding it high in the air.

"You there!" Captain Hall pointed at a man across the room from me. The man looked behind him and then pointed at himself.

"Me Sir?" he asked nervously.

"Yes young man, you. What is that you are holding up?" The young man looked up and smiled.

"Well that's the overcoat Sir." He said confidently. Captain Hall dropped his head and swung it from side to side.

"Lord in heaven, would someone please help this boy find his overcoat?" Private Johnson ran over to the young man grabbing his overcoat and handing it to him. "That young man is your overcoat. What you are holding in your other hand is your trousers." The young man turned a blush of red with embarrassment and quickly dropped them to the ground.

* * *

The very next morning we were awoken by the sound of a bugle blaring loudly and drums pounding in the early hour mists. Our tents were ransacked by Sergeants and Corporals alike who yelled and barked at us to get up, get dressed, and get on line. I didn't know what they meant by getting on line but I saw some of the other boys running to stand in formation in front of a Sergeant with a grey beard. I followed them and found a spot I felt comfortable with, or at least the spot I supposed nobody would yell at me about. More of the boys rushed in and soon I was surrounded. Suddenly I felt something pressing hard against my shoulder. I turned my head to see Corporal O'Brian pressing a small wooden cane deep into my arm.

"There you are boy." He said quietly. "You didn't think we were done, did you?" I swallowed my spit nervously and tried to ignore him as it seemed the Sergeant was about to say something important. "Oh don't you worry. I'm gonna keep my eye on you boy. I'll find you when you least expect it. Embarrassing me like that in front of the Captain. You got balls boy but it's gonna cost you. Just you wait and see."

"Corporal!" The Sergeant called out. Corporal O'Brian dropped his cane and marched away to the Sergeant's side. The other two men who had attacked me the night before flanked the Sergeant as well; they were also Corporals. The two striped devils were not much older than us but they had a hate in them something fierce, as if their daddy beat them too damn much. They liked hurting people and now that we were here all they wanted to do was hurt us.

"Atten-hut!" The Sergeant commanded. I quickly stood up straight and held my arms tightly against my body. "Good morning gentlemen and welcome to the Eighth Volunteer Cavalry of Tennessee or as we like to call it, the Eighth. I am Sergeant Loyod and I am here to train and prepare you for battle. We have two weeks' time to turn you farmers and tradesman into soldiers; soldiers of the Union Army. As you are volunteers you are not held by the same rules of fully fledged Union soldiers. If you do not wish to serve you may return to your homes, forfeit your earnings, and carry out your days in dishonor amongst braver men; or you can stay with us, train and fight. Maybe even return home as hero's." The Sergeant stopped speaking and looked amongst the ranks waiting for someone to fall out of the formation but his speech had done the trick and scared anyone from leaving out of fear for being called a coward. "That's what I thought. Very well if you are staying then we are going to train and train hard. Before our time here is up you will learn to follow orders, to march, to shoot, and most importantly you will learn to kill and survive." Sergeant Loyod turned his back to us and faced the woods in the distance. "Just beyond those trees and over the river lies our adversary. Some of us may even have kin fighting for the Rebs; but keep one thing in mind, they will not hesitate to gut you with an Arkansas toothpick. What I am asking is if you are prepared to kill your brothers. Can you do that?"

"Yes Sergeant!" we replied loudly.

"I said can you do that?" he asked again.

"Yes Sergeant!" we replied even louder. Sergeant Loyod lifted a worn wooden cane and bounced the other end in his open hand.

"We shall see. We shall see. Very well, this is Corporal O'Brian, he will assist me in my duties to make you into soldiers. I have authorized

Corporal O'Brian to beat you within an inch of your life should you disobey an order or otherwise vex me. Is that understood?"

"Yes Sergeant!"

"Right! Corporal carry out the training of the day."

"Yes Sergeant!" The Corporal turned to us with sharp eyes and a devilish smile. That son of a bitch made me terribly nervous and I dreaded the thought of what he was going to make us do.

"Alright you sorry sons of bitches git your haversacks. Make sure you got everything in'em. Today were going for a little nature walk." I didn't like Corporal O'Brian's tone. He seemed overly chipper about the idea of going into the woods. Suddenly the other Corporals ran into our ranks yelling and screaming swinging their canes about. We dispersed like chickens and I ran back to my tent grabbing my haversack and tossing everything inside as quickly as possible.

"Git your asses back to formation, let's move!" one of the other Corporals ordered. Once I had my things I ran back to the formation and threw the straps of the haversack over my shoulders. The weight was more than I was used to and the straps seemed to cut into my armpits. How far was I going to carry this?

"Corporal Burleson!" O'Brian called out. "Take the front of the formation with Corporal Uankey. I'll hold the rear and pick up stragglers."

"Yes Corporal." Burleson was a heavy set short man with big arms but was no lazy slouch. He moved quickly and with purpose while Uankey was thin and pale but had an anger chiseled into his face like a kid who got hit with his daddy's belt one too many times.

"Company, right face!" We turned right, well, at least most of us did. The Corporals quickly pounced on anyone that had turned the wrong way striking their legs with canes to correct them. They went back to their positions after some yelling and brawling. "Forward march!" We stepped off down the dirt road. It was still very early, the sun hung low against the horizon but it was already terribly warm and humid outside. July in Kentucky was never known for being forgiving and I readied myself for one miserable day in the heat. Burleson soon led the formation to the right once more until we stopped in front of a well-guarded wooden building. Cannons were lined out front appearing freshly painted and perhaps never used in battle.

"Company halt!" Burleson ordered. Uankey ran forward speaking with one of the five armed guards in front of the building that stood next to piles of cannon balls. Handshakes and nods were exchanged all around until he ran back towards us. "Listen up Company. This is the ordinance depot; we're going to issue you your rifles. These rifles are to be yours from now until the end of your enlistment or death. Now I know most of you are familiar with shooting varmints' in your back woods so these rifles shouldn't be much different. Git in a single file line and follow directions given." We quickly melded into one line in front of the building and slowly made our way forward. I looked around the man in front of me and could see volunteers being issued their rifles one by one. I was excited and ready to get my hands on a new rifle. I only ever shot paws and his was in some pretty poor shape. Finally, it was my turn and I stood in front of a seemingly uninterested private with a dead look in his eyes.

"Name?" he asked seeming apathetic.

"Anderson J. Roach." He filled out a small chit and handed it to me without even looking me in the eyes.

"That's the chit for your rifle. Don't lose it. We're issuing you a sixty-three Springfield. You know how to shoot a musket don't cha?" I looked the rifle up and down running my hand along the fresh barrel.

"I sure do."

"Good, don't get yourself killed son. Next!" I stepped out the other side of the ordinance depot and fell back into formation with the others. We waited for a time until all the rifles had been issued.

"Alright now, stop messing around with your rifles. We're not shooting until tomorrow. Atten-hut!" Corporal O'Brian ordered. We quickly stood at attention with rifles at our sides. The Corporals now carried their own rifles they had removed from the depot. Their rifles appeared very worn with most of the barrel finish coming clean off and the hammers seeming nearly broken. "Pay attention, the next command is going to be, shoulder arms. When you are given this command, you will lift your rifle up to your shoulder like so and hold it in place with one arm. Is that understood?"

"Yes Corporal!" the company replied in unison.

"Shoulder arms!" We swiftly lifted our rifles upward and leaned them against our bodies. "Left face!" Seeing our rifles raised high above our heads was exciting, we finally looked like real soldiers. I couldn't wait to carry this rifle everywhere I went. "Forward march!" back down the dirt road we went with Corporal Burleson leading the formation. I was at the rear now with O'Brian close on my heels. I pretended not to notice him hoping he wouldn't notice me either. Soon we passed the Officers' quarters, called the white house by some. It seemed quiet and more than likely the Officers still slept at this time of day. We reached a smaller dirt path and the Corporals picked up the pace. Corporal Uankey looked back and started waving his right arm about while holding his rifle with the left.

"Let's go you dogs! Move it!" As the minutes passed and the sun rose the day grew hot very quickly. The light of day beat hard on my freshly issued uniform and sweat came out of every pore. The Corporals barked insults and made us pick up the pace as we approached a dry creek bed just below the camp. Our footsteps were loud against the stony ground and nearly sounded like a cavalry charge.

"Halt!" commanded Corporal O'Brian. Our formation stood in the center of the creek bed and we waited there for a moment catching our breath. I heard the crack of branches in the trees that lined the ridge above us and I gazed up curiously thinking a large deer may be watching over us overhead. Without warning the deafening crack of rifle fire broke out and echoed on the stone ground. Smoke billowed from the trees and I could see the angry fire of muzzle flashes bearing down on us from both sides. "It's an ambush! Take cover!" Corporal O'Brian commanded in a panic. The formation split apart in all directions scattering like frightened rabbits. With no powder or shot we had nothing to fire back with and quickly it sunk in that we would most certainly die in this place. As I found cover behind a large boulder I could feel my heart and hands grow cold as the blood rushed to my heart. My eyes searched frantically trying to find something else with which to defend ourselves.

"We need shot!" a young man yelled in desperation. I dropped further to the dirt and quickly dug in where I was. I looked back and saw several boys had dropped their rifles and ran in terror in the opposite direction. Dark figures emerged downward from the tree lines behind us and pressed closer to finished us off.

"Were surrounded! They're everywhere!" I cried out in a panic. Then I noticed the men were in blue Union uniforms; Corporals and Sergeants from the Union Army. Had we been betrayed? Did they turn on us? They carried canes as our Corporals did and quickly rounded up the boys that ran off beating them with their staves until they lay prostrate on the ground begging not to be hurt anymore. The rifle fire ceased and the smoke slowly cleared as our own Corporals began to laugh hysterically. Those sons of bitches, it was a trick!

"Get up! All of you! Now!" Cautiously we stood from our hasty hiding places with looks of embarrassment and confusion written on everyone's faces. "Get in formation!" Corporal O'Brian ordered. We formed up without further delay and the boys who had been beaten senseless for running were dragged to the front of the company. Sergeant Loyod was amongst the other Union veterans that held a young boy by the collar who kicked up dirt as he was thrown to the ground with the others.

"Take a good look!" Sergeant Loyod said pointing his cane down at the five boys. "Take a good long look at these yellow belly cowards. Not one of them worth their weight in salt. These are the men that will get you killed on the battlefield. While you are firing your rifle, manning the picket lines doing your duty as soldiers of the Union Army it's men like these who will flee. They will drop their weapons and run; leaving you behind with less rifles and less shot going down range at the Rebs. It's because of men like these that you will die much sooner than you had intended. I know many of you are good god fearing men that believe that when it's your time to go it is your time to go. After spending many days on the battlefield myself I have learned several important facts; god will not protect the stupid or the cowardly. If you cannot perform your duties in an effective and expedient manner you will die. If you drop your weapons and run from battle either the Rebs or I will kill you. So, what's it going to be?" We were silent and did not respond to his question. I knew full well that these boys were in for the ass whoopin of a lifetime. I did not intend to join them nor did I wish to face a coward's death. "You will fight and you will hold the line! You will hold the line until we order you to retreat or until we are dead to the last man. Is that understood?"

"Yes Sergeant!" we replied in unison. Loyod swung his cane over his head and downward quickly striking a boy that lay in front of him on the back. He cried out in pain until the Sergeant grabbed him by the collar and pulled his face up to his. The boy was terrified babbling like a fool with tears and snot streaming down from his face.

"You git your ass back in formation. If you ever run from a fight again the last thing you will see is the flash of my muzzle in your fucking face. Now all of you, get up and get back in formation! Corporals, resume training. Whip these boys into men! We got thirteen days, let us not waste any time." The Corporals raged against the boys screaming at them to pick up their rifles kicking dust and dirt in their faces. They were forced to the front of the formation and I heard some say that they would be forced to fight first when we encountered Johnny Reb. One of them looked back at me, his eyes welled up with tears and blood streaking down his forehead. At first I felt sorry for the boys and the beating they took but now after Loyod's speech I didn't like these boys too much. What if it was me they were fighting next to and they just left me to hold my own against a wave of Rebs? The boy shot me a long pathetic look but I gave him no reason to think I pitied him so he turned away and looked forward as he was sniffling and spitting blood in the dirt.

"Aye Sergeant!" Corporal O'Brian replied. "Right lads, you heard him. Atten-hut! Forward march!"

\* \* \*

We woke early once more to the startling sounds of bugles blaring in the humid air. The Corporals raided our tents again yelling and screaming throwing our belongings about. I left all my clothes on overnight except my socks and boots to let my feet dry out. I rose quickly pulling my socks down from a string I had hung them from overnight. They were dry and mostly clean, still the best pair of socks I had ever owned.

"Roach!" Corporal O'Brian yelled as he charged at me like an angry bull. The other men scattered from my tent and ran out as they saw the Corporal in all his fury come for me. The camp seemed empty and quiet now that everyone but O'Brian and I had left for formation.

"Yes Corporal!" I said nervously standing upright. He leaned in closely and I could feel his hot rank breath coating my neck. The smell offended me so much that I turned my head away in disgust.

"Oh boy, I told you I'd get even with you. Sergeant Loyod ain't here to save your sorry ass this time." His fist found its way to my gut and I fell to one knee when struck but quickly stood upright again for fear of seeming weak or submissive. "You should stay down boy, otherwise it's going to get much worse for you."

"I'm no coward Corporal." He struck me again this time in the face. My eyes welled up and I spit out blood after he knocked one of my bad teeth loose.

"Did I tell you to fucking speak boy? Hmm? I think you have gone and lost your mind boy. Until you get out there on the battlefield and prove yourself you will always be a coward. So, I'm gonna make sure you never make it to the field." A terrible blow cracked across my left knee and I fell screaming in absolute agony. He lifted his cane over his head and I raised my hands from my leg to stop him. Suddenly I was freed of his shadow and I saw his eyes grow wide as he was dragged backward by a shadow and thrown outside the tent into the cold dirt.

"Stand down Corporal!" It was Sergeant Loyod. O'Brian stood quickly and charged at me. Loyod swung his fist striking Corporal O'Brian square in the face sending him crashing to the ground. O'Brian was knocked out cold and didn't make a sound. Loyod turned back to me taking three steps or so and extending his hand. "Are you ok son?" he asked. I nodded quickly.

"I think so Sergeant."

"I don't know what you did to piss him off so bad but he's got a special kind of hate for you. Can you stand?" he asked me. I pushed my body up putting my weight down on my good leg and then slowly let my weight down on the other. I fell quickly to the ground as the pain hit me like a sack of potatoes being thrown by a bull.

"No! No!" I yelled out gripping my knee tightly.

"Stay here Private. I'll fetch the physician." Sergeant Loyod ran off all the while I lay there in terrible pain rolling back and forth on the ground. I feared the worst wondering if they were gonna take my leg off or if I would take fever from an infection and die. I heard footsteps running towards me and a pale man with no hair and a gaunt sort of face reached Corporal O'Brian. Loyod gripped the man by the shoulder and shook his head then pointed towards me. The gaunt pale man entered the tent and sat down next to me with a calm face.

"What seems to be the matter son?" he asked in a kind manner.

"My leg." I said with a trembling voice. "He caned my leg. It hurts something bad." The man lifted my pant leg and started running his thumbs up and down around my knee. "Stop!" I cried out in pain as he pressed hard against the spot where I got hit. "Please stop!"

"Easy boy, easy. I'm Doc Farmer. Looks like you got yourself a real nasty knock but you're going to be just fine. Nothing is broken, maybe a fracture but it's not broken. You're just going to have to stay off your feet today. Do you understand?" I reluctantly nodded worried about missing the days training. Doc Farmer turned his gaze to Sergeant Loyod. "Perhaps you want to get your rabid dogs under control. Discipline is one thing but debilitating your own regiment?" Sergeant Loyod looked away and rolled his eyes.

"Yes Sir, but what about my training?" I asked. The man laughed deeply and placed his hand on his forehead.

"Well unless I'm mistaken the war isn't going anywhere son. Those Confederates took a terrible loss at Gettysburg and yet the war continues. Take the day to recover and you can try again tomorrow. I'm sure Sergeant Loyod can manage without you for just one day." Sergeant Loyod stood just outside the tent and spoke to Doc Farmer just before he left. After he departed Loyod walked up to me with an uninterested look.

"Well lucky for you Doc Farmer tells me that you are injured and not just hurt. Otherwise I'd tell you to get your ass back in formation. Just remember that when were out there, beyond the river, Johnny Rebs not gonna care that you twisted your knee. You're gonna need to fight regardless of your state; bullet wounds and all. We're doing rifle drill today. I will send another Corporal to teach you the basics while you rest. Tomorrow we fire the rifles and you need to be ready. I can't have you fall behind or you'll have to rotate to another Company and that could take a few weeks or even months." The Sergeant had a sense of urgency in his voice; a tone that suggested that I had to keep up if I didn't want to get left behind.

"Are we heading out soon?" Sergeant cracked a weak smile and gripped my shoulder.

"Were always heading out Private. Now get some rest. We need you up and ready tomorrow." Loyod stood scratching at his grey beard and then marched outside the tent with one hand firmly on his sabre.

"What about Corporal O'Brian?" I asked curiously. Sergeant Loyod cleared his throat and spit on the motionless Corporal just outside my tent.

"Leave him. Maybe a nap will take the fire out of his blood. I'll send someone to fetch him before he wakes up. Corporal O'Brian is a good fighter, a good soldier, but a terrible human being." I smiled and Loyod marched away until the sound of his footsteps faded away in the distance. My leg ached and pounded and I was frustrated that I couldn't just get up and get back to training. Leaning back, I stared blankly at the roof of my tent that flapped in the cool breeze of the morning. Thoughts raced through my head about what the others might think of me, that maybe they thought I was a coward or some kind of sissy boy but soon my mind gave way to the calming of my body and a warm darkness fell over me.

\* \* \*

"Roach." A voice called out. "Private Roach, wake up." A hand gripped my shoulder and shook me gently from side to side. My eyes opened to find the sunlight pouring straight into the tent. I covered my eyes and blinked quickly trying to shake off the blindness. A young man with Corporal stripes stood above me. He had a bright red moustache and a strange accent I had never heard before."

"Yes Corporal." I responded in a daze. My clothes were drenched in sweat and the heat was overwhelming today.

"I brought you some water. Drink up." The Corporal handed me a canteen and I gladly took my share of water before handing it back to him. "Now listen up boy, Sergeant Loyod said you're going to miss out on rifle practice and drill. You'll be a little behind the rest of the men so tomorrow morning when you wake take this with you." The Corporal reached behind him and handed me a small drum and two wooden sticks. I gazed upward at him naturally confused.

"I don't understand Corporal. How is it I'm supposed to fight with this? Ain't we supposed to shoot tomorrow?"

"You're not. Tomorrow you will receive a lesson on drumming with the other drummer boys. Every unit has at least one drummer boy and in this case, it looks like you're it." A drummer boy? This can't be right?

"How the hell am I supposed to fight with these?" The Corporal stood upright and left the tent. "Corporal!" He never came back and he never responded. I lay back down and closed my eyes once more to get some rest as the warm darkness came over me again. I slipped back into a dream of spring fields covered in daisies, my father working the crops and my mother cleaning linens down by the stream. I was back home; a breeze blew in from the north like it always does in the afternoon pushing the leaning trees even further from their roots. The sun shone bright and its warmth pressed hard against my neck.

"A.J.!" my mother's voice called out. She stood upright from the stream with a basket of cloths in her hands. "A.J.!" I ran towards her feeling light as air, it seemed like it took forever to get to her and with each step I took the sky grew dark and angry. In the distance, I could hear the crack of musket fire and the yelling voices of strangers. "Come here A.J." my mother's voice called to me. Fire sparked against the oak wood in the distance and suddenly the forest was ablaze.

"Maw!" I yelled in a panic. "What's happening?" I reached her at last but could not get close enough to touch her. "Maw, what's happening to the forest? What's going on?" Mothers eyes grew cold and tears streamed down her face.

"Why did you leave A.J.? Why did you leave your maw and paw?" She looked down and blood began to soak through the chest of her blouse.

"Mother!" She dropped the woven basket of clothes to the ground and a long dark spike exploded through her chest where the blood had trickled. A bayonet was driven through her body and suddenly standing behind her was a tall man in a tattered grey uniform, his face covered in dirt and only the white of his eyes and the yellow of his teeth could be seen clearly. "Mother, no!" She dropped to the ground and fell on her face. Just behind me I heard another yell, in the remoteness of the fields; it was father fighting off three men who pressed him against the log house. They stabbed him repeatedly until he fell to the ground. I gazed back at my mother's murderer as he placed his foot on her back and relieved her of the bayonet. He brought the blade close to his face and licked the blood from its broad side.

"Mmm." He moaned. "She tastes good Billy Yank. Your next!" He charged! I scrambled back and fell...

"Wha! Oh Jesus!" I sat upright and looked about in a panic realizing I was in my tent still at Camp Nelson. It was dark and the other men were all back in their cots sound asleep. It was midnight, I had slept through the whole day. My thoughts weighed heavy on my mother and father from that point on. I was worried that the Rebs had in fact rolled over our farm and killed maw and paw. The look in their eyes, the desperation. It all seemed so real; but it wasn't, it was just a night-mare. Maw and paw were probably sound asleep just like these boys in my tent. I took a deep breath and went back to sleep. Tomorrow was another day and now I felt resolved to carry out my duties, no matter what they were.

# Four
# Drummer Boys – 8<sup>th</sup> Cavalry, Camp Nelson Kentucky – July, 1863

I was startled awake once more to the sound of bugles. Boys hopped out from their cots in their drawers and threw on their pants, boots, packs and rifles before heading out. I did the same but instead of keeping my rifle at the ready I slung it round to my back and grabbed the stupid drum and sticks the Corporal had left behind for me. My knee was sore this morning but sturdy and much healed since the day prior. The caning left several black bruises up and down my leg but I was already a day behind the others and did not care to fall back any further. Rushing out the tent I fell into formation with the drum strapped around my neck and hanging in front of my stomach. The boys around me started to snicker and make fun of me behind my back. It became so loud that I was about to turn around and confront the cowards but then Sergeant Loyod emerged with his loyal dogs walking quickly behind him.

"Aten-hut!" We quickly snapped our feet together looking straight ahead. "Roach!" The Sergeant called out.

"Yes Sergeant!"

"Git over here." I ran outside the formation and quickly rounded to Sergeant Loyod who stared down at a parchment of paper. Without looking at me he said, "March on over to the Officers' quarters. You'll find the other drummer boys there along with a Corporal Dunham who's gonna instruct you. When you're done git your ass back here. Ya hear?"

"Yes Sergeant." Without delay I turned away from the formation and headed through the cool fog to the White House just a short walk down the road. I tried to be brisk about it and not attract any unwanted attention to myself as I feared the Corporals may find an excuse to leave the company formation and chase me down. To the right of me I marched past the road that led to the negro soldier's tents. It was loud down there too with the sound of marching footsteps and the clamor of negro boys grabbing their equipment. At the head of the road leading to their camp were three negro soldiers standing guard with a picket in the road. Seemed they didn't want anyone wandering to the negro side of camp despite the fact that we were fighting together and it seemed strange to me. If we were fighting together why didn't we train together? It wasn't much longer after the negro side of camp that I reached the Officers' quarters and on the grass across the road were ten white men, a colored boy, and a Corporal I assumed to be Corporal Dunham waiting in formation.

"You Roach?" he asked in a deep voice through a bushy salt and pepper beard.

"Yes Corporal." I said as I saluted.

"What the hell are you doing?"

"Saluting Corporal?" The whites of his eyes turned blood red and the vane in his neck began to bulge outside his high collar.

"Do I look like an Officer to you? Am I wearing gold boy?"

"No Corporal."

"Then put your fucking hand down and get your ass in formation with the others. Jesus, Marion and Joseph! Save the salutes for Officers, not for me. Lord knows I don't need one of those Rebs pickin me off from the trees 'cause they think I'm a Captain after you saluted me."

I thought salutes were used to report in but now I see that they were reserved for Officers only as a sign of respect. The Corporals fear of getting shot for being saluted made me wonder if we would salute at all outside Camp Nelson. Reb soldiers and more particularly spies were everywhere these days and who knew who was watching from afar.

"Ok gentleman, listen up. I am Corporal Dunham and I have been given the task of training you to be drummer boys. Now it is my personal belief that Drummer boys are dumb, useless, and have no place on the battlefield but the Officers seem to think that custom is more important than practicality. So, here we are." Corporal Dunham knelt and picked up more drum sticks from the ground and handed them out. "Each of you will have one drum and two pairs of sticks. I'll say it again, each of you will have one drum and two pairs of sticks. Now why would I give you two pairs of sticks?"

"In case we lose one?" a boy blurted out.

"You lose my governments sticks and you'll be in for a world of hurt boy. You guard those sticks with your very lives. Anyone else got a better idea."

"In case one breaks." I called out.

"Exactly. The battlefield is large boys, large and loud. Messengers and couriers take too long to get word from one place to the next and they often die. Drums and bugles are the most effective way to keep the battle lines moving together."

"If we're going to be on horseback why don't we have bugles instead of drums?" another boy asked. Corporal Dunham lowered his head shaking it side to side.

"You are a curious bunch. I'm surprised the other Corporals haven't knocked the snot out of you yet. Look, we ran out of bugles and that's why you have these smaller drums made for horseback. Just be happy you're not carrying those drums the infantry boys got. Those poor bastards will sweat until the cows come home. Now, you have nearly forty commands you will need to master today before I can release you back to your units. We will begin with the four primary commands you will use the most often." Corporal Dunham knelt lifting a drum placing the strap around his neck allowing it rest on his stomach.

"The four primary commands are march, attack, halt, and retreat. I will first demonstrate march." Corporal Dunham pulled up his arms and with the flick of his wrists he pounded on the drums over and over as we quietly listened. When he stopped, he rested his arms atop the drum. "Did everyone catch that?"

"Yes Corporal!" we replied in unison.

"Good, now together. One, two, three." We pounded the drums keeping up with Corporal Dunham's cadence. Several of us seemed to be out of step and so he slowed his tempo so others could catch up. Slowly we caught on and the beats of the drum ran together smoothly and efficiently like a well-oiled rifle. Corporal Dunham suddenly stopped and we stopped along with him. "Very good. Now what was that command?"

"March!" we replied. Corporal Dunham nodded his head in agreement.

"Very good. Each drum command is unique so the soldiers on the battlefield and the Officers can clearly recognize them in order to take proper actions on the field. If you make a mistake or fail in your assigned task you won't just get yourself killed but the other men in your regiment as well. Is that understood?"

"Yes Corporal!"

"Next we will try attack. Now this one really gets the boys fired up so when you're doing this one put some effort into it. Drums can't kill the enemy but they can bring the men together and rally their spirits to fight on. It's a rolling cadence that goes up faster and faster. Give it a listen." Corporal Dunham raised his arms again striking his sticks together twice then vigorously beat the drum skin. The beat rolled up just like he said going faster and faster. I could feel the sound almost pushing me, urging me to move forward. It was obvious why this was the command to attack the enemy. "Ya'll got that?"

"Yes, Corporal." we replied.

"Good, alright then follow me. One, two, three." We slapped our sticks twice and then beat the drums with all our might. I was the one out of step this time and couldn't seem to get back on track. "Stop!" Corporal Dunham ordered sounding frustrated. "Stop, stop, stop." He walked up to me and gripped my wrist. "You see this, you see how rigid your wrist is. It's like a corpse on a cold day, rigid and inflexible. Loosen your wrists, relax. You want them to roll back and forth quickly otherwise you're gonna mess up the command. Try it again."

"Yes Corporal." I replied. I struck the sticks together and then began the roll up for the attack command. With my wrists loosened I was capable of striking the drum skin faster and faster. Corporal Dunham nodded his head with the beat and then placed his hand on my shoulder.

"That's good Private. Alright then, together again." We struck our sticks together and commanded the attack with a vigorous roll up. The drums were loud and made the air around us seem electric. Corporal Dunham stopped and we followed suit. "Good, you're learning quickly. Next is the Halt command and it's a little different. This time you are actually going to strike the rim of your drum followed by a slow cadence. Do not strike the rim too hard or you'll break your sticks. Alright, now watch me." Corporal Dunham began striking the skin, then rim, then back to skin until he struck the skin in repetition six times before repeating the cadence. "Does everyone understand?" We nodded enthusiastically.

"Yes Corporal." We replied.

"Good, follow me. One, two, three." We began striking skin, rim, skin, rim and then the succession of slow drum skin strikes. It was loud and boring, perfect to get everyone's attention to stop marching. I felt confident with these commands and was ready to test them on the battlefield. "Alright good, everyone stop. Now on to retreat. This is an important command to remember for several reasons. First and foremost, if you hear it you better repeat it quickly and then get your ass out of there before you get overwhelmed by a bunch of uncivilized types. Secondly, not all retreats are used to run from a battle."

"How's that Corporal?" I asked.

"Well I'm fixin to tell you if you'd keep your flap shut Private. Some retreats are used to get the boys back to picket lines, trenches or tree lines so we can regroup when the battle formation turns to disarray. We are stronger together and you will help the boys stay together, one drum beat at a time. The retreat is a steady and fast successive strikes of the skin. Pay attention." Corporal Dunham pounded away at the drums without delay. This command sounds like an alert or panic to alarm the men on the field. "Ready?"

"Yes Corporal."

"Follow me. One, two, three." We sounded the retreat with our drums and stayed in perfect harmony with Corporal Dunham. He quickly stopped to allow us to move on to the next set. All day we went on banging the drums, trying new commands and then every once in a great while, Corporal Dunham would pick on one of us and test our memory by making us stand in front of the formation and demonstrate a command. The hot Kentucky sun cooked us under our dark hats and sweat permeated my clothes. All we had were a few breaks between sets to drink water and eat a few salty crackers. The day was long and yet somehow sunset approached before I knew it.

"Alright gents, that's all I can teach you." Corporal Dunham said with tired breath. He pulled the drum strap away from his body and wiped the sweat off from the back of his neck. "I'll let your Sergeants know you have been properly trained. Now go back to your companies and do them proud.

"Corporal?" the negro boy in the back raised his hand.

"What is it boy?"

"Beggin your pardon Corporal but if we get stuck in a fight do we drop the drum and run?" Corporal Dunham smiled and wiped the sweat from his brow now flicking the fluid from his fingertips.

"If you find yourself in a position of life or death you pick up a weapon and choose life. God will take care of the rest. Now go on, all of you. Git." We left the formation without delay and headed back to our companies. I looked back at the other drummers I had spent the day with knowing that I would probably never see them again. I think most of us were destined for death carrying these drums around but under god's good graces perhaps a few of us would be permitted to stay on this green earth a while longer. As I walked back to camp I watched the sun settle behind the rolling hills and saw the clouds and horizon set ablaze the brightest of orange you had ever seen. The wind began to rise cooling the sweat on my brow and for a moment I forgot that there was a war out there in the fields and forests. Quickly the sun fell dipping behind the rolling hills, giving way to shades of pink and dark purples eventually fading to blue. Not wanting to get caught resting I lengthened my stride until reaching the field of tents. Eighth Cavalry, Company F was still in formation and appeared to be preparing for dismissal. I decided to take the long way around so not to get sucked in to any work details. Just one more left turn and then straight ahead to my tent.

"Just where the hell do you think you're going runt?" A familiar and unfriendly voice called out from behind me. I stopped in my tracks and looked back without turning my body. It was Corporal O'Brian and his boys. That son of a bitch had a fiery look in his eye and he was looking to start some trouble for certain.

"What do you want Corporal? I ain't lookin for a fight I just want to get back to my tent." Corporal O'Brian snickered as he cleaned his teeth with a wooden tooth pick. He flicked it away and walked towards me with his hands firmly on his hips.

"You hear that boys. Private Roach here says he ain't lookin' to get into a fight. Is that right boy? Is that what you say?" I looked the bastard dead in the eye holding my resolve firm. His breath was rank' the smell of whiskey that flowed like fire from his mouth.

"No Corporal, I don't want no trouble." Suddenly he lunged his hands towards me and snatched the drum from my grasp.

"Well lookie what we got here boys. Ol' Private Roach got himself a musical instrument. I guess they figured you were no good at fightin' so instead they want you in the back with the rest of the yellow belly cowards. Ain't that right boy?"

"Give it back Corporal." It didn't matter what I did. He was set on making my life more difficult than it needed to be. I could feel my anger rising like a storm in my head and the more he taunted me the worse it became.

"What'cha gonna do boy? You gonna strike a Non-Commissioned Officer? Good way to git yourself thrown in the hole. I know you ain't never been in the hole before. Not a pretty place for someone as soft as you. It's dark, hot, and after a good while you start to hear and see things that ain't there. Go ahead boy, you wanna hit me. Do it, pick up those little lady fists of yours and land it right here." He leaned forward taunting me more and more pressing his right cheek outward towards me. I clenched my fist so tight my knuckles cracked and before I knew what happened I lunged forward and gave him a good one across the face. The Corporal fell like a stone down a well and his fellow Corporals looked on in utter shock. "You done it now!" The Corporal said through clenched bloody teeth. "You don' it now you sum bitch!" He balled up his cheek and spit a load of blood on the ground in front of me. "Grab him boys. Time for some reflection in the hole!" The Corporals lunged at me and I stepped back to throw another punch.

"That's enough!" a voice commanded. It was the Sergeant Loyod with one hand on his sabre and another holding an oak club that looked like it had hit its fair share of Union boys. The Corporal sprang up quickly and stomped towards Sergeant Loyod pointing back at me with a rigid arm and finger.

"Sergeant that Private struck me. I want him fried up in the hole for two weeks for assaulting a Non-Commissioned Officer and insubordination!" Sergeant Loyod lowered his shoulders and cocked his head seeming unconvinced at the Corporals poor attempt at victimhood.

"I watched the whole thing Corporal. Far as I can tell you deserved the ass whoopin you got." Corporal O'Brian stood there in disbelief at the Sergeants estimation of quarrel and shot me an evil look over his tense shoulder. "Besides, we don't have time for him to sit around in the hole. We leave tomorrow morning and we need our drummer.

I suggest you get your shit squared away before we head out to the field. I'm taking Private Roach out to the rifle range to get some shot time in. Roach, meet me at the range with your rifle in fifteen minutes. We don't have much light left so move yur ass."

"Yes Sergeant." Sergeant Loyod gave me a nod and I returned it in kind as he turned and walked away. Corporal O'Brian ran up to me putting his face right next to mine, his lip twitching uncontrollably. Hot foul-smelling breath covered my neck and I leaned back to give myself some much-needed space.

"You listen here boy. When we get out to the field you better watch your back because one day you may find yourself alone in a trench or hiding behind a picket somewhere and when you turn around your gonna find me with a pistol pointed at yur back. The only thing they'll know is that you got yourself killed by some Reb. Ain't nobody gonna know any better. So, you watch yourself." The Corporal pushed me back with both hands and walked passed me hitting my shoulder with his. I was more than happy to see go on his way but now my mind weighed heavy on the barrel of the Corporal. I never thought that in a war against the Confederates I'd have to worry about my fellow soldiers trying to kill me out of spite. Without delay I threw my drum and sticks down to the tent floor, grabbed my rifle and ran as fast as I could to the range. On my way through the myriad of tents I passed Billie who raised his hand up in the air excitedly as I approached.

"A.J., where you goin? Gone ta fight dem Rebs all by yourself?" Without stopping I replied;

"Gonna go shoot at the range. Back in a hot minute!"

"Well don't go shootin your thumb off! I need someone to watch my back." He joked.

"You got it!" I replied. As I approached the open range further down the road Sergeant Loyod stood there smoking his corn cob pipe staring out into the distance. Smoke billowed like miniature ghosts around his beard and dark blue hat.

"Bout time you showed up." Sergeant Loyod remarked without turning his head. "You ready Private?"

"Yes Sergeant." I unslung my rifle from my shoulder and pointed the barrel to the dirt.

"Alright then." He reached over on a bench next to him and slid a small container towards me. "Here's your shot, powder, and wad. You know how to shoot that thing?" I nodded confidently.

"Yes Sergeant."

"Coon hunter?" he replied sharply.

"What was that Sergeant?"

"You a coon hunter son? You know, Racoons, you hunt them back on the farm?" I smiled and nodded.

"Every chance I got Sergeant." He smiled beneath his bushy beard but quickly wiped it away.

"Very well Private. Pick up that stick and make it sing. I want to see a clean shot on that target. That's fifty yards. If you can handle that we can move on." Sergeant Loyod crossed his arms, perhaps doubting my skill with a rifle.

"Yes Sergeant." I quickly put the butt of the rifle down on the ground and grabbed the top of the barrel with my left hand. With my right I reached over and grabbed the cartridge set out for me and tore the top of it with my teeth spitting the spare paper away. I poured the contents of the cartridge into the barrel and made sure the bullet didn't slip away. Straight down the barrel it went and I grabbed the ramrod and pressed the cartridge all the way down tapping it at least three times so I wouldn't get a misfire. Reaching over to the bench I grabbed the primer and affixed it below the hammer that I had cocked back. Raising the butt of the rifle to my shoulder I aimed in on the black and white target in the distance. Breath in, breath out, breath in, breath out; a natural pause came in my breath and I squeezed the trigger. A loud bang exploded in the evening air lighting the dimly lit ground around me. The shot cracked through the sky and quickly met its mark hitting dead center. Sergeant Loyod pulled the pipe out of his mouth and leaned forward squinting at the target.

"We'll all be damned. Who the hell taught you the nine count?"

"My paw did." Sergeant Loyod uncrossed his arms letting them fall comfortably to his side.

"Well good thing for your paw. Looks like he taught you to shoot as well. Ok gunslinger, let's see how you do putting a few volleys down range in rapid succession." Sergeant Loyod pulled a fancy looking silver pocket watch from his breast pocket and held it out in front of him. "I need you to load, aim, and fire at least three times in one minute and this time I want you to hit the target at one hundred yards. You think you're up to it." I nodded without any reservation.

"Yes Sergeant."

"Alright Roach, let's see what you got. When I say go, you go. Ready, set, and go!" I quickly grabbed the cartridge and went to work, fire, reload, fire, reload, fire, reload, fire. "Stop!" My hands were greasy covered in sweat and powder; sweat ran down my forehead as I took a deep breath to calm my pounding heart. I moved so fast that I lost count of my shots.

"How'd I do Sergeant?" I said exasperated. He scratched his head and looked at his pocket watch with surprise.

"My damn watch must be slowing down."

"How you figure Sergeant?" Was he disappointed?

"Private, you pulled off four shots in one minute and hit center mass on a target at one hundred yards each time. Nobody in my regiment has ever done this their first time on the range."

"Must have been luck Sergeant." I replied humbly. Sergeant Loyod scoffed at the remark.

"Alright smart ass. You ready to go again." I happily nodded.

"Yes Sergeant." As I placed the butt of my rifle on the ground he reached over and snatched it from my hands.

"Let's try something a little different this time." He reached over the bench and grasped a leather cloth that was draped over something. Removing the cloth, he exposed a shiny new rifle I had never seen before.

"Is that one of them repeaters?" I asked excitedly. Sergeant Loyod lifted it up in the air and smiled looking up and down the barrel.

"A Henry Repeating Rifle. Ain't no other like it. Just got the shipment in yesterday to replace our Spencer's. The entire company got to shoot them after they qualified on the Springfield."

"Why'd you have me shoot the Springfield if we were gonna use the Henry, Sergeant?"

"If you drop your rifle, lose it, break it odds are you're gonna find a Springfield lying in the dirt next to a corpse somewhere. Better to know how to shoot it and not have to than have to and not know how." He had a good point. I bet not all the boys knew how to load and fire a musket. "Now, I want you to take this, load and fire until this box of forty dead men is empty. You got me Private?"

"Yes Sergeant, but, how do I fire it?"

"Real simple Private. These here are your rounds, just drop them down into the magazine, sixteen rounds in total. Once you're done just close this cap off, cock the rifle and you're ready to fire. You with me so far?"

"Yes Sergeant, but what about the powder?" Sergeant Loyod laughed.

"It's in the casing, understand?"

"Yes Sergeant."

"Alright Private. Give it a go." I gently took the rifle from Sergeant Loyod's grasp and quickly went to work loading the rifle, sixteen rounds in all. I cocked the rifle with relative ease to load a round and aimed in. Round after round I sent down range hitting my target with deadly precision. In no more than a few minutes I had fired all forty rounds into the targets. I pulled the rifle back and looked over the now warm barrel and smoking bore. It was a thing of beauty and I felt like my rifle and I were going to have a long-lasting relationship.

\* \* \*

The days passed faster and faster as we toiled in the heat of day and darkness of night. Each and every day there was drill practice, bayonet training, and rides on horseback in and around camp. We became better brothers through our training and teamwork in just over a week, but our attitudes towards the war had changed little. We were determined that we would decimate the Rebs and nothing, not even Satan himself was going to stop us...

* * *

Bugles blared early in the morning as they always had. Startled I opened my eyes and sat upright sleepily gazing outside the entrance of the tent. The sun had not yet risen over the horizon and even the birds in the trees were not chirping. I was used to early mornings on the farm but this seemed unnatural to be woken up so soon before the daylight each and every day. I stood with numb legs and quickly donned my uniform over my long johns, slung my rifle and grabbed my small drum letting it rest firmly on my hip. As I withdrew from the tent with the other men, voices clamored everywhere and bodies rushed hurriedly past. I found Fox Company and quickly fell into formation with the others.

"Roach!" Sergeant Loyod approached looking worse for wear. No doubt he had been up late drinking and smoking. "You're gonna be in the front with the Officers and I. When we get on horseback; I expect you to drum a slow cadence to keep us in step for a time until I tell you to stop. Is that understood?"

"Yes Sergeant." I replied. I quickly left my spot in the rear of the formation and headed to the front next to our flag bearer who carried the company standard. It was a simple flag that looked like it was stitched together by one of the maids in the Officers' quarters. A dark blue fabric with a large white "F" on each side of it. The ends of the banner were worn and tattered and several spots of the flag appeared to be bleached from long campaigns in the sun. It had seen better days but to me it seemed like a symbol of pride carrying a flag that had seen previous battles, perhaps even something to bring us a bit of luck.

"Atten-hut!" Sergeant Loyod commanded. We quickly snapped to attention. Sergeant Loyod spun around and saluted a newly arrived Captain. "Sir, all troopers present and accounted for!" The Captain returned the salute and then promptly dropped his arm with Sergeant

Loyod following suit. Sergeant turned to the right and joined the formation leaving the Captain at the forefront.

"Company, at ease!" The Captain commanded. We relaxed and looked on at the Officer waiting for him to speak. "Gentleman, I am Captain Masengill, your Company Commander. I know your time here at Camp Nelson has been brief but our country, your country needs you out in the field. The Rebs have been stabbing, murdering, and killing their way into Union territory. They have stooped as low as you can possibly go. We are no longer simply fighting our brothers. We are fighting criminals; men who no longer are bound by the rules and etiquette of warfare. Towns within Tennessee are being ransacked for supplies, women are being defiled, and children are being slaughtered. We move to kill them sons of bitches and to put them down like the dogs they are!" We cheered happily and raised out hats in the air. "As Cavalry, we will be the tip of the spear bringing the fight to the enemy swiftly, keeping the Rebs off the flanks of our infantry so they can move forward and engage the larger of the Confederate forces that remain. I'm proud to have each and every one of you under my command and expect nothing but the best from you. Before we head out you will be well fed; it will probably be the best meal you will have for some time so eat well. You will receive provisions, ammunition, swords and horses then we shall mount up. Are you ready Gentlemen?"

"Yes Sir!" we cried out in unison.

"That's what I like to hear. Now let's go get them sons of bitches. Sergeant Loyod." The Sergeant returned to the front of the formation and saluted the Captain. "Take command of the troops and carry out the orders of the day. I want the Company ready to deploy in two hours' time."

"Yes Sir!"

# Five
# Road to Williamsburg – July 1863

Captain Masengill led us on a dusty ride some ninety miles south of Camp Nelson through the baking sun. Rumor was that the Rebs were crossing over from Tennessee in droves making incursions to steal supplies and attack our telegraph lines making it difficult to get messages quickly to the boys about the Rebs whereabouts. Williamsburg was our destination but we stopped in London Tennessee where another hasty Union camp and supply depot was up and running. The order to dismount could not have come sooner and I was personally relieved to get down from Abigail. She snorted loudly when I got down and was clearly relived to no longer cart me on the trails. It was early in the morning and likely we would only get a few hours of sleep before it was time to move out again. I did not doddle nor did I take the time to set up any kind of tent as some of the men were doing. I tied a worn-down Abigail to a sturdy oak branch near a patch of grass and quickly set down my bed roll on a soft patch of dirt and leaves. Oak leaves were sharp and tended to stick to the skin but the wool bed roll kept the little buggers at bay. A fire was quickly made near the Officers tents that had been erected by several privates and shortly thereafter a few riders approached followed by several troopers on foot. I overheard them call themselves the Forty Fourth from Ohio. Infantry from the sounds of it but I stopped paying attention shortly after their arrival and quickly dozed off to a warm and comfortable sleep.

* * *

I was awoken by a firm hand on my shoulder that gripped tightly. It was still dark outside and I must not have been asleep any longer than three or four hours. The Officers fire raged just to the side of me and all the Eighth was being roused to move out. In the greater distance, I could hear sporadic rifle fire; faint pops and cracks in the shadows. More than likely just small skirmishes but my mind wandered to dreams of giant menacing armies the likes of which no one has ever seen just waiting to pounce us on the lonely roads. I had been in plenty of fist fights with the boys back at home but never had I been to war. I thought the worst and imagined cannons as far as the eyes can see raining down hot metal on us in a relentless manner and murderous armies emerging from the shadows, streams, and forests. I shook my head to erase the thought from memory. We still had two more days of riding before we reached Williamsburg but kept a wary eye for Rebs hiding out in the bush along the way.

"Roach!" Sergeant Loyod bellowed from his half erected tent. I stood and quickly pulled back on Abigail's reins to make sure it was still good and tight before I marched over to him.

"Yes Ser…" I had to clear my throat and repeated myself. "Yes Sergeant!" The Sergeant was prostrate, giving orders from the dirt.

"It's time to rouse the troops. Get on the drums, call to revile." He said with his cavalry cap tilted over his eyes.

"Yes Sergeant." I swung my drum to the front and pulled my oak sticks from my leather belt and pounded away at the skin.

"Reveille, reveille, revile!" The Corporals called out frantically. Left and right men darted upwards from their resting places like seedlings sprouting up from the earth.

"Fox Company! Formation! Fall in!" Sergeant Loyod commanded as he slowly stood from his resting place. The men scrambled forward and formed up just in front of the Officers fire. The brass were still on the opposite side of the tents checking their maps and working out their plans for the day. "Gentleman, we have another long day ahead of us. We finished thirty miles of riding yesterday. Today the Officers want our company to cover forty miles. Word is that the Forty Fourth Ohio Infantry is engaging a mixed Confederate regiment of cavalry and infantry led by a Colonel Scott. It is said that Scott and his men are heavily entrenched in the tree lines and we aim to drive them out. Corporals, account for your men and report back to me. When we have an accurate count, we will break for chow and then mount up. Is that understood?"

"Yes Sergeant!" We replied. Sergeant Loyod left promptly, no doubt to get some food and maybe even coffee if it was available. As for the rest of us it was probably gonna be water and whatever the cook slopped up in his cast iron pot. The Corporals promptly finished their count and headed out to chow as quickly as they could. I was starting to think the only motivation for getting promoted was being first in line for breakfast. I could smell bacon, sausage, and even fresh coffee as we waited anxiously in line.

"Hurry up!" Corporal O'Brian yelled back to the rest of the company while stuffing his face full of bacon. "No lollygagging! Git yur chow and git yur ass moving!" O'Brian's gaze caught mine while I waited in line and his eyes squinted a bit before turning his head forward. It wasn't going to be long before I had to face him again but this time he was occupied more than at Camp Nelson and perhaps this lack of idleness would keep him off my back a few days longer.

"Hey, Roach. Roach!" A voice called out a few men behind me in the line. It was Billie, Billie Jones. I hadn't seen his face since our first formation at Camp Nelson. He joyfully skipped ahead a few men trying to politely cut in line and got right behind me. "So you the drummer now?" I reluctantly smiled.

"It would seem so." Billie shot a crooked smile, his cold blue eyes reflected the cook's fire as he rubbed his chin vigorously.

"So you spend your time at the front with the Officers. What's it like?"

"What do you mean Billie?"

"Do the Officers tell you stuff or you just over hear them?" I shook my head.

"The Officers keep pretty much to themselves. I don't hear much from them. Mostly just Sergeant Loyod barking at me to beat the drum from time to time. What about you?"

"Aw heck man. I just spent the last thirty miles staring at the back side of a horse and listening to the boy next to me humming Maryland the whole damn way. I had half a mind to put a ball in his head just to shut him up." The chow line moved slowly until I finally reached the cook. I held out a small metal plate and he reached deep into a cast iron pot and used a wooden spoon to scoop out a generous helping of grits.

"What happened to the bacon and sausage?" I asked frustrated. The cook cocked his head and smiled at me.

"Meats are for the Officers and Non-Commissioned Officers. You boys get grits today. Just be happy you ain't eating salted pork and crackers." He ran his fingers back through his thick wiry black hair and wiped them off on a bloody white apron.

"Any coffee?" I asked reluctantly? The cook pulled a corn cob pipe out of his fat mouth and blew his tobacco smoke in my face.

"Get out of here boy before I spit in your breakfast." I didn't argue with the man any further and walked back to my horse. I found a log right next to the girl and took a seat. After I got a few bites of the grits down into my belly footsteps came up behind me and Billie sat down on the log next to me.

"Grits ain't so bad. At least he cooked'em in the same pot as the pig. It's got some flavor to it." I smiled and took another bite of my food.

"I guess I shouldn't expect the going away meal they gave us at Camp Nelson. Would have been nice though."

"Shoot no!" Billie exclaimed. "This here is solider food. Out here we will only get the very worst unless we come across some Reb supplies. I hear they carry fresh salted pork in all their carts and whiskey in every oak barrel." Billie crammed a large helping of grits in his mouth and chewed noisily.

"If they carry pork and whiskey on all their carts how do they get water and ammunition?" Billie slapped his knee replying with a mouth full of food.

"Those back-water boys just drink from the swamps and soak their beards in the river. They wring'em out in their canteens just to get a fresh drink." I stared at Billie for a moment unsure if he was being honest or trying to tell a joke. His crooked smile cracked again and he began to laugh aloud. "I'm just pulling your leg friend." I smiled and then pulled my canteen up from around my neck to take a drink. Canteen water tasted like metal after sitting in the container for so long. I drank until the canteen was empty and smacked the side to get a few more drops out of it.

"I need to get some more water. How bout you?" Billie tapped on his canteen as it made a loud hallow sound.

"Yup, sounds about empty. Let's git down to the river an git some more water. The Sergeant will probably make us ride out sooner than later. Don't want ta be caught on the road without any water." We stood up bringing our plates with us to wash them out. Reaching the base of the river we walked upstream until we passed up most of the camp. Getting water downstream could be dangerous and make you sick. Better to walk a little further and keep it clean. I knelt next to the water with my back against an oak tree and Billie on my right. "How many do you reckon were gonna ride up on when we get to Williamsburg? A hundred? A thousand?" Billie asked as if I knew something he didn't but I did hear rumors.

"I heard it was thousands but you know how everyone loves to tell a good story. I don't believe nothin' until I hear it from the Captain himself." The sound of the river was calming as the stream moved gently by. I took a deep breath in and stretched my back to take out the ache from the long ride. A faint crack erupted in the distance across from the river; a twig snapping loudly under foot. We gazed across the gently moving water wary of anything that may be watching us. It was only then that I realized we had left our rifles back with our horses and we were not alone.

"You heard it to?" I asked Billie. He nodded his head quickly as he shifted the whites of his eyes side to side in the darkness.

"Yes Sir I did. What you suppose it is? A rabbit maybe or wild dog or a squirrel?" I shook my head slightly. Most beasts were smart enough not to go trampling through the woods unless they want to attract a predator or hunter.

"That branch was too big for a rabbit. A deer or horse maybe?" As we gazed into the dark forbidding forest shadows slowly hovered and darted between the trees, inching their way towards us. I caught the reflection of fire off a pair of eyes and then the glint of a rifles barrel. "Rebs!" I shouted. Gunfire cracked loudly lighting up the dark forest and the river bank below. "Run Billie! Go, go!" Dirt flew up from the ground and into my eyes as the shot barely missed my body. I rubbed it out as I darted up the bank and scurried down the other side. Cavalry men ran in our direction with rifles drawn.

"Where's it coming from?" A private shouted. I pointed back behind me.

"There, across the river! Johnny Rebs!"

"How many?"

"Six, maybe ten!" I wasn't for sure so I gave a number I thought made sense. Billie and I reached our horses and grabbed our rifles to join in the pursuit leaving the horses behind. Rifle fire still cracked all around but this time it was Union fire hurling itself across the river at our attackers. The water was no deeper than our knees and we hurriedly made our way across following the sounds of rushing footsteps. Then all at once, everything fell silent. There were no more footsteps, no more shots, just the eerie quiet of the wood.

"Halt!" Sergeant Loyod commanded quietly. Not a sound was uttered, not even the birds or the crickets made a noise.

"Did they git away?" The Sergeant shook his head keeping his rifle pointed out in the distance.

"No. They're hiding out. That's for damn sure. Split up, you boys go north and the rest of us will go south. Push east and flush'em out. We're gonna bird dog them before they have a chance to escape." I moved southward with Sergeant Loyod taking slow steps in the dark careful not to snap any twigs beneath my foot. A faint noise caught my attention sounding itself repeatedly. It was heavy breathing in the darkness muffled by the sounds of crickets and moving creek water. I turned back and waved my arm to the Sergeant to come over. He and a few men get close to watch my back as I approached a small dirt embankment. Another step and then I placed my foot on a twig that snapped loudly echoing on the forest floor. "Damnit." I whispered quietly. I shut my eyes tightly in frustration and then heard the rustling of feet through the brush. Opening my eyes I saw a dark shadow dart away between the trees.

"There he goes!" I raised my rifle, aimed in, and pulled the trigger. The butt of the rifle kicked hard against my shoulder as fire and sparks lit the surroundings of the wood. A dull smack sounded noisily and the shadow fell hard to the ground.

"Great shot!" Sergeant Loyod exclaimed. "Let's go pick'em up before his friends do." We ran forward quickly approaching a dark lump lying flat on the ground. "Get a torch over here!" A bright fire bounced up and down through the woods until a Private carrying the torch could be clearly seen. I knelt and looked over the man while the torch lent its flickering light. The shot went right through the center of his back; a clean kill if I ever saw one. I turned his still body over to see the face of the merciless soldier I had killed only to be greeted by the dead and cold face of a boy, no older than thirteen years of age. His expression maintained the last few moments of sheer pain he must have felt when the lead ripped through him and for a moment I felt dread knowing what I had done to him. I wanted to go to war against the Rebs and kill southern fighters, veterans. Never in my wildest dreams did I ever think I'd be shot at and shooting back at boys in grey.

"You got him dead to rights. That boy never saw it comin!" Billie exclaimed with excitement in his voice.

"Who were they?" I asked Sergeant Loyod. The Sergeant rifled through the boy's pockets and checked the patches on his clothes.

"Best I can tell they were part of a scouting party. They may have a larger force nearby but if we're lucky they were just stuck out here on their own. Get back to the horses, we need to move out now before the others send for reinforcements." Sergeant Loyod slapped my shoulder. "It was a good shot Private. Keep that up and you just may make it out of this war alive. Now let's go." Sergeant Loyod grabbed the boy's rifle from the dirt, stood up with the others and began to walk away. I looked back at the boy as the torch light faded in the distance seeming to drag his poor soul with it.

"What about him?" I asked. "We can't just leave him here." Sergeant Loyod quickly stopped in his tracks and turned his head back.

"The hell we can't. He ain't one of ours Private. Leave him where he lies. The Rebs will come back for him. Or they won't..." I turned back and saw the ashen pale face of what once must have been a bright and warm expression. This wasn't right, this boy didn't belong here. He should have been out chasing squirrels and shooting coons with his friends. What was he doing fighting with the Rebs?

"It ain't right Sergeant. He needs to be buried proper. A Christian burial." I argued. The Sergeant stopped in his tracks with his shoulders raised up high. He spat at my boots and stared me dead in the eyes.

"It ain't right?" Sergeant walked up to me leaning his face in closely to mine. "It ain't right? I'll tell you what ain't right, these sons of bitches leaving our boys to rot in the sun letting the crows pick at their still warm corpses. I've traveled hundreds of miles in this war and I've seen the way they treat our dead. I ain't bout to break a sweat over one dead Johnny Reb; especially not the kind that would ambush us in the dead of night. You best stow away that bleeding heart of yours or its gonna git you killed." Sergeant Loyod spit at my feet once more and glanced at the boy's body. "They can all rot in hell for all I care. Now git your ass to your horse Private. That's an order."

"Yes Sergeant." I marched past the Sergeant as he followed me with his eyes and then walked close behind me. I could feel his anger bearing down on me and I did not wish to incur his wrath any further. We quickly reached the river where several of the Officers waited patiently on us. I knelt on the opposite side finally filling my canteen.

"We got one Captain." said Sergeant Loyod with pride. "Private Roach is a dead shot for sure. Put one right through the back of his heart." Sergeant Loyod handed the rifle over to the Captain who seemed to gladly accept it as a trophy. He smiled and gazed back up.

"Where's Roach?" The Captain asked. I quickly stood and capped off my canteen.

"I am here Sir." Running across the stream I stood in front of the Captain and crisply saluted him which he returned in kind.

"Well done Private. He extended his arm for a hand shake and I gladly accepted it. "I don't believe we have met Private. I am Captain Massengill, Company Commander of Fox Company."

"Good to meet you Sir."

"You're the drummer boy aren't you?"

"I am Sir." I replied reluctantly.

"Well, that may not last long. Were due to pick up some more recruits just before we get to Williamsburg. With a shot like yours I'm gonna need good gunfighters out there. Do you know how to handle a pistol?" My eyes opened wide and I nodded excitedly.

"I do Sir."

"Good, go and see Sergeant Loyod about issuing you a pistol. We have some spares with the Officers supply wagon. Make sure you get yourself a good holster and belt to go with it. No sense in riding with a pistol tucked in your waist band. You'll lose it the moment we have to charge some Rebs in the field."

"Yes Sir. I will Sir." Captain Massengill nodded.

"You are dismissed Private Roach. Carry on." I saluted the Captain before I departed and headed straight away to Abigail where Billie seemed to be waiting in anticipation of a good story.

"What did he want?" he asked anxiously.

"Who?" I pretended to not know but I knew exactly who he was talking about.

"The Captain? Captain Masengill. What did you two talk about?" Billie leaned in closer and raised his eyebrows.

"He's giving me a pistol." I said with a sort of matter of fact tone in my voice.

"You, a Private? You get a pistol. Hot damn! He's proud of you for puttin down that Johnny Reb the way you did." I didn't reply or even glance at Billie. I felt nothing but shame for killing that poor boy. For so long I thought they were just evil men, even monsters, but now I saw the war for something it really was, ugly and cruel. "What's wrong with you? Ain't you happy?"

"Nothing. Just leave it be Billie." Billie cocked his head at me and gave me a peculiar look. He clearly did not understand my grief.

"Don't tell me you're upset bout killing that Johnny Reb back there? That boy and his friends tried to kill us. If it wasn't him it was gonna be us. You get me?" Billie was right. I too quickly forgot the shots that barely missed us along the river bed. It was probably the boy that took the first shot not knowing that an entire company would be hot on his heels. With this in mind I realized that it very well could have been me shot dead on that river bank laying face first in the water. The river would have swept my cold frigid body away and the war would have just gone on without me. I smiled and looked back up at Billie who had his arms crossed in disappointment.

"You're right Billie. That boy shouldn't have been there in the first place." Billie slapped me mildly on the back.

"There ya go. Now get gone and go git yur pistol before we take off." Most of the company was already mounted and I quickly grabbed Abagail by the reins and made my way to the Sergeant whose tent had already been taken down and packed up. He knelt over his saddle pack stuffing it with fresh provisions for the long ride ahead.

"Sergeant." He stood up slowly and turned around with an approving expression like a father who saw his son shoot down a deer for the first time.

"You're here about the pistol." I nodded.

"Yes Sergeant." He took a step to the right and knelt grabbing a pistol stashed between piles of wood next to a smoldering fire. "I heard the Captains orders and already grabbed it for you. This is a Colt Eighteen-Sixty. You ever used a pistol before son?"

"Yes Sergeant but never a revolver. Just them single shot wonders back at home. Paw keeps one stashed away under his pillow in case there's trouble." Sergeant Loyod pulled the pistol from the holster and opened it up revealing the shot chamber.

"Six shots but you gotta load it before we go to fight otherwise you won't have time to get all six in. Load it from front to back, powder, ball, and wad. Percussion caps go on the back to be struck by the hammer. You following me so far Private?"

"Yes Sergeant."

"Don't use it like a rifle, it won't shoot as far. Use it when the Rebs are close or you're going into a building. Point straight at'em and pull the trigger. Nothing else to it." He handed the pistol to me and I closed the breach moving it around to inspect how it worked. "Here's your holster and sixty rounds. Should be enough to get you through a few rides. There's two spare cylinders in there to. Get them loaded up so you can just swap them out in a gun fight. You good?" I looked up at the Sergeant and smiled from ear to ear.

"Yes Sergeant, I'm good."

"Well don't look so damn happy. You're gonna have to carry the damn thing now. Git on your horse and get in formation. You're still my drummer till we get to Williamsburg." I wrapped the belt around my waist quickly securing it and holstering the pistol in place. The weight of it against my hip felt just right.

"Yes Sergeant." I couldn't help but smile at the fact of being the only Private in the Fox Company to carry a pistol. I wasted no time mounting my horse and getting back to the dirt road falling in formation towards the front with my drum at the ready. Sergeant Loyod pulled his painted horse in front of Abigail and pulled on the reins to calm her down.

"Get the men to attention Private. It's time."

"Yes Sergeant." I wrapped the reins around my arms, slapped my horse a few times so she knew the sound was coming and then banged on the drum skin. The remainder of the Eighth fell in quickly and steadied their horses waiting for the next command. The Officers rode slowly past showing no sense of urgency to ride out and Captain Massengill was flanked by two Lieutenants who I had yet to meet. They were very young clean shaven men, probably no older than twenty. They spent some time conversing as they looked over some papers, most likely a map and then the Captain pulled a shiny silver pocket watch from his jacket. He looked back to Sergeant Loyod flagging him to come over. Snapping the reins he and his mare quickly made their way to the Officers huddle at the front of the formation. I tried to listen in but they were very soft spoken this morning and the sound of anxious horses shifting their hooves behind me drowned them out. No doubt Billie would ask me later what they had discussed but I would know even less this time than the last. Sergeant Loyod returned another salute to the Officers and rode straight back at me.

"Alright Private. Move us out."

"Yes Sergeant." I banged on the skin and gave the command to march forward. Leather reins snapped and cracked in the morning air and over one hundred horses moved together in a slow mass down a winding dirt road. I swung the drum down to my side and out of the way of my pistol in case I needed to get to it quickly. Two more days of riding before we made it to Williamsburg. I felt fortunate not to be amongst the men in the Infantry who spent all day and night on their feet. Abigail was my savior indeed and as far as I was concerned the finest damn quarter horse in the Union.

\* \* \*

Despite my best hopes the day did not pass quickly as we sweat like railroad workers clear through our blue uniforms. Every now and then we would pass some Federal men marching in small units along the seemingly unending road. Billie cracked a joke about falling off the edge of the world which made me drift into deep thought about how far the road actually went. Even with the solace of green trees and majestic scenery of the fields there was death up and down this dirt road.

Some men of other regiments had died of exhaustion, others of infection or disease, their bodies left on the side of the road with their hats placed carefully over their expressionless faces waiting for the undertaker to carry them off. The smell of corpses was not unknown to me nor the sight of a dead body but never in my life had I seen so many scattered over such distances. There were places where the air was thick with death and one had to cover his nostrils so not to gag and vomit at the atrocious odor. I turned back to see several cavalry men had affixed handkerchiefs over their mouth and nose to keep the smell at bay. As I considered doing it myself I could see that the Officers and the Sergeant had not performed this act themselves and so I felt compelled that this would not look favorable to them. Sergeant Loyod had spent some time speaking with me throughout the day and gave me even further reason to feel fortunate to be part of the cavalry. He spoke of a foot disease that many infantryman men came down with on long marches. Their feet would become infected and turn black as it mercilessly ate into their flesh. If not properly treated the infection would strike the man with a most terrible fever and he would most likely die within a day. The Officers waved down Sergeant Loyod again and he rode up to speak with them briefly before returning to me.

"Call the company to halt Private. We're stopping here." He commanded of me.

"Yes Sergeant." I pulled my horse to the side of the road and wrapped the reins around my arm quickly before swinging the drum to the front and banging the skin. The men halted their horses as a cloud of dust knocked up from the horses' hooves enveloped us and waited for additional commands.

"Listen up, thirty-minute reprieve. Water and feed your horses down at the river. Fill your canteens up stream, eat some rations and attend to anything else you require. Be quick about it. We need to be ready to move again before we can set up camp about ten miles south of here."

"Yes Sergeant." Was repeated by many men through the ranks. The look of relief washed over the men's faces like a child told to break from his chores. It was not only the ride that wore us down but the sheer boredom of long quiet rides. We were told to keep our mouths shut as much as possible and not to make too much noise during movements. With all the noise the horses made I didn't see why it matter so much. The Confederates could probably hear us a quarter mile out.

"You four." The Sergeant pointed at several men just behind me who had already dismounted their horses. "Come here." The men walked their horses forward and stopped just in front of me. "You four are on watch. You have five minutes to water your horse. Get yourselves about half a mile from here and spread out but make sure you can still see one another. If you see any Johnny Rebs fire a shot in their direction, then ride back here like the devil was on your heels."

"Yes Sergeant." The men reluctantly replied. They mounted their horses and rode off in the distance kicking up dirt under the afternoon's sun.

"Private!" Sergeant Loyod snapped at me.

"Yes Sergeant."

"What are you waiting for? Git your business done before we ride off. I don't want to hear you complaining later when your horse drops dead or you run out of water."

"Yes Sergeant." I hopped down from Abigail and briskly pulled her over to the river. She was breathing hard and spitting out the dust that had collected around her nose. I wiped down her muzzle until her hide was free of the dirt then rubbed the white line that went from the top of her head to her nose to keep her calm. When we reached the bank of the river she suddenly sped up ahead of me and nearly dropped her whole head in the river taking in as much water as she could handle. I gave her a few minutes to drink and rest before walking her back up to a dead oak tree that lay flat along the river and tying her to a thick branch. I walked up the stream a few strides until I was clear of the other horses and filled my canteens. Pulling my hat off my head I dunked it in the river and let it soak before throwing it over my head.

It was so damn hot outside and this river was just what I needed to cool off. As drops of water ran down my face and the back of my neck I looked across the river spotting leaves and watching them gently flow downstream.

Dragonfly's and small birds dotted the riverbank and for a moment you could almost forget that there was a war going on. There was so much peace in this place, it seemed plentiful for all men. Lincoln told us we were going to war to abolish slavery. So much death over a disagreement on what to do with the Negros. We had a few colored fellas in our unit but most of them were with the supply wagon, the cooks, and watching over the Officers necessities. I walked back to Abagail and reached into one of my leather riding pouches and pulled out some salted jerky and two crackers. We would eat better once we stopped at our next camp but my stomach made angry noises and I needed to get something in there. I heard last night some of the back woods boys had headed out from camp and hunted down some coon and even hog. If I was gonna get anything worth eating out here I'd need to go out and hunt it myself or have something worth trading for. I sat next to Abagail on the oak log and she repeatedly bumped here muzzle into me.

"Stop it." I protested but she kept bumping into me. "Abigail, I said stop you dumb beast." She wouldn't stop, she wanted something that I was eating. The horses ate a lot of oats and grains back at Camp Nelson but now they were forced to just eat green grass. She wanted the crackers I had and I was reluctant to hand them over but she kept giving me that look like she had been mistreated in some way. "Oh fine!" I handed over the crackers and she quickly cut them up with her teeth and swallowed every crumb. "You happy now?" She nuzzled my face again with her nose and I gave her a friendly pat down before pushing her away. "I know girl. I'll get you some better food once we get to camp. I promise." She breathed out hard and shook her head shaking off the flies that buzzed incessantly around her ears. I leaned forward and pulled off my riding boots and socks letting my feet air out for a minute for fear of getting that foot rot Sergeant Loyod went on about. My eye lids started to fall as a cool breeze ran across my feet and face. I let my eyes close gently and took in a deep breath.

\* \* \*

"Roach." A voice called out and a hand fell firm on my shoulder. "Private Roach." I looked up to see a boy red of hair and pale of complexion looking down at me. He carried his rifle at the ready and had a panicked look upon his face. "Sergeant Loyod is waiting for you. Better get up and go see him now." I fell asleep against that damn log was so comfortable. My heart started pumping fast in my chest and I threw my socks and boots back on as quickly as I could. Scrambling to my feet I untied Abigail from the log rubbing my eyes with my palms.

"C'mon girl." She pulled back on the reins not wanting to leave. "I said c'mon girl. Git now!" I pulled harder and she followed me. Back into the oak forest and towards the road I saw Sergeant Loyod waiting impatiently for me with crossed arms standing next to his horse as he placed his riding gloves back on.

"I wouldn't fall asleep next to the river if I was you." he warned.

"What do you mean Sergeant?" He reached into his riding bag and pulled out an arrow.

"An Indian arrow? Where'd you get this Sergeant?" He pointed back to where I had fallen asleep and smiled.

"Along the river right by where you were napping. You recognize it?" I shook my head as he handed it over and I gladly grasped the arrow bringing it near my face to examine it closely.

"I ain't seen many arrows before Sergeant. We kept clear of Indians in my family." Paw never spoke well of Indian folk. Always telling stories of raiding parties killing and raping; hurting good innocent folk. He used to say, *the only good Indian is a dead Indian.* Maw didn't like hearin' paw talk like that but she didn't say nothin' bout it.

"It's an arrow of the Cherokee nation. One of three Indian tribes that sided against us with the Rebs. They like using the arrows, keeps things nice and quiet like. I've lost a few boys to the rivers before at the start of the war. They swim up on you like snakes and fill you full of flint before they scalp you and swim off. Sometimes they take a knife and slit your throat when your asleep and send your body down river." Sergeant Loyod snatched the arrow out of my hand and placed it back into his riding pouch. "Don't sleep next to the river. You got it Private?"

"I got it Sergeant." I nodded.

"Good, get the men to attention and back in formation. We need to form up and ride out quickly. We have ten more miles to cover before sunset and I don't want to be stuck riding at night. You never know who's out there watching." I mounted Abigail and quickly slapped the drums. The men all sprang up from their resting places and rode out to meet us on the road. We waited for the Officers to arrive which now seemed like a normal state of affairs. The Officers were always talking, always planning so naturally it took them longer to do anything than the rest of us. Captain Masengill rode up with his Lieutenants in tow and turned his horse around to face the men.

"Move out!" he called out. This was the first time I had heard the Captain call out any orders aloud. Usually he let Sergeant Loyod or the drums do all the talking. I followed up with the march cadence of the drums and rode forward following behind.

\* \* \*

The sun fell heavy against the open fields and lit the sky ablaze as the Tennessee sky seemed to do every evening. The winds picked up from the north and kicked hard against our sun burnt faces. It had been a long and arduous journey. We stopped at a creek just outside of a town called London. Atop a hill I could see torch lights in the distance and the familiar hums of evening night life. The smell of burning oak, beef and pork wafted in the air along with the sounds of men and women laughing happily in the local saloon.

"Do you miss it already?" Sergeant Loyod asked as he walked behind me. I shook my head without a single thought about it.

"I never spent much time in a real town Sergeant. My family are farmers, always farmers. We woke early to tend the farm and went to bed late when we were done tending the farm. I went down to the general store and the lumber yard from time to time but only with my father when he made long trips to town."

"Well, tonight's your lucky night trooper."

"What do you mean Sergeant?" He extended his arm and opened his hand.

"Give me your drum and your sticks." Without hesitation, I pulled the drum strap up over my head and handed it over along with the drum sticks that were tucked under my belt. Sergeant Loyod took them without protest and placed them on the ground next to his horse.

"Did you find a new drummer Sergeant?" I asked curiously.

"No, but you will. I'm sending you down with Captain Masengill to London town. The Officers will bring their horses and a few men with the supply wagons. I need you to help resupply and bring the recruits back up here with you. The youngest of the new recruits will be the new bugle boy."

"Bugle Sergeant?" I was confused, why wouldn't they use my drums?

"Were in town now Private. We can pick up supplies including a bugle. There is a small Union Depot here that will give us everything we need. Stay with the Officers until they are done with their business and whatever you do, don't come back without supplies and new recruits."

"The recruits ain't going back to Camp Nelson?" Sergeant Loyod shook his head with an expression of disappointment as his brow hung dark and heavy over his eyes.

"No private, they are not. Not everyone gets time to be trained like the Eighth. Besides, tomorrow we're going to round up the Rebs in Williamsburg and we need all the bodies we can muster. Now get a move on. Captain Masengill and the other Officers will be waiting on you. Officers are to be waited on, not to be kept waiting."

"Yes Sergeant." I rode off towards the supply train and then tugged on the reins to stop Abigail.

"Is there a problem Private?" Sergeant Loyod snapped.

"No Sergeant, I just wanted to say thank you Sergeant." Loyod's frustration faded to a weak smile.

"Get the hell out of here." I smiled and smacked the reins against Abigail's neck. She rode off quickly and I leaned forward trying to keep up with her. As the men pulled off from the road and set claim to their sleeping quarters for the evening I found Captain Massengill atop his horse next to five supply wagons. The wagons were driven and maintained by the Negro's but since we were going in town it looked like the Negro's were being kicked off the wagons and replaced with white Private's and Corporals. Not all towns were friendly to the colored and I think Captain Massengill was trying to avoid any misunderstandings while we gathered supplies.

"Private Roach, I'm glad you could make it." I saluted promptly and the Captain returned the salute.

"Reporting as ordered Sir."

"Very good. As you can see I've ordered the Negros to remain at camp. Now I am not a man to care one way or another about the color of a man's skin. I find myself more concerned with the content of one's character. However, Williamsburg still has many loyal sons of the south amongst them and I aim not to upset them. The presence of Union soldiers alone tends to raise the displeasure of the locals. Now, when we arrive in town I expect you and the other Privates to meet up with the local recruiter, collect the new recruits and whatever supplies they may have on hand. I want to be in town for no longer than two hours' time. Do you understand?"

"Yes Sir."

"Good man. Now remember Private, we Officers have business of our own to attend to amongst the civilian population. Do not leave without us unless forced to do so by the barrel of a gun." I had a bad feeling about running into trouble in town but the Officers seemed rather calm about the whole thing. If they were confident I supposed I should be all well.

"Yes Sir." I replied.

"I also wanted to introduce you to Lieutenant Campbell and Lieu-tenant Taylor." I presented a crisp saluted which was quickly returned by the young Officers.

"Good evening gentlemen."

"Good evening Private Roach." Lieutenant Campbell replied. "I see you have your pistol on hand." I nodded.

"I do Sir."

"Sergeant Loyod has told us good things about you. We have all agreed that it would be best to keep you in our company in the event of un-pleasantries." Lieutenant Taylor remarked.

"I'm at your service Sir."

"Alright, enough of the courtesy. We have work to attend to. Move out!" Captain Masengill ordered. Reins and whips were cracked over the horses and the wagons creaked forward through the soft trodden dirt paths. Down a gentle hill we rode past oak trees and poison ivy vines that lined the dark foreboding path. At the bottom of the hill all the trees had been cleared out nearly two hundred yards from town and we approached a cluster of lamps and torches where men armed with rifles and shotguns stood at the ready. "Halt!" Captain Masengill ordered. "Private Roach, you come with me and keep your hand close to that pistol. I don't know how welcoming the town's officials will be."

"Yes Sir." We rode forward slowly leaving the Lieutenants and the supply wagons behind. I could hear the wagon drivers cocking their rifles and readying a spare they kept in the back of the wagons. My heart began to race thinking we were sure to get into a skirmish but the Captain seemed as cool as a Tennessee autumn.

"Hold on there!" A voice called out carrying a dimly lit lantern. "State your business here." He demanded.

"I am Captain Masengill, Company Commander of the Eighth Cavalry, Fox Company. This is my supply train; we are here to meet with the Union recruiter and resupply." Three other men stepped forward carrying civilian weapons, mostly shotguns and single shot pistols.

"Do you have any paperwork that might lend some credibility to your business?" The watchman asked.

"I do indecd Sir, but before I present them may I ask who you are?" The man spit in the Captains direction at the feet of his horse and gazed upward with the fire of his lantern reflecting brightly from his eyes.

"I am the law here young man. Sheriff Roberts of London. Sworn to uphold the law and protect the good folk of this town." By the sound of his voice the Sheriff did not seem to doubt his complete authority in town and was little intimidated by our party. From what I could see of the Sheriff he was a short and fat man but the shadows that curved along his face showed and dark and wicked man seeming sort of man.

"It's a pleasure to make your acquaintance Sir." Captain Masengill replied with courtesy but the man just spit again in the Captains direction.

"Uh-huh." He replied. "Look Captain, we got us a lot of good upstanding folk in this town, good southern god fearing folk you see. Many of them don't take kindly to your type wandering about and it would upset them an awful lot if I just let you pass during the evening hours when folks are out tryin to have a good time." I could see the Captain was becoming frustrated. I gazed behind us to see the Lieutenants keeping their hands dangling over their pistols.

"And what type might that be Sheriff?" The Sheriff spit his chew again.

"The kind in Blue Captain."

"I see. And what about the Sergeant that occupies the local recruiting post? Is he not a welcome guest of your town?"

"Oh, you mean Sergeant Howard? Well, we have a sort of understanding if you catch my meaning." The Captain nodded.

"I see. And this understanding you have with my Sergeant, is this something that perhaps you and I could share as well?" The Sheriff looked back at his men who lowered their rifles from their shoulders and suddenly seemed at ease with our presence.

"Well then, I don't see why not. I'm sure we are both fine Christian men. I'm sure we can come to a mutual understanding." Captain Masengill sneered and reached into his jacket and the men behind the Sheriff raised their rifles and beaded down on him quickly. Captain Masengill opened his free hand and lifted his head.

"Calm yourselves gentleman, my pistol is firmly on my hip. I'm just reaching for some of that understanding your Sheriff and I are coming to." The Captain slowly pulled a leather pouch from his jacket and handed it down to the Sheriff; he snatched it from him eagerly. "Does that seem to be enough understanding for my men and I to do what we need and leave in a few hours?" the Sheriff opened the pouched to reveal green backs from the Union.

"I don't know if this is the same understanding I was talking about there Captain. You see, round here were used to the kind of understanding that comes in blue or maybe even something a bit heavier." Captain Masengill nodded and reached into his case removing a leather pouch and tossed it down to the Sheriff. Roberts bounced the pouch in his hand making the familiar chime of coin.

"You can keep them both." Captain Masengill remarked. "Think of it as a sign of goodwill." Sheriff Roberts nodded his head and looked back at his men who lowered their weapons once more.

"Yup, that'll about do it. Thank you for your patronage Captain Masengill and welcome to London town. Your path is temporarily clear." The Captain turned back and waved the wagons forward. Once they caught up I slapped the reins and rode forward with the Officers. I looked back to see that we were clear of the Sheriff and his men before opening my mouth.

"Captain Sir?"

"Yes Private?"

"Why didn't you order us to shoot those men?" I asked quietly. The Captain laughed and threw me a quick glance with a crooked smile.

"Shoot them? Private, do you know how many of those good old boys in town would come after us if I laid their brothers low? The whole damn town would hunt us down and shoot us in the knee caps just so they could tar and feather us before they strung us up on that old oak tree. No Private, shooting them would not be a wise strategy."

"Yes Sir." Despite being from New York Captain Masengill seemed pretty knowledgeable on how to deal with the locals. London approached quickly and my eyes grew wide as I soaked in the sights of the biggest city I had ever seen. A long finely beaten dirt road drove straight in-between stores, saloons, and manors of all sorts that split down other roads with more buildings finely lit by lamps outside of each home. We approached a brightly lit building on the corner that was busy with London's night life. As we rode closer I saw men standing outside wearing cowboy hats and leather dusters leaning against the hitching posts and walls of a saloon. They sneered at us and spit in our direction at the dirt grumbling under their breath. I stared inside the building to see a loud and bustling scene filled with locals of all types, merchants, farmers, businessmen and of course, ladies of the night. The whores lined the alley just behind the saloon and they whistled as we rode past but I pretended to ignore them. A small building directly next to the saloon was labeled the recruiting post and inside sat a solitary Sergeant at a writing desk with a single lit lamp. We pulled up to the hitching post and dismounted from the horses. I didn't wait for the Captain and quickly tied Abigail off to the post.

"Sergeant!" Captain Masengill called out as he removed his riding gloves and tucked them under his belt. "Sergeant Howard!" The Sergeant jumped up seeming startled and ran outside quickly to greet the Captain. As he exited the door he placed a pair of fine copper bound spectacles to his face. Only one other time had I seen a man wear such a contraption on his face and for some reason it made the Sergeant appear smarter than he probably was. He locked his gaze on the Captain and popped smartly to attention rendering a proper salute.

"Captain Masengill! Good evening Sir." Captain Masengill seemed to return this salute with a greater level of enthusiasm than I was used to seeing.

"Good evening Sergeant." The Captain lowered his salute.

"What are you doing in London at this time Sir?" Captain Masengill looked up and down the road both sides and with a serious expression said,

"Perhaps we should go inside and chat. Do you have whiskey in your supply Sergeant?"

"I do indeed Sir."

"Wonderful." Captain Masengill looked back at me. "Private, you can join us inside. The rest of you, watch the wagons and the door until I return." The men on the wagons saluted and the Lieutenants saluted as well.

"Yes Sir." They said as we walked into the recruiting post. The room was small and simple with a few recruiting posters on the wall and dry rations boxed up in the corner. Sergeant Howard scrambled quickly to grab another chair for the Captain while I stood firm in front of the door. I didn't understand why he didn't bring Lieutenant Campbell or Taylor inside but I assumed it had something to do with him wanting me to stand guard so I did just that.

"Have a seat Captain." Sergeant Howard said as he brushed the dust away from the chair.

"Don't mind if I do Sergeant." The Captain sat down heavy in the chair and kicked his dusty boots up on the desk while Sergeant Howard opened a drawer and nervously fumbled through some belongings until he came upright with a half full bottle of Tennessee brown and two dirty glasses that were stained on the bottom. The Sergeant pulled the glasses to his jacket and hurriedly began to wipe them down but the Captain pulled the glass away from him to Sergeant Howard's shock.

"Captain Sir that glass is dirty. Let me clean it up for you." Masengill shook his head and raised an open hand.

"Nonsense Sergeant Howard. I'll not have this glass cleaned, it'll take away the flavor. Now pour me a shot before I die of thirst." Sergeant Howard smiled and quickly poured until half his glass was full. Captain Masengill seemed displeased and snatched the bottle from the Sergeant. "Now is that any way to treat your superior Officer?" The Captain poured the Tennessee Brown heavy until it reached clear to the rim of the glass. "Now that is how it's done Sergeant." Sergeant Howard smiled and nodded.

"Yes Sir. I do say you know how best to pour a glass of whiskey. Now Captain, what can I assist you with?" Sergeant Howard leaned forward to listen intently to what the Captain had to say.

"Were set to assist in an engagement against the Rebs south of here sometime tomorrow."

"Williamsburg Sir?" The Sergeant asked.

"That's right Sergeant. The Ohio Infantry has asked for our assistance and we aim to do just that. Those grey jacketed bastards have been sniping at our men from trees, bushes, buildings, stables, and all sorts of places that no honorable man would strike another man from. Bottom line is the Infantry does not have the speed nor the numbers to flush old Johnny Reb from the bush." He lifted his glass and took a hearty drink, nearly half of the whiskey he had poured down his throat and then slammed the glass down heavy on the worn oak desk. "I aim to change that."

"Well yes Sir. How can I help you?" Howard said nervously as he continued to rifle through some papers.

"I need your bodies Sergeant, as many as you can spare for the Eighth. Do you have your most recent list of volunteers?" The Sergeant looked at Captain Masengill as if he was perplexed or confused by the request. He glanced over at me, smiled, and then turned back to the Captain adjusting the spectacles on his face.

"Well, yes Sir Captain Sir, but those boys are bound for Camp Nelson to get properly trained and outfitted before they head out to the field." Sergeant Howard placed his hands on the desk and began tapping his fingers up and down making a sort of drummers tune.

"I asked for the list Sergeant, not your excuses." Sergeant Howard nodded and pulled his desk drawer open again reaching for some papers pulling out a solitary piece that he reluctantly handed to Captain Masengill.

"Yes Sir. Here's the list." The Captain dropped his feet from the desk and sat upright to read the list under the light of Sergeant Howard's lamp.

"Hmmm." Captain Masengill muttered. "What are all these names crossed out for?" Sergeant Howard looked nervous and sweat began to drip down from his face causing his spectacles to slip further down his nose. He pushed them back up again and leaned in to speak.

"Those are the boys that deserted Sir." He blurted out as he nervously adjusted his spectacles closer to his eyes.

"Deserted?"

"Well, defected Sir. Those boys got swept up by the Confederates and they ran off to fight with them." Captain Masengill let the paper fall to the desk and slammed his fist down.

"How the hell did you lose them?"

"That's just it Sir, there's a lot of folks around these parts that don't sit right with the North. A few Confederate soldiers came through these parts just a few days ago, offered good coin same day for anyone that would fight on their side."

"Sergeant Howard..." The Captain said with frustration in his voice. "Does the town not have a telegraph available for your use?" he nodded repeatedly.

"Why yes Sir it does." The Captain clenched his fists.

"And are you not capable of sending messages when Rebs come waltzing through London in your presence."

"Why yes Sir but..." Captain Massengill stood and lifted his glass polishing off the last of his whiskey and then threw the glass against the wall shattering it to a thousand pieces.

"Then why the hell is this the first time I'm hearing of this? If the telegraph was broken you could have sent a rider and if there were no riders by god you should have gunned them down yourself! Forty-two? Forty-two! Forty-two boys that could have fought with us are now gonna fight against us because of you! Because of your incompetence!" The Sergeant began to stand but kept his head and shoulders lowered perhaps out of fear. I felt a bit tense standing at the door but felt no inclination to become involved in the conversation. If what had transpired was true than Sergeant Howard seemed beyond saving.

"Captain Massengill I understand your upset Sir but I can't send no messages out of London. The locals, why the Sheriff himself would hang me from the old oak tree just outside of town." Captain Masengill lunged forward gripping Sergeant Howard by the collar and pulled him in closely.

"Good, then at least you would die a hero of the Union and not the sniveling Non-Commissioned Officer I see before me. The Private here has more back-bone than you." Captain Massengill released him and Sergeant Howard rubbed the scruff of his neck roughly to wipe away the pain. "Where are the other fifteen boys Sergeant?" Howard lifted his arm and pointed outside.

"I got them put up in the hotel across from the saloon Sir. Just waiting to be picked up."

"Well, wake'em up and get them outside. They're going to spend the night in camp and report to me going forward. I don't need any more boys wandering off to fight for Johnny Reb."

"So they're not going to Camp Nelson Sir?" Sergeant Howard asked nervously.

"No Sergeant, they are not! We have enough supplies, weapons, and horses to support their immediate needs. I will however require that you direct my wagons to the depot so we can pick up additional provisions." The Sergeant stood there for a moment seeming almost unable to move. "Well Sergeant, what the hell are you waiting for?"

"Yes Sir, right away Sir." The Sergeant leapt up from his chair and headed out to the street towards the hotel. Captain Masengill began to laugh under his breath and pushed Sergeant Howard's glass towards me.

"You ever drink Tennessee Brown Private Roach?"

"Can't say that I have Sir." He motioned with his head towards the glass that shone brightly under the light of the lamp.

"Take it. It's yours. Tomorrow you will be baptized under fire. If tomorrow were to be your last day I wouldn't want you to go to the gates of the almighty without having tasted whiskey. Saint Peter himself might turn you away." I tried to keep my bearing but cracked a smile out of the corner of my mouth and reached for the glass. I lifted it up to my nose and breathed deeply, it was strong and made my head shake and the hair on my arm stand up straight. "Go on." The Captain urged. I lifted the glass and threw it back swallowing as fast as I could. It burned something awful going down and I closed my eyes and gritted my teeth. When I breathed out if felt like fire coming out of my throat. "That's a good man. Now, let's get outside with the horses and get ready to leave. Wouldn't want to overstay our welcome." We stepped outside as the wagons rode past to the supply depot and quickly mounted our horses once more riding towards the hotel. Boys were already lining up outside yawning and stretching; awakening from their presumably peaceful slumber. I had been in the Union Army for no more than three weeks but already I felt like a veteran compared to these soft looking things. "Private Roach?"

"Yes Sir?"

"You stay here and keep an eye on the boys. Can you read?"

"I can Sir." I replied confidently.

"Very good. Take this register and call out the names to get a proper head count. Make sure everyone not crossed off on the list is here and able bodied." I took the register in hand and looked it over briefly. It was a simple enough task for me to complete on my own.

"Yes Sir I will." The Captain stomped loudly into the hotel and disappeared from sight. I looked down the list and began calling out the names of the boys who responded quickly and sharply. It wasn't long before all the names were checked off. "Alright boys, just wait here for the supply train and we'll be off." The streets were now dead quiet, not even the saloon itself made a peep and the moon hung high on a cloudless evening lighting the town streets below. I got back up on Abigail and waited patiently for the Captain and his Lieutenants to return while the boys leaned against the outside of the hotel making jokes and placing bets on how many soldiers they'd kill the first chance they got. I felt stupid after hearing them banter on because no more than a few weeks ago that was me. I was sure that I would single handedly win the war and kill hundreds or even thousands of Rebs but now I had seen the road, seen all the young bodies rotting in the sun looking like bad beef and getting picked apart by the crows. Nothing good was about to happen for those boys once we got out to the road. Some of them would die from the heat, some would die from sickness or infection, and some of us would die tomorrow fighting Johnny Reb.

I didn't really smile that much anymore, at least not like I used to. I felt like my happiness had been taken from me. Something inside had changed and I didn't know if it was for the better or not; perhaps it was just part of becoming a man. Nearly half an hour had passed and the wagon trains pulled up. The lead driver waved me over and I gave Abigail a little love tap to move her towards him.

"You seen the Captain?" The wagon driver asked me. I shook my head.

"No, he went inside about thirty minutes ago following the Lieutenants. Haven't seen him since." The driver smiled and wiped his lips with his sleeve.

"Must be in there giving the ladies a good time. I don't like this town much. Not after that meetin' with the Sheriff. I think it best we git gone sooner than later." Just then loud footsteps came walking outside. Captain Masengill appeared adjusting his belt and pants then straightened out his hat. Lieutenant Campbell and Taylor pressed through the swinging doors just after him both appearing flush in the face. Taylor in particular seemed worn and almost pale as a ghost. Campbell turned to notice Taylor's expression and gave him a nudge with his elbow. Taylor came to and adjusted himself before they both went back for their horses.

"Private, is everyone accounted for?" Captain Masengill asked as he wiped the sweat of his brow with a white handkerchief.

"Yes Sir. All fifteen."

"Very good." Captain Masengill turned back towards the boys placing his hands on his hips. "Gentlemen, and I do use the term loosely, may I have your ears. I know you had planned to go to Camp Nelson to get some training before you headed out but that won't be happening. It won't be happening because we need you, we need your help. I am Captain Massengill, Commander of Fox Company or Company "F" if you will. Going forward you are under my command and the command of my Non-Commissioned Officers, Sergeants, Corporals and so forth. Is that understood?"

"Yes Sir." They responded nearly in unison.

"Very good. When we get to camp just over yonder the quartermaster will issue you uniforms, weapons, and supplies. Is there anyone here who does not know how to fire a rifle?" Not one of the boys raised their hands and most of them seemed overly confident in their marksmanship skills. "Are you sure, because if you can't load and fire a rifle I need to know here and now before I put you on the back of a horse." The boys remained silent. "Very well. Private Roach, see to it that they get on the wagon train."

"Yes Sir. You heard the Captain, get on the wagons. Let's go." The boys quickly pushed off from the hotel walls and climbed into the back of the wagons. Their faces beamed with excitement at the idea of a grand adventure that lay before them. If only they knew...

"Private Roach, did you see where Sergeant Howard went to?" Captain Masengill asked. I looked up and down the road and shook my head.

"No Sir. I haven't seen him since we left the recruiting post. I thought he'd be here." Captain Masengill seemed suspicious and whipped his horse around kicking the beast forward while looking intently in windows and down alley ways. I followed him and the sound of voices from behind the hotel caught our attention. Captain Masengill raised his gloved hand in the air with a closed fist signaling me to stop. I did so and listened as the quiet voices became louder in my ear. Three, maybe four men and one of them sounded an awful lot like Sergeant Howard. The Captain dismounted and I followed suit quietly jumping down from Abigail. We crept down a dark and narrow alley between two buildings and as the voices became louder the Captain drew his pistol and I did the same. We reached the back corner of the building and listened in intently to the voices bouncing and echoing softly off the walls.

"But I can't." said a voice that sounded like Sergeant Howard's. "If I try to give you any more boys they'll find out and hang me for certain."

"If you don't do as your told I'll gut you like the gutter fish you are. Is that what you want boy?"

"How much did we pay you? How much did good old General Lee pay you to do the good Lord's work? He kept you fat, happy, and drunk and this is the best you can do for the south land? This is how you repay our generosity?"

"Now boys, let's not get hasty. I got plenty more boys coming through town next week but I can't give all of them to you. Let's just put away the knives and work something out. I got rations and ammunition back at the post. You can take all of it."

"Oh were gonna work something out alright. Were gonna take everything you got and then were gonna take just a little more. You get me boy?" Captain Masengill charged around the corner and I followed him to see Sergeant Howard pinned against the wall by three men in Grey coats. Startled they turned back quickly, one with a large bowie knife in his hand and the others slowly reaching for their pistols.

"What the hell is this?" said the one with the knife. "Did you tell him about us?"

"I didn't, I swear! I didn't tell them nothing."

"He's lying! Well looks like we got ourselves a good old fashioned standoff." Captain Massengill pulled back the hammer on his pistol.

"Sergeant Howard, under the authority of the President of the United States I am taking you prisoner to hang for your crimes of treason." The man with the bowie knife took a large step forward bending at the knees somewhat seeming ready for a fight.

"Oh he ain't goin nowhere Captain; and neither are you and your boy." A loud crack and a puff of smoke exploded as Captain Massengill pulled the trigger of his gun. The other two pulled their pistols and I drew down on them in parallel with the Captain. When the smoke cleared the three men had fallen and we had emptied our pistols entirely into them. The Captain wasted no time and grabbed Sergeant Howard throwing him to the ground on top of the Rebs quivering bodies and pistol whipped him. Sergeant Howard's spectacles flew off his face and he screamed putting up his hands in surrender.

"Please Sir no! I had no choice! They would have killed me…" He sobbed like a child begging not to be beat by his parents. I felt no pity for this man and even looked forward to what was to come next.

"And how many of our men have you killed by sending boys to fight for the South? Huh? You fucking yellow belly coward! I should gut you here and now!" Other soldiers rounded the corner and ran up behind us. I turned quickly with pistol at the ready but when I saw blue uniforms I dropped my guard.

"Captain what happened?" Lieutenant Campbell asked.

"Looks like we have a traitor boys. Get him and these bodies in the wagon as fast as you can. The Sheriff will be down on us soon after those shots." I grabbed the feet of one dead man and helped carry him out while Sergeant Howard was forced into the wagon train by Lieutenant Campbell.

"I didn't have a choice Captain! Please you have to…" The wagon driver hit Sergeant Howard over the head with the butt of his rifle sending him crashing face first to the wagon floor.

"That'll shut you up!" The wagon driver exclaimed. After I finished helping get a body in one of the wagons I ran back to Abigail who waited steadfast for me to return. She was a little jumpy at first but I had no time to console her now. I snatched the reins and jumped on my saddle.

"Let's go Private. The Sheriff will be here any moment. Yah!" We rode like the devil out of town through the opposite end as quickly as possible. When the last building passed, we took a wide trek back to camp and in the dark distance behind us we could see lamps, torches, and hear the echoes of men yelling and arguing in the gloom. The Sheriff and his men must have finally found the pools of blood where his Confederate allies once lay. Under the cover and protection of the oak wood the sights and sounds of London disappeared and soon we were approached by the watch of the Eighth that bared down with their rifles until they could recognize us.

"We heard gunfire. What happened?" A watchman asked me.

"We came up on some Rebs." The watchman's eyes grew wide.

"How many? Should we get in formation?" I shook my head.

"No. It was just three of'em but the town Sheriff and his posse are Southerners. They'll be looking for us near town."

"You think they'll ride up here on us?" he asked nervously.

"You have nothing to fear Private." Captain Masengill replied. "If the Sheriff rode up on us it would be his final act as Sheriff of London, or as Sheriff anywhere for that fact." I pulled Abigail off to the side and let the wagon train pass by so I could meet up with Captain Masengill. The wagon driver that held Sergeant Howard had already stopped and with the assistance of several other Privates, dragged Sergeant Howard out of the backside along with the dead Rebs who were laid out next to each other.

"Sergeant Loyod!" Captain Masengill called out loudly. Other men of the camp repeated his call until it made its way down the regiment to the Sergeant. A dark figure came running forward and the gold stripes on his sleeve cut through the darkness. Sergeant Loyod saluted Captain Masengill.

"Captain Masengill Sir. We heard some shots in the distance and sent scouts. Is everything alright?"

"Private Roach came through for us once again Sergeant." Loyod peered at me over his bushy grey mustache. "Our recruiter in London was found to be collaborating with the confederates and recruiting men to send their way. We killed the Rebs but Sergeant Howard remains unharmed." Sergeant Loyod looked over the bodies that now appeared ashen pale and motionless beneath the lamp light. He pointed to the watch;

"You men, search them. Turn out their pockets. I want to see everything on their person." The watch lay their rifles next to the bodies and began searching them one at a time stripping off their duster jackets, boots, hats, and then pulled their pockets inside out. By the time they were done twelve knives, two pocket pistols, and a few coins were recovered.

"Sergeant." A Private called out.

"What is it Private Michaels?" The short young man held up a piece of parchment covered in writing.

"This one had this in his pocket." Sergeant Loyod took the paper and began reading it over his eyes bouncing back and forth as he followed the words. The more he read the angrier the expression on his face became.

"Get Sergeant Howard up here!" Howard was pulled forward by ropes that bound his hands and neck.

"Let go of me! I'm innocent! Why won't you listen to me?" Sergeant Howard begged but his pleas for mercy fell on deaf ears. Private Michaels came up behind Howard and struck the back of his left knee sending him to the ground. Sergeant Loyod bent down and pulled Sergeant Howard up by his salt and pepper hair. Howard strained his neck and breathed rapidly as the vein in his forehead bulged outward.

"What the hell is this?" Sergeant Loyod demanded holding the paper rigidly in front of Howard.

"I don't know, that's the first time I've seen that! I swear to god!" Sergeant Loyod pulled his hand back and gripping the paper in his fist punched Howard clean across the face. Howard's head swung back and when he brought it forward he spat out blood and coughed a few times.

"You swear to God? As far as your concerned right now I am the father, the son, and the holy spirit! Don't lie to me you traitorous piece of shit! What is this? Tell me now or so help me I'll tie each of your limbs to the horses and let them rip you to pieces. What is it?" Howard's eyes welled up with tears and he sobbed like a grief-stricken widow.

"Please! I didn't have a choice. They would have killed me if I didn't do it!"

"Do what?" Sergeant Loyod demanded. "Do what god damnit?"

"The Confederates have been entrenched in this town since I've been here. They pulled me out of the saloon on my first night, beat the hell out of me, cut my chest with a knife and they swore they would cut my balls off if I didn't cooperate!"

"What did you do Howard?" Sergeant Loyod asked with his thumb pressed against the man's left eye. Loyod pushed harder and harder into Howards skull as he screamed in absolute pain.

"They made me recruit for them and give them Union supplies!" he confessed.

"Why didn't you report this? We could have sent help, cleaned the town out?" Sergeant Howard shook his head repeatedly as blood trickled down his face.

"No. It's no use. The Rebs are everywhere in this town. There's no safe place. No refuge! All my telegrams were intercepted, and my letters read before they went out in the post. The Sheriff has that town under his control. There ain't nothing that he doesn't know." Sergeant Loyod pushed Howard's head into the dirt and released his grip of Howard's hair.

"Take a look for yourself Sir." Loyod handed the paper over to Captain Masengill who quickly examined it with a stern expression.

"Well I think this is all very plain." Captain Masengill stepped in front of Howard. "Get him on his feet!" The watch lifted the beaten and bruised Sergeant Howard upright and made him face the Captain. "Sergeant Howard, by the authority given to me by the President of these United States; Abraham Lincoln, I hereby sentence you to hang by the neck until you are dead. This sentence shall be carried out immediately."

"No! No, you can't!" Howard's tears sprang forth like a spring in the mountains but Captain Masengill stood firm in his resolve.

"Do you have anything to say before this sentence is carried out?" Sergeant Howard lifted his open hands begging and pleading for mercy.

"No, please! Captain, it wasn't my fault; it wasn't my fault!"

"Very well, gag him! Find a large oak next to the road and string up the dead Rebs next to him. We need to send a message to the Sheriff and London."

"No! No!" Sergeant Loyod pulled a rag from his pocket and forcefully crammed it into Howard's mouth. I helped the watch move the

Confederate bodies next to the big oak and dropped them hard in the dirt again while other men came up with rope and lamp lights. They didn't waste any time wrapping the ropes around their necks, tying them off and lifting their bodies clean into the air. Three dead Johnny Rebs now swung high back and forth casting a ghastly shadow against the giant oak. I glanced at Howard whose skin had turned pale white, beads of sweat running fast down his forehead as his eyes bounced about quickly probably searching for some means of escape or a sign of mercy.

"Tie him up." Captain Masengill commanded. Sergeant Loyod grabbed the rope and tied it around Howard's neck himself while the men of the Eighth Cavalry continued to pile in behind us conversing back and forth with one another in anticipation of the hanging.

"Private Roach, get over here and hold him still." Without hesitation, I stood in front of Howard and gripped his jacket tightly to keep him from falling over. He looked at me with desperation, blood shot brown eyes and tears falling from his face. Loyod finished the hangman's knot and slapped Howard on the side of the face.

"Traitors go to hell Howard; I hope you're ready to meet Satan cause god ain't gonna save you. C'mon Roach." Sergeant Loyod fell back into the ranks holding the other end of the rope. "Ready Sir!" Loyod called out to Captain Masengill.

"Very good Sergeant. Sergeant Howard, by the authority given to me by the President of these United States; Abraham Lincoln I hereby sentence you to die by hanging for the crime of treason. This is your last chance Sergeant Howard; do you have anything to say before you meet your maker?" Howard lowered his head in hopeless shame and remained silent. "Very well. Sergeant Loyod, carry out the sentence."

"Grab the rope lads." I fell in with several other men who gripped the rope and pulled it until the slack had given out. "Pull!" Sergeant Loyod commanded. We walked backward quickly and Sergeant Howard's body was raised effortlessly in the air like a specter in the night. Private Michaels and Sergeant Loyod tied off the rope around the base of another tree securing it snugly. I watched in dread as the traitor

Sergeant Howard danced the hangman's jig. His legs and feet kicked and kicked and kicked swinging from side to side trying desperately to find something to prop themselves up on. His head went from pale, to red, blue, and then purple. His eyes and veins of his neck bulged outward twitching every which way until suddenly his head stopped moving. His legs no longer kicked and his feet twitched beneath his body; liquid came flowing down his pant legs and dripping to the ground. A foul smell filled the air and Howards pants had darkened with the last of the excrement in his body.

"Roach." Sergeant Loyod pulled my attention away from the final moments of Howard's death.

"Yes Sergeant." I said softly as I found it difficult to pull my eyes away.

"Is this the first time you've seen a hanging?" I swallowed my spit and cleared my throat.

"I've seen men hung up on a tree Sergeant but I've never been there to watch them die. Not like this."

"They always piss themselves when they die. There's nothing glorious in death son. It's an ugly and foul thing. Just remember that." Loyod lowered the bill of his hat and slowly walked away seeming disinterested now that the deed had been done. I turned back to see the orange glow of the lamps and torches casting the shadows of the dead as giants against the mighty oak. One by one men of the Eighth walked away from the grim scene and headed back to their duties but I did not turn away, I barely blinked as I looked upon the now deceased Sergeant Howard in the face. I saw, or at least I think I saw his eyes move and I wondered if for a moment, Sergeant Howard was still alive; but perhaps it was merely the light of the flames playing tricks on me. When I departed my little log home, this is not what I had envisioned war would be like. I had yet to be in battle and already death was everywhere and hung heavy in the air thick as pitch fog. Tomorrow would be a grim day indeed.

# Six
# The Scott Raid –
# August 1st, 1863

"Fire!" Cannons roared spewing fire and iron from the top of a gradual slope pounding the small town of Williamsburg and the surrounding tree line that was rumored to be infested with Confederates. I waited patiently in the early morning air lined up with the rest of the Eighth as Captain Masengill and his Lieutenants spoke with the Officers of the Ohio Forty Fourth Infantry unit that had been holding back the Rebs. Each time the cannons roared Abigail flinched a little and I leaned on her patting her neck down giving reassurance that everything would be fine.

"It's alright girl. Those cannons aren't meant for us. Quiet now girl." She shook her head and snorted loudly in protest. "Steady girl, I need you steady today." Beyond the four blistering cannons and rummaged wagons were what looked like hastily dug trenches with only a handful of boys sitting deep inside their fighting holes staying well clear of the cannon fire. Just beyond that in the flatter part of the field were pickets where the majority of the Ohio Forty Fourth maintained a ragged looking fighting line. I looked up and down the picket lines expecting to see more men but it appeared to be no more than seventy to a hundred soldiers all huddled behind the wood planks with gaps between the men every ten or fifteen paces. They seemed to be in poor shape with little provisions, terribly tattered clothing and low ammunition.

"Fire!" The Artillery Officer called out once more; his bright red shirt making him stand out from everyone around him. It was a wonder to me that a sharp shooter had not yet made his mark on him. Each cannon fired with near perfect timing one after the other. Some shells struck in open fields and others cut through oak trees as a sickle cuts through the grass. The crack of timber was explosive and echoed loudly against the valley floor that trembled. I could hear faint voices in the distance, yells, screams, and commands but still could not see the enemy force. Captain Masengill and his Lieutenants rode towards us after meeting with the Commanding Officer of the Forty Fourth.

"Gentleman, semi-circle, let's go!" Captain Masengill ordered. He brought our horses in closely and Abigail bucked a little as we were squeezed by the herd. "Listen up, this is going to be a delaying action. Colonel Gilbert of the Ohio Forty Fourth was ordered to hold this position; unfortunately, they are down to just one hundred men with few provisions and the only thing keeping them from being overrun is the cannon fire. Their supplies and communication lines have been sabotaged on a number of occasions and they are unable to maintain artillery suppression beyond this afternoon. We will flank the enemy position heading south and then swinging east until we can engage them head on and hopefully without warning. While we take attention away from the men at the picket lines they will begin to retreat back to their cannons, pack up what they can and head back for our camp outside of London. Once the Infantry is clear we will retreat and run straight across the field until we can meet up with and escort these boys back to a more defensible position. Is that clear?"

"Yes Sir." We said in unison.

"If you become separated or lost ride north-west until you find a Union regiment that can get you back to us. If you are injured do not ask or plead with the Rebs to help you. I have on many occasions watched them sweep up the fields. The only medicine they will offer is a bayonet to the chest. These are not gentleman soldiers, remember that. I wish you all the best and may god watch over you." Captain Masengill swung his horse about and rode to the front of the column.

"Fall in!" Sergeant Loyod ordered. We fell back in and formed a column two by two. "Forward!" The horses galloped and I gave Abigail a light kick and snap of the reins to move her onward. The dirt and dust kicked up heavy with the sun beaming down on our left. My sabre bounced and rattled next to me and I reached down with my free hand to tighten the strap. The rattling stopped and the sabre ceased banging my thigh. It wasn't long before we turned east under the cover of the thick Tennessee woods with the battlefield and picket lines to our left where I saw the boys of the Forty Fourth looking on in quiet desperation at our action. The guns still roared mercilessly and now I could hear the cannon balls whistle as they ripped through the sky before crashing down on their victims. Some distance beyond the pickets Captain Masengill slowed our pace and turned us north. This was it, through these trees and beyond a few berms would be the Confederate troops waiting to hard-heartedly greet us with lead and steel. Clenched fists went up in the air signaling for us to hold and stay quiet. I could see Captain Masengill un-holster his pistol and move forward with Sergeant Loyod scouting ahead while the Lieutenants maintained the column. They disappeared over a small incline and behind a few trees. My heart started to pound hard in my chest not knowing if they would be killed or if we would be set upon by hundreds of blood-thirsty grey coats. My mind wandered to the worst places and I closed my eyes for a moment to shake it off. When I opened them, the Lieutenants had dismounted and were laying down in the dirt at the top of the berm trying to get a better vantage point. Horse hooves beat loudly on dry twigs and then the Captain and Sergeant rounded the corner on foot walking their horses back.

"You ready?" A voice said softly behind me. I looked back to see Billic leaning down on his horse.

"Billie." I smiled and reached my hand back for a hearty handshake. "About as ready as I'll ever be. I'm just prepared to get this thing done." Billie smiled back at me.

"I know what you mean. Good luck Roach. I got your back."

"Thanks. Good luck Billie." I turned my head forward and saw the Lieutenants pointing to each far side of the formation instructing us to get into a fighting line and break up the double column. I pulled Abigail to the left and rode out to the far side nearest the edge of the tree line. Our line stretched for quite some distance across the wood; nearly one hundred men and horses in all. Captain Massengill removed his sword and we followed suit pulling swords, pistols, and lever action rifles. My arms felt cold and lifeless as the blood pounded heavier in my chest. I gripped my sabre and pulled it skyward, though I don't know how it did not fall from my grip. My hand seemed weak as the handle of my sword felt as if it pressed tightly against my bones. I gave Abigail a light tap and we began a slow march forward over several small inclines and around trees. I peered through the forest and saw nothing of the enemy and wondered if they were hiding, waiting and ready for us. Musket shot could be heard in the distance getting louder, louder, and louder. I glanced to the left and could see the boys of the Ohio Forty Fourth just ahead in the distance taking fire from the Rebs. The further we pushed our horses ahead the more apparent the voices became. A cloud of smoke and gun powder filled the air concealing us further but we could not see the enemy either; in fact, it seemed we would not see them until we were on top of them and they on top of us. My mind wandered to the thought of bayonets bristling forth from the bushes and trees and the fear of being skewered by a hundred blades.

"Charge!" a brave voice commanded. I could not see or notice who had called the command but all at once the horses sped forward and now we were dashing through the forest weaving in and around trees through the heaps of dense smoke. Cavalry bugles blared and trumpeted their fight song and it gave me courage as Abigail pulled me into the unknown. Without warning, without a fair glimpse, grey clothed figures appeared before us and darted in and out of view until I could clearly see trenches with men resting against the berm. I pulled my blade back quickly and swung downward as Abigail ran straight into the fray. The first of the Rebs did not see me until I was right on top of him. Abigail stepped on his head crushing the boy beneath her feet not even giving me the chance to swing my sword; the brief sound of his skull cracking under her weight sent a cold chill down my spine.

The next few boys stood and tried to give way to our charge but they were too late. I swung my blade and glanced a man against his neck as he tried to run away. The blood sprayed on my face and into my eyes. I had to wipe it away to see anything and as I did so I could feel Abigail barrel through at least two more men as they yelled and scrambled for their lives. Gun fire began to shift from the Ohio Forty Fourth to us but our charge was so quick and so fierce that I had already found myself in the center of their camp. A melee broke out and pistols were drawn to deal with the hordes of grey jackets pouring out of the bush. The cloud of smoke grew more intense and we could only see twenty feet from our faces or so. It was unnerving as bayonets appeared out of nowhere and my revolver was suddenly empty with no time to reload. I holstered it and pulled my sabre once more kicking Abigail hard trying to keep speed on my side. On the opposite end of a supply train, muzzle fire intensified and poured down heavy on us like a thunderous hail. Abigail cried allowed as a shot hit her front shoulder spattering blood on the ground.

"Yah! Yah!" I called out as I kicked Abigail and slapped her reins urging her to move quickly. I rode straight for that train wagon. Shot cracked and whipped in the air all around dropping branches and leaves from the sky; they fell gracefully like tiny dancers amongst the chaos. A man in a long pointy hat came around the corner with a bayonet and as he raised it I swung fast and hard with my sabre nicking the top of his head. We rode past and I looked back to watch the man fall holding the top of his head and staring at the blood in his hands. Two more Rebs just behind the wagon were reloading in a panic and then swiftly cut down by Lieutenant Campbell who opened up on them with just two clean shots from his pistol. A shot rang out behind me and hit the tree just next to my head. Abigail whinnied and jumped up on her hind legs. I pulled her reins to the left and she swung around back down to the ground. Behind a pile of fallen logs was a Confederate reloading his musket. I kicked Abigail hard repeatedly and she thundered forth. The solider looked up at me and saw me charging forward with sword drawn, the panic in his eyes all too apparent as he fumbled with his musket ram rod trying desperately to get it down the barrel. At last he plunged the rod down packing the shot, wad, and powder. He removed the rod letting it fall to the ground and lifted his musket cocking the hammer back. Abigail leaped over the gap and I swung at the man striking his hand against the musket. Fire roared upward as he pulled the trigger on the way down screaming at the site of his now missing fingers. I leapt down from Abigail and approached him as he cupped his bleeding hand.

"Damn you stupid Yank!" he threw his head forward spitting in my eye and reached down for the bayonet on his belt. I stepped onward and grabbed his shoulder with my free hand running the blade of my sabre straight through his gut. His hand that gripped the handle of the bayonet went limp and fell. He gazed up at me with blood shot blue eyes and a face stained crimson. "Damn you Yank. Damn you…" The weight of his body fell like a bag of stones sliding clean from my blood drenched sword.

"Roach!" Lieutenant Tyler cried out. "Get back on your damn horse!" he ordered. No sooner than he finished his command a shot went clean through the side of his head. It appeared as if something had kicked him as his body flew to one side and off his horse. On the way down his foot was still caught in the stirrup and the spooked beast rode off in terror dragging the young Lieutenant across the unforgiving debris laden field of battle. The solid lines of Reb's began to give way to our advances and the once organized regiment became a scared rabble running in every direction for refuge or a new firing position. In the chaos, the bugle sounded dull but I recognized the terrifying call for retreat. I turned my girl around and rode her out as quickly as I could. The smoke flew past as shot rang behind striking the trees and ground all around. Soon the smoke cleared giving way to trees and open fields and I could see other riders ahead forming into a single line and swinging quickly right, straight into the valley. Sergeant Loyod was at the forefront and I looked back to see the Captain Masengill pulling up the rear with sword still swinging in hand. The picket line was empty now with the Ohio Forty Fourth already pulling back from the elevated position and back onto the road headed for London town. We road hard and I kicked Abigail as wildly as I could; she sped up huffing and puffing. My hat fell back and flew off my head into the grassy field but I cared not to retrieve it for doing so would surely risk my life more than I cared to. Riding beyond the pickets I saw blue coats lying face down in the field as if they were taking naps on a warm sunny day. I looked away from the corpses as we were nearly out of range of the muskets but again I dared not to stop for any reason. Surmounting the hill, we pulled up in time to see the last of the wagons pull out with the cannons hitched to the rear; their wheels squeaking noisily down the road. Sergeant Loyod turned about lifting his arm and pointing to the men to keep riding forward. By the time I reached him he had pulled nine other men and horses to the side with him and then he pulled me to the side as well.

"Listen men, I need you in these trenches to put down some fire. The infantryman are tired and worn from battle. They will be slow to get down the road and if we don't hold back the Rebs just a little longer they'll run up on us and try to cut every last one of them down."

"But Sergeant…"

"What is it Michaels?"

"There's only a dozen of us. We don't even have any cannons. How are we gonna to hold them back?" Sergeant Loyod rubbed his bushy beard and wiped the sweat from his brow.

"We just are Michaels. We're not going to stay here long. Just long enough to let them know there's still some danger in advancing. You got those Henry's, time to put'em to work. Is that understood?"

"Yes Sergeant!" We said in unison.

"Good. Now get your horses to lay flat and get your asses in the berms. I want you to load and fire until we are out of ammo." I hopped down from Abigail and checked the bullet wound in her shoulder. It wasn't bad but would need to be cleaned later if she was going to be any good to me. Wrapping my arms around her neck I pressed my head into her face and forced her to lay down on her side. She didn't seem to particularly like it but she was well trained from Camp Nelson and laid down just the same.

"Stay here girl. I'll come back for you." I pulled my repeating rifle from its holster and all the extra ammunition stuffed away in my riding pouch then made my way to the trench. Sergeant Loyod dug himself in deep on the far side with each man falling in. Private Michaels fell in next to me and sat quietly as he stared blankly ahead into the fields. It seemed that his nerves had taken hold of his courage. "Hey." He was startled and jerked his head to me gazing at me with glossy frightened eyes. "Load your weapon Michaels." I said gently. Michaels nodded his shaking head and without a word began loading his Henry.

"Listen up boys. When those bastards come out of the wood don't open fire till they reach the pickets. They think we've already made it down the road but were gonna show them better. Wait for my signal to fire. Once we start firing, give'em hell and don't stop until you're out of ammunition. Once you're out, get on your horse and get the hell out of here."

"Yes Sergeant!" We replied. I finished loading my rifle and then moved on to my pistol. I pulled it from the holster and yanked out the cylinder to get it reloaded.

"How did you get one of those?" Michaels asked with a shaky and shrill voice. I glanced at Michaels and then looked up and down the dark shiny barrel of my Eighteen-Sixty Colt.

"I shot a boy, in the back, in the dead of night. Captain Masengill gave it to me." He seemed surprised by my response.

"That was you? Back at the first night of camp?" I nodded and broke open the pistol breach to start loading.

"It was me and a Private named Billie. We went down to the river to water the horses and fill canteens. They started shooting at us so we gave chase. It was just a couple of boys. Sergeant Loyod thinks they were scouts."

"What do you think?" Michaels asked curiously.

"I think they were just a couple of boys who happened to be on the wrong side, probably lost in the woods." I was lying just to cover up my shame. The boy I shot didn't look much different from Michaels; a small frame, young, innocent.

"Lost?" Michaels giggled a little.

"What's so damn funny?"

"Ain't you heard about the Rebs? Those boys is born in the wood, in the swamps. They never get lost, they never go hungry, and if you get lost and they start tracking you, ain't nothin in the world gonna keep them from shooting you full of lead." I shook my head and grinned.

"Those are just old wives' tales. They're not what everyone says they are."

"How do you know?" Michaels was sure of himself.

"Cause I killed one. He was a boy, a young man just like us probably even younger. He didn't belong out there. He shouldn't have died like that."

"What about Howard and those three Johnny Rebs you flushed out with the Captain?"

"That was different. Howard was a traitor and the other three were no boys. They were veterans of the Confederacy, tough as nails with the South running through their blood."

"Here they come!" Sergeant Loyod alerted us. I laid down flat and dug my elbows deep into the dirt. I lifted the barrel of my rifle and beaded down on the tree line where small figures slowly emerged making their way through the brush and the tall grass towards the pickets. "Hold your fire until I give word." I kept my finger far from the trigger worried my heart would pound harder and I might flinch firing a shot and giving them just enough time to get away and regroup. I glanced away from my sights and looked at Michaels who shook like a leaf next to me with his finger right over the trigger. I slowly reached my hand out and gripped his shooting wrist pulling his finger clear from the trigger.

"Calm yourself Michaels." He looked over at me with pale skin and an open mouth.

"Ain't you scared?" he asked.

"Yeah, yeah Michaels I'm scared." I looked back down my sight to see infantry and cavalry slowly amassing near the picket lines. They surveyed the hillside and did not seem to spot us. Some of the Confederate soldiers put down their rifles and knelt next to the bodies of the dead from the Ohio Forty Fourth. They pulled boots, belt buckles, jackets, weapons, stripped the bodies bare of anything they could use. Some of them were even relieved of their clothes entirely leaving their bright white skin to burn in the sun. It was disgraceful.

"Why ain't we firing Sergeant? Look what they doin to our kin! Bunch of heathens!" a Private called out angrily.

"Hold your fire Private. Just wait a little longer. We need more of them out in the open. Just wait." Out of the cover of the trees came a large group of mounted soldiers. Two of the riders carried flags and they turned outward following the picket line. When they turned, I could see a smartly dressed Confederate Officer in a clean grey uniform and plenty of gold piping along the sleeves.

"Is that a General?" I asked aloud.

"I'll be damned." Sergeant Loyod said.

"What is it Sergeant?" I asked.

"That's Colonel Scott. He's the Commanding Officer of these men. He's been entrenched here for months taking out railways, telegraph lines and stealing our supplies. If we can take him out they may have to pull back entirely." Sergeant Loyod adjusted himself in the dirt. "Get ready." He said calmly. We all moved slowly in the dirt adjusting our weapons and our aim. I looked over the line of rifles to see Sergeant Loyod's mustache curling upward along his face.

"This is it." I said quietly to myself.

"Fire!" A shot rang out that cracked like lighting from Sergeant Loyod's rifle and we repeated the sound over and over sending shot after shot down at the Rebs. It was clear that they were not aware of us being on the hill. Rebs scrambled up for their rifles as we rained down merciless fire. Bodies fell, horses jumped upright frightened throwing their riders from their backs. Many of them swung behind the pickets or lay down behind the corpses of the Ohio Forty Fourth propping their bodies up on their sides to soak up the lead. I slowed my fire now as I watched rounds strike our fallen comrades and I felt guilt for desecrating their bodies further. Dirt flew up from the berm in front of us as return fire impacted and shot whipped and cracked above our heads. "Don't stop now boys, keep it up!" Sergeant Loyod ordered as he swapped his rifle for his pistol aiming high above the Rebs since they were too far out of range for his Colt. Our Henry's made quick work of them putting down fifteen rounds per rifle as quickly as we could cock the guns and pull the trigger. The Confederates rallied at the pickets and their line of infantry filled the gap laying down heavy fire on us. To the right of the fighting line Cavalry was beginning to gather preparing to charge up the hill and run us down. Dirt kicked up again in my eye and I dropped below the berm just as another round impacted near my head. I wiped the dirt out so I could see and as I looked left and right I noticed most us had huddled behind the dirt either to reload or take cover. "Load your rifles! One more volley together and then we're off!" My heart pounded hard and as I reached for my ammunition, my hand shook something awful. I could barely feel the lead between my fingers and as I loaded the rounds; at the top of the magazine tube my bullets kept getting stuck on the rim. It seemed like forever had passed until my rifle was fully loaded again.

"Ready!" Michaels replied aloud as he cocked his rifle. The other men repeated his call one by one until Sergeant Loyod held up his fist.

"Take your positions!" Loyod commanded. We turned and lay against the berm sighting in. The Rebel Colonel had disappeared into the woods for sanctuary and the Reb infantry and mixed cavalry were bearing down on us making their way up the gentle slope.

"Damnit!" Sergeant Loyod cried out in anger. "Looks like we're not getting Scott today!" The Cavalry line held firm until a sword was raised high in the air. Commands were given but I could not hear them in the distance over the deafening fire. "Let'em have it! Fire! Fire! Fire!" I squeezed the trigger and watched a grey coat fall into the grass. I cocked the rifle quickly expelling a hot shell that left a trail of smoke in its wake. Turning my rifle to the Cavalry that now charged ahead of the infantry I put a round into a horse's chest. The beasts front legs collapsed and the rider flew forward knocking and tangling up several other horses and crushing their riders. I kept firing into the line of cavalry maybe hitting two more until I ran out of rounds. I closed my eyes and mouth as something warm and wet splashed my face followed by a scream. I wiped it from my face and saw the blood covering my hands. Michaels curled up next to me holding his shoulder screaming aloud with his rifle in the dirt. I picked it up and fired off the last of his rounds until it was empty.

"They got me!" Michaels screamed over and over. "They got me! Oh god I'm gonna die!" I grabbed his arm and threw it around my shoulders.

"You're not gonna die boy, now let's go!" I stood us both up and we ran for the horses.

"Retreat! Retreat! Get back to the horses!" Sergeant Loyod and the others stood with him and ran back. I helped Michaels get up on his horse; wrapped the rein around his good arm and slapped the back of the steed to get him moving. The shot intensified all around and I could hear the yells and commands of the Rebs getting closer and closer. They screamed and hollered as they approach making sounds like wild savages. I leapt atop Abigail without placing my boot in the stirrup and gave her a good kick. She grunted loudly and dug in her back legs taking off at great speed. I held on to the reins for dear life knowing that if I fell Johnny Reb would hang me from one of those Oak trees.

"Go Abigail go! Ride, ride, ride!" The others were not far ahead kicking up a cloud of dirt and dust covering some of our trail. I looked back and watched the infantry disappear behind the hill and trees. The Confederate Cavalry would not be far behind so I turned away and did not look back. Abigail rode faster than she had ever done before and as the trail passed before us she showed no sign of tiring. The trees began to thicken up providing some comfort in its protection and in the distance, I could see the black of a cannon facing us and a wagon train with Infantry of the Ohio Forty Fourth running slowly next to it. Captain Massengill was pulled off the side of the trail with pistol in hand nodding at each of the men as they rode past.

"Are you alright son?" Captain Massengill asked Private Michaels who still gripped his arm tightly with a bloodied hand. Michaels winced and took a deep breath.

"Shot in in the shoulder Sir."

"Very well son, get to the Physician as soon as you can. Get that shoulder seen to. I need you back in the fight. That's an order."

"Yes Sir." Michaels rode ahead and around the wagon train through tall dry grass.

"Private Roach." I wiped my brow with my hand a quickly saluted. "Yes Sir?"

"I'm glad to see you still amongst us. Did your boys give it to them good back there?" I nodded.

"I believe so Sir. They never saw it comin. The Reb infantry must have taken the hill by now but I don't know about their Cavalry. Sergeant Loyod is a hell of a fighter Sir."

"Very good. Keep your pistol loaded and a watchful eye on the rear. I've got a few boys in the back of the wagons ready to open fire if needed. They won't be running us down today." Captain Masengill seemed confident that the Cavalry would have no chance to make an advance on us and he was probably right. I looked off the trail and saw nothing but large trees and thick brush. It would be impossible for them to mount anything other than a two by two column making them vulnerable. I loaded my pistol as best as I could while Abigail bounced up and down. Turning my head, I took a long look down the trail behind us and waited anxiously for the Reb's to storm forward like dogs from hell. They never came.

\* \* \*

We rode for nearly a day and all the way back to London. Captain Masengill felt it was the only place that we could reinforce and give the Ohio Forty Fourth enough time to recuperate and resupply. My neck, hands, and jaw line were burned from the hot Tennessee sun. My hands raw from grinding against the leather reins and my lower back as stiff as a corpse. Once again I felt fortunate to not have been Infantry as I past solider after solider resting against trees due to exhaustion, borrowing water from anyone that still had it or running at the wagons to see what they had kept in the back, but the wagons were empty and even the drivers seemed to be dying of thirst. As I arrived back in our camp just outside of London town we were being greeted by local folk with water, food, and medical provisions. Michael's horse stopped just ahead of mine; he dipped down and fell hard to the dirt below. I jumped off Abigail and ran to his side worried that he may have expired.

"Michaels, you alright?" He rolled on his back, his face pale, covered in sweat and his eyes wandered about. He lifted his hand with his fingers outstretched and I gripped them tightly.

"I just need some rest." He said meekly.

"Step aside! Step aside!" A woman's voice called out from behind me. I turned my head only to see a streak of gold rush by my face. I stepped back to see a young woman leaning over Michaels inspecting his wound. Her complexion was light and fair, long blond hair that she had tied up in a ponytail and a long neck line. She turned her head towards me and stared with her chestnut brown eyes and ruby red lips. I opened my mouth but for the life of me nothing came out. I just stared and stared at her eyes and counted the freckles that ran along her cheeks and on her nose. She grinned a bit, gazing back at Michaels and took a deep breath before her smile subsided. "Has he been riding the whole day with this wound?" My throat grumbled a bit and I swallowed what spit I had in my dry mouth. She cocked her head at me and parted her lips.

"Ehm…" I couldn't seem to get any words out.

"Solider? Are you able to speak? Have you been hurt?" I cleared my throat again.

"No mam. Ehm…yes Mam I can speak."

"I asked you a question young man. Did he ride all day?" I nodded and a stupid smile crept up my face. No matter how hard I tried I couldn't wipe that smile off.

"Yus, ehm…yes mam he did. Took one shot to the shoulder. We didn't have time to stop and patch him up properly."

"Ok, he lost a lot of blood, he needs water, rest, and we need to get that lead out of his arm and clean that wound. Help me get him up and to the infirmary." I nodded again and threw his good arm around my shoulder to walk him over to the tents. The woman stood revealing a blood covered apron and hands stained red. She must have been working all day treating the wounded. "This way soldier and be careful with him." I assisted Michaels with walking until we reached a white tent that held three other wounded men. Just outside the tent a small hole was dug in the ground where bloodied severed limbs rested freshly sawn off from their former owners. A small crimson tinged cot was cleared off and the woman pointed me in to lay him down.

"Easy…" Michaels whispered. I helped him down until his head rest firmly on the cot. Placing my hand gently on his chest I patted his head twice.

"You're gonna be alright friend. I'll come check on you later tonight." Michaels nodded and just closed his eyes.

"Don't take my arm miss. Please, I need'em." Michaels blurted out begging to be spared the saw. I turned away trying not to look the woman in the eye and then she grabbed my wrist pulling me towards her.

"Where do you think you're going?" I pointed my thumb back towards the road where I had left Abigail.

"I need to get to my horse and check in with my Sergeant. He might have orders for me." She shook her head seeming to disagree with my current course of action.

"Oh no you don't. Your horse and your Sergeant can wait. I need you here to hold him down while I dig that bullet out. It's going to hurt him something awful and I can't hold him down myself. The longer we wait the greater the chance I'll have to cut it off entirely." I wasn't about to let Michaels get his arm lopped off if I could help prevent it.

"Alright then miss. I'm all yours." I stepped back inside and placed my rifle down on the floor. "Where do you need me?" She pointed at Michaels side.

"Just get right next to him there. I'll need you to keep his head and chest down." I moved over next to Michaels who gave me a frightful but tired look. His skin had turned such a worrisome pale white.

"It's gonna be alright buddy." I kept trying to reassure him but had no idea what I was taking about. The woman gathered some cloth and tied them tightly around Michaels arm at several places until he could no longer move it.

"Drink this." The woman handed a bottle of whiskey to Michaels and put it straight up to his lips.

"I ain't never had whiskey before mam. I don't think it's right." He muttered.

"Well there's a first time for everything ain't there. Drink, it'll help with the pain. Michaels took a deep drink and then began to cough loudly. She took the bottle from him and started pouring it directly into his wound; Michaels yelled and writhed in pain.

"It burns!" he cried as he tried to sit up. I pressed down on him harder and harder trying to restrain him from hurting himself.

"Alright, hold still now. This is going to hurt but I can't have you moving or I might nick an artery." She took a small sharp blade and cut at the wound first on one side and then on the other opening it up wider. Michaels screamed and kicked with all his might trying to free himself of the cot, but he wasn't going anywhere. She finished with the knife and placed it down on a small table where she kept her tools. Then she retrieved small metal pliers running them over a lit candle for a moment and then plunging it deep into his arm. Blood spilt out wildly as she twisted and turned her pliers until suddenly she stopped. "I got it! Hold still. Don't move." She urged as she slowly removed the pliers and in the grasp of her tool was a small bullet. She quickly dropped the bullet into a metal pan that sounded noisily as it fell. "That's the worst of it I promise. We just need to clean you out and sew it up."

"Do you want me to stay?" The bangs of her hair fell in front of her eyes as she leaned over Michaels with a needle and thread, she pulled her bangs gently back behind her ears to look at me.

"Hold him in place just a little longer while I stitch him up." Her damp blood-stained hands worked gently weaving the needle and thread in and out of Michaels skin. He clenched his teeth and breathed heavy, wincing with each pull. She reached the end of the wound and pulled tightly closing it up. Leaning forward she pinched the thread between her teeth and cut the thread loose. "There, you're all done Private." Michaels nodded and smiled through quivering lips.

"Thank god..." Michaels eyes rolled into the back of his head and he fell asleep soon after or passed out. I couldn't tell which was which.

"Is he alright?" She placed her fingers on his throat and then on the inside of his wrist holding it in place for a moment before she placed his hand back down gently against the cot.

"He'll survive, he's just exhausted." She walked outside lifting her apron wiping Michael's blood from her hands. I followed her out to get some fresh air, the tent had a stench that seemed to hang heavy in the air. She released her apron letting it fall atop her light blue dress and placed her hands delicately on her hips.

"Thank you." I said. She looked back at me seeming surprised to still see me.

"For what?" she asked curiously.

"Taking care of Michaels. We had a rough go earlier today. Michaels stayed behind with a few of us to hold the Rebs from advancing. He was probably the most scared of all but he still fought plenty brave."

She nodded looking up at the clear blue sky through the cracks in the tree branches.

"Do you have a name or just go by Private?"

"Roach Mam, Private Roach." She giggled and bit her upper lip a bit.

"Roach, you mean like the bug?" I smiled.

"Yes mam. Just the same." She pulled her hair behind her ear and smiled.

"Well, do you have a first name?"

"Anderson Mam." I replied quietly.

"Please don't call me Mam. Mam is a name for my mother. Makes me feel old."

"What can I call you?" I asked curiously.

"Jenny." Her name rang in my head pretty as a bell. Even in this mess her eyes were warm, her smile comforting, she seemed to float above the ground and light up the dark oak wood.

"Jenny? That's a pretty name." She shot me a disapproving gaze.

"Are you being familiar with me Anderson?" She made me nervous, but in a good way. I wasn't sure how to answer but didn't want to stop talking to her neither.

"No Mam, I mean, um, Jenny."

"Where are you from Anderson? You sound like a local boy." She had me pegged, dead to rights. Probably thought I was as dumb as a rock to.

"Yeah, I'm from Granger County. Just a few days' ride from here. How about you? You don't sound like you're from around here." She shook her head smiling and covering her mouth.

"No, certainly not. New York is my home state but were a long way from there, aren't we?"

"You mean like the city?" She giggled and nodded.

"Yes Anderson, like the city."

"So what brings a city girl down South?"

"My father is a Surgeon, my mother a nurse. So, I followed the family profession and became a nurse myself but I'm trying to become Physician."

"A woman? Do they allow that in New York?"

"Well, officially no. That's why I came down here. I heard the Army was short on Physicians and Nurses, I thought perhaps I could help and maybe get the hands-on practice I needed. I was hoping that when I returned home I could be granted a license or perhaps my own practice for supporting the war effort." She was a smart one for sure. Pretty and smart don't come around often in my neck of the woods making Ms. Jenny seem all the more desirable.

"Well, I hope it works out for you Jenny."

"Did you get drafted or volunteer?"

"Oh I volunteered." I said proudly. "I'm with the Eighth Tennessee Volunteer Cavalry. Were all volunteers in the Eighth."

"That's quite noble of you. And why did you volunteer?"

"Well I could have stayed home, farmed the land but my big brother and several of my friends already signed up at the start of the war. I was too young so I had to wait."

"So you felt like you had to join; because of your brother and your friends?"

"A little bit yeah, I was also bored and thought this might be fun. I didn't want to settle for the farming life. It's been hard on my family and getting harder still."

"Fun? So, what do you think now?" I dropped my head shaking it back and forth energetically.

"No. I don't think it's any fun. This killin and people getting hurt all the time. I grew up with a lot of Southern folk in my town. They ain't that much different from you and me."

"And the slaving? Doesn't that make us different?"

"My family never owned any slaves. Slaves was for the rich folk. I don't have anything against the Negros. They work hard and now they fight hard, two long years of war already is enough."

"You know in the city there are colored folk with more money than whites. More education and property too?" I was fairly surprised by Jenny's statement and found it hard to believe but I had never been to New York and I had heard about the things that Lincoln was saying. I'd imagine anyone in my town would be shocked to see a Negro walking around in a fine suit.

"That would be a sight to see. Nothing like that around these parts but I guess that's what we're fighting for?"

"Roach!" a voice called out. I thought it was the Sergeant Loyod but could not make out where it came from.

"I need to go Ms. Jenny. It was nice to have met you." I turned and began walking away back to Abigail.

"You will come back, won't you?"

"Jenny?" I wasn't sure why she'd want me back.

"To check on your friend, Michaels. You will come back to check on your friend won't you" I lifted my arm and attempted to tip my hat, realizing I had lost it in the battle I tried to play it off with a smile that I could not hold back.

"Yes Ms. Jenny. If we don't push out tonight, I'll come back to check on Michaels. Take good care of him. He done good by us today." Jenny held her hands together and nodded her head watching me as I turned away. My heart pounded loudly in my chest and despite being surrounded by death I could only think about her and her alone. I worried for a moment that maybe I was too forward or familiar with her or that perhaps she was a distraction for me.

"Private Roach." It was Sergeant Loyod that I heard. He extended his arm for a handshake and I gladly took it. "How's Michaels?"

"He's well Sergeant. The Physician just got that bullet out of his shoulder and sowed him up good. I think he's going down for a long nap."

"Good, that's good. I know things got a little hairy back their but you and the other boys did a fine job holding Johnny Reb back. The Ohio Forty Fourth or what's left of it expressed their deepest gratitude. If not for us those boys would have been pinned down and fought until the last man. Had we shown up a day later I do say we would have arrived to sky full of vultures and a field of corpses."

"What about the men that were left behind? The ones at the pickets?" Sergeant Loyod looked down and then gazed up from under the brim of his faded cavalry cap.

"The Rebs won't just let us go back to collect those boys. We'll have to send another regiment after Scott and his men clear out. Perhaps in the mornin' or the day there after." My blood began to boil. What kind of men would keep other men from collecting their kin?

"Why the hell not Sergeant. Wouldn't we let them collect their dead?" He nodded.

"In most cases Private yes, in most cases. You gotta understand son were not fighting against a nation. These are defectors, traitors to the United States of America. Two years of fighting and their numbers ain't growin'. They will do whatever they can to keep their way of life alive. Although I don't agree with them I sure do admire those sons of bitches for their fighting spirit. It's a helluva thing to fight against ones brother. A helluva thing."

"Are we moving out Sergeant?"

"Not anytime soon. I don't have any orders at the moment other than to assist the Ohio Forty Fourth until their ready to march. They'll need to rest, resupply and get more men under their command. Until further notice we are to hold this here patch of dirt."

\* \* \*

I fell asleep shortly after getting some rations and woke up several hours later. The campground was quiet for once, less festive than what it had been the previous nights. The men were weary from battle and the heat, most retired to bed early. I rose slowly from my bed roll and rubbed my eyes so hard I could hear them squeaking in my skull back and forth, back and forth. A few voices spoke softly in the darkness with their silhouette's sedentary around a camp fire where only a handful of men sat. I pushed myself laboriously off the ground, my joints cracking as my muscles burned on the way up. Abigail was asleep standing up next to me and it looked as if many of the other horses were tied up near her to keep company. Somehow I had set up my bed in the makeshift outdoor stable. The perfume of fresh manure was overwhelming and I longed for some fresh water to wash the stink off. Stepping towards the bonfire I began to recognize a few of the profiles that lingered amongst the light. Sergeant Loyod was leaning against a log with a bottle in hand, Captain Masengill stood upright with a leg propped on that same log and from what I could make out the remaining Officers and Sergeants of the Ohio Forty Fourth. My steps were loud as I pressed down on the dried oak leaves with my boots. Captain Masengill was alerted to my presence and turned to gauge what was approaching him. He seemed relieved when he recognized my face.

"Private Roach, you are welcome to join us if you dare." I shook my head to Captain Masengill's invite in protest of his hospitality.

"I wouldn't want to be presumptuous Sir."

"Nonsense private. You have spilt blood with both myself and Sergeant Loyod. Let's face it son, you're one of us now." Sergeant Loyod lifted the bottle above his head.

"Have a seat Private, we won't ask you again. That's an order." I quickly took the bottle and stepped over the log making myself comfortable next to the inviting fire.

"Yes Sergeant." Another nameless bottle of Tennessee Brown sat in my hand. I took a deep swallow and bared my teeth afterwards at the burn going down. It didn't matter how much I fought it, the beverage was always like fire and still tasted like drinking a tree.

"You drink about as good as a lady." Sergeant Loyod was poking fun at me but I paid it no mind. Captain Masengill lifted his arm in the air with an open hand that demanded a drink and so I handed him the bottle.

"Now, now, Sergeant. I've seen Private Roach work that pistol. He's not exactly a shy man when it comes to pulling the trigger. Are you Mr. Roach?" I shook my head.

"No Sir. I'm not shy to shoot a man down when he aims to put me six feet under. I just reckon its good common sense to protect one's life and the life of the men in his company." Captain Masengill nodded and pointed directly at me.

"You see Sergeant Loyod, the young man seems to have a good head upon his shoulders. Perhaps we should be promoting him. He may one day make a fine Sergeant in our Company." Sergeant Loyod grunted and scoffed under his breath. Across from the fire Corporal Uankey was fast asleep. Sitting next to him was Corporal O'Brian who glared at me through the flames of the fire. It seemed his dislike for me had yet to fade and in fact it seemed to only grow. It had been some time since we shared words and I hoped that would continue.

"Although I do not disagree with you Sir, these boys are all volunteer and not proper military men. More than likely he will return to turnip farming or some other common trade after the war." Captain Masengill turned his head to me.

"Private Roach?"

"Yes Sir?"

"What is it that you do, or did in your home town?"

"I was a farmer Sir. Same as my father and his father before him. We have always been farmers Sir. It's true as the Sergeant said, it is common work but its honest work Sir." Captain Masengill smiled and nodded his head several times and then indulged in another drink of the bottle before passing it off to the Officers of the Ohio Forty Fourth.

"Well, we shall see Private Roach. We shall see. You might get to liking military life. We may make a proper soldier out of you yet. If you can stay alive that is." The men of the Forty Fourth in our presence laughed at this remark by the Captain. It seemed that war gave men a dark sense of humor, particularly for the infantry whom face it more closely and more frequently than the cavalry.

"Yes Sir." The Captain was beginning to slur his words. It was obvious he was drunker than a skunk and he would aim to keep me there in his verbal crucible for as long as he wished. I strained to think of a clever way to dismiss myself but with most the camp asleep I found it problematic to imagine my escape. Turning my head, I saw the watch in the distance on several sides of the camp pacing back and forth with faintly lit lamps that looked like fireflies floating about carelessly in the dark of night. "Beg your pardon Sir?" Captain Masengill halfway spit out his drink back into the bottle.

"No, you most certainly may not Private Roach." I lowered my shoulders and took an apologetic half step back.

"Yes Sir." He raised his arm with the bottle in hand leaning it towards me.

"Take another drink Private Roach. I am not yet done with you." I stepped forward taking the bottle from his hand and placing the fire back to my lips. The drink did not burn nearly as much this time and the last drink started to settle into my body relaxing my muscles and bones. Sergeant Loyod cocked his head back towards me and started laughing aloud.

"What is it Sergeant?" I asked.

"It looks like you are a solider after all. Being able to shoot Johnny Rebs is a start but a true warrior of the United States knows how to drink and hold his liquor." He reached out his arm towards me and I quickly handed the bottle to him relieved to once again be free of it.

"Sir?" I asked once more.

"What is it Private Roach?"

"I was told to bring food and water to the watch Sir." Captain Masengill took the bottle and drank the very last drop. Lifting his arm quickly he threw the bottle into the fire smashing the glass into thousands of pieces and sending embers streaming high into the sky.

"Very good Mr. Roach. It appears that we are done with the bottle and thereby done with you. Carry on soldier."

"Yes Sir." I saluted crisply and the Captain in his drunken state gave me a halfhearted salute before he caught himself falling to the ground. As I left the company of Officers and Non-Commissioned Officers I heard faint words and then an eruption of laughter. They were in good spirits and I suppose it was better than the alternative. I'd seen Sergeant Loyod in all his fury swinging that oak stick around cracking knee caps and backsides. Many troublesome boys had come across Sergeant Loyod and many of those boys were pained to become men by his sheer will of force. Stepping away into the dark of the forest I minded my steps carefully to avoid stepping on any of the men strewn about the camp floor. Just ahead I saw a faint light sitting outside the tents of the infirmary and then voices just beyond it near some thick brush. Something about the voices gave me an uneasy feeling. It wasn't what I could hear and I did not yet recognize whom they were but the tone felt almost perilous. I walked just a few steps more so I could clearly hear the conversation in the gloom of night.

"C'mon girl, I know you're sweet on me." A man's hoarse voice said forcefully.

"I most certainly am not. You would do well to remove yourself Sir before you find yourself on the other end of a court martial." It was Ms. Jenny. Her voice was commanding; telling the man how it was going to be, but I could still hear a faint fear in it. A worry that perhaps she was not as strong as she hoped.

"Now is that any way to speak to the future father of your children?" She scoffed and I could hear her kick dirt under her feet.

"Children? With you? I'd rather die before I let you lay a hand on me. Your children will probably have the faces of cattle." I heard a loud scream that quickly fell under a muffle and the struggle of oak leaves and dirt under foot. She was being attacked! I ran past the lamp light and the tents to see two dark figures tangling in the brush. My eyes adjusted and I saw a man standing behind Ms. Jenny with his hand firmly over her mouth and the other one pulling at her waist. He began forcefully pulling her further into the brush when I drew my pistol and stepped behind him pressing the barrel heavy into the back of his head just behind his ear.

"Let her go." The man was startled but seemed to recognize the feeling of a gun bearing down on him as he did not panic once he realized the situation he was in. He leaned his head back just far enough so his eyes could raise and see me. He smiled with rotten browned teeth in his mouth, his breath foul floating on the thick Tennessee evening air.

"Well hey boy. You know I didn't mean nothing by this. I'm just trying to show this here little lady a good time you know?" I cocked back the hammer and pressed the barrel harder into his head pushing him forward. He took a deep breath and shrugged his shoulders.

"Let her go or I'll blow your brains all over the camp." He still didn't move and refused to let Ms. Jenny free. His grip seemed to tighten, his position on the matter appearing firm and resolute.

"Now look here boy. Things don't have to get nasty. We can settle this like men. How's about I take my turn and then I'll let you have yours. Or, if your set on having it clean I'll let you have her first. How's that sound?" Without hesitation, I lifted the pistol and hit him hard with the bottom end. He dropped heavy and limp to the ground like a sack of rocks and for a moment I worried I had killed him. Ms. Jenny stepped away from her attacker placing her hands over her mouth as she gazed over his now limp body. She was still very much frightened and began to sob. I holstered my pistol and reached out to aid in her comfort.

"No!" she exclaimed. "Don't touch me." She pulled away from me turning from side to side erratically then stepping up to the fallen soldier and kicked him in the side repeatedly with a mad bulls' rage.

"Ms. Jenny it's alright. He ain't gonna bother you no more." I reached out to her again and she pushed me away striking me in the chest with both hands.

"Don't touch me, just…just give me a moment Anderson." Jenny paced back and forth with her hand on her head; her arms shaking like the leaves of a tree on a windy afternoon. Suddenly she stopped and gave the unconscious man another kick to the side and then shot me a plain gaze as if she was in shock. "What have we done? What do we do?" I pulled the hat off my head and scratched at my hair for a minute.

"I dunno, leave him? He's probably drunk. Just let him sleep it off." She turned her head looking back at the infirmary and started walking away. "Where you goin'?" I asked curiously.

"Give me a hand. I have an idea." I walked on over wondering what she was up to when she grabbed one end of a stretcher. "Get the other side." Without question I walked around brushing the side of her dress and catching the sweet smell of wildflowers as she pulled strands of her golden hair behind her ears. Leaving the tent, we quickly knelt next to the man placing the stretcher close to his body. "Get his back off the ground, roll him towards you." I did exactly as she said and she pushed the stretcher under his body. I let him drop hard back down to the ground not caring much for his welfare and grabbed the handles. "On my count, one, two, three, lift." Up we went with the man's body. Ms. Jenny led the way towards the main road where the watch and supply trains stood silent. She led us towards an empty wagon and we loaded the man in the back sliding him in until his body was secure. Jenny reached up grabbing the man's wrist placing her fingers just below the thumb.

"What are you doing?" I asked suspiciously. "You're gonna git us into a heap of trouble." I warned fearing the Sergeant or worse that the Corporals may come around the corner at any moment.

"Go wake up the driver and bring him to me." I still had no idea what Ms. Jenny had in mind but I didn't think I had time to ask questions. I looked back at the camp fire to see it had mostly died out and smoldered dimly in the distance. Sergeant Loyod and a few other men appeared to be passed out drunk but Captain Masengill was nowhere to be seen. I could only hope he decided to retire to his tent so not to find me in this compromising position. I found the driver sleeping on his chair with a blanket draped over him and shook him gently by the shoulder but the man did not move. I shook him again, harder this time over and over until he stirred and sat upright pulling the blanket off himself quickly.

"What is it?" he said looking straight up. I saw gold stripes peek out of the blanket, a Corporal, just my luck. He fixed his eyes on me and looked me up and down; his face went from worn and weathered to mean. "Private. What the hell are you doing waking me up in the middle of the night?"

"Apologies Corporal. The Physician would like to see you."

"Phy… who? Physician? Well what the hell does she want?" he muttered.

"She wants you to get down here." Ms. Jenny said with authority in her voice. With her hands on her hips she practically stared the Corporal down from his resting place.

"Mam, I meant no disrespect by it. It was a long day and I did not get much rest."

"Do you see this man?" She pointed to our adversary as he remained unconscious in the back of the wagon.

"What in the heck happened to him?"

"He is very ill. Captain Masengill wants you to take him to the nearest Hospital and leave him to be treated."

"Hospital? This man? He don't look to sick to me. Looks to me like he's sleeping."

"I assure you Corporal, what was your name?" The Corporal straightened out his cap and uniform.

"Corporal Dunham Mam." He replied hesitantly.

"I assure you Corporal Dunham that this man is very ill indeed and very near death. I am unable to treat him in these conditions. Now, are you going to ride out or should I wake the Captain so he can give you the orders himself?" Corporal Dunham suddenly seemed very nervous and even a few drops of sweat began to fall from his sun burnt forehead.

"No Mam. No need to raise the Captain from his beauty rest. I'll do just as you said." Corporal Dunham jumped back atop his wagon and dutifully gripped the reins.

"Thank you Corporal. Take your time now. Wouldn't want you to get lost." He smacked the reins against the horses and set off in the darkness with a lamp at the front of the wagon that swung from side to side. I stood in amazement watching the wagon roll away and returned my gaze to Ms. Jenny.

"I don't think I've ever met anyone like you?" Jenny smiled.

"Like what Anderson?" she held her hands together in front of her and batted her eyes giving the impression of innocence but I now knew better.

"Forgive me for saying Ms. Jenny but your trouble." She laughed quietly and covered her mouth to conceal the noise.

"You're not the first person to call me that. I've never been one to follow the rules. Following the rules never really seems to get us to where we want to go." I was excited and felt like I had gotten away with murder. She was clever, beautiful, and one of a kind. She turned to me and leaned forward kissing me on the cheek. I felt my face become flush, my heart pounded fast in my chest and my legs became weak as all their strength was taken away. In her presence, I could feel a fire in my heart and I was as jubilant as I had ever been.

"What was that for?"

"Thank you, for saving me back there. If it weren't for you I'd probably be in pretty bad shape about now. I hate to think what that man would have done to me had you not shown up."

"When do you suppose the driver is gonna figure it out?"

"The nearest hospital is seven miles from here. If we're lucky he'll sleep until he gets admitted. If not he'll wake up the Corporal and head straight back down here."

"And then?" Images of being questioned by Captain Masengill and Sergeant Loyod filled my head. Despite their recent curtesy and fondness of me I did not want to get on their bad side.

"You worry too much Anderson."

"You don't think he's gonna tell on us?"

"If he goes to the Sergeant, the Sergeant will go to the Captain, and the Captain won't do a damn thing. I'm too valuable to him and his men to send me away on the words of a scoundrel."

"What's a scoundrel?" Jenny giggled.

"It's a bad person Anderson, a criminal." I nodded.

"I like some of them fancy words you use. Did you learn those from New York?"

"Heavens no. New York isn't much better than this place; in many cases it's worse. No, I learned them in school. Didn't you go to school Anderson?" I shook my head.

"Me? Yeah I went to primary school but only a few times out of the year. I spent most of my time workin' the farm from sunrise to sunset. I know more about the back end of a shovel than I do about much anything else." Jenny smiled and showed no sign of disapproval or ridicule.

"Well, in either case I don't think he will trouble us anymore." She sighed deeply and placed her hands behind her back. "Well, it has been an eventful evening. I should head back and go to sleep before someone becomes suspicious. This isn't how I had planned our first evening together."

"How did you plan it?" She shrugged her shoulders and swayed from side to side.

"I'm not sure, but maybe this was better than what I had hoped for." She leaned forward and ever so softly kissed me on the lips. It was the first time a woman had ever done so. All worry and anxiety simply melted away and the only thing on my heart and soul was Jenny.

"Thank you Anderson. I hope you come visit me again. I'm usually outside the infirmary every night, so if you're ever lonely, you know where to find me."

# Seven
# Battle of Blountville – September 22$^{nd}$, 1863

The month near London passed by quickly with few skirmishes to speak of. We spent most of our time on watch, clean our rifles, and gathering food where we could. A few Sergeants of the Ohio Forty Fourth taught me and Billie had to play poker. Oh, what a joy it was. We'd spend hours on end playing poker; betting on rations or other trinkets we picked along the way. Sitting around the camp fires we'd eat our square meal, make jokes and tell stories about life back at home. I made more friends along the way but old Billie and I were inseparable. He'd take a bullet for me and I'd do the same for him. Then there was Ms. Jenny. I so did look forward to the evening when the sun would set and the air would cool our troubles away. Each night she waited for me and if I wasn't on watch I would meet her at the burning lamp light near the infirmary.

Jenny and I would talk for hours on end. As the nights passed we became closer and closer. Several of the men began to talk amongst themselves about our relationship so we tried our damnedest to be discreet. Then one evening when I was about to kiss Jenny goodbye as I always did she pulled me excitedly into her tent and closed the flap and blew out the lamp light.

"I love you Anderson." She said to me.

* * *

"Men, gather round. Gather round now!" Captain Masengill ordered waving his riding gloves lazily in the air. It was apparent that our Captain was weary, no doubt our movement further into Southern controlled territory had made his duties all the more trying. "Have a seat men, just have a seat anywhere. I want to speak to you for a brief moment if I might." I gave Abigail a gentle pat on the nose.

"Stay here girl, I'll be right back." She dragged her front hoof on the ground a few times. She was anxious. She knew we would be riding out to battle soon. We had been in so many skirmishes that she no longer seemed to mind the sound of musket fire or the deep roar of cannon. In fact, she seemed to prefer these darker times that we had embarked on. I had grown fond of this beast and her fast legs that carried me over the fray. She got me out of the worst fights and was always steadfast, never questioning where I commanded her to go; a loyal beast through and through. Sitting down amongst the men Billie quickly found a spot next to me.

"Hey boy! How you holding up? You git any of your rations back from last nights game?" I was about to respond until Sergeant Loyod stepped forward giving us a mean glare. He wasn't in the mood for any childishness or idle banter.

"Alright men, settle down now, settle down. Now listen up, General Burnside aims to deprive the Rebs of what remains of their supply lines. General Burnside seems to think that we are the solution to this challenge. Gentleman, today you will be fighting for salt."

"Salt?" Billie blurted out seeming confused. Captain Masengill nodded.

"Yes Private, salt. Beyond a bridge across the mighty Holston River lies a salt mine used to preserve food for the Reb troops. Just beyond that is a mine that produces gun powder and lead. If we ride ahead and take this position, we can cripple their ability to wage war against us. They will be almost entirely defensive in an effort to save their re-sources. This could be a major turning point in the war and I'm proud to be here with you today. Since the Scott Raid we have lost more than a few friends to battle and disease, you have engaged the enemy gal-lantly and tirelessly and carried out your duties as commanded. Today will not be any different. We will go out there, find the enemy, close on their position and kill them. We will suffer casualties, some of us will die, but in the end, we will be successful in this endeavor and perhaps bring a speedy end to the war. Our company will move out, clear the roads leading to Blountville while the artillery pounds the hell out of that town. Make no mistake gentleman, this is the South. The Johnny Rebs are thicker than fleas and meaner than rabid dogs. They are heavily entrenched and they will not give up their territory without a fight. We clear the roads and the outlying structures around the town and let the cannons do the rest. Is that understood?"

"Yes Sir!" we replied in unison.

"Very well, saddle up men. It's going to be a glorious day." Captain Masengill seemed confident as always but this was the first time we would head straight into a town for fighting. I didn't particularly like the thought of Rebs shooting at me from every window and every rooftop. Billie hit my shoulder from behind;

"What's wrong boy? You look spooked." Billie asked me with squint-ing eyes.

"Nuthin." I didn't even make eye contact and looked away just so Billie wouldn't read my face.

"What you worried about? We've been in harder fights than this. Like Captain said, were gonna let the cannons do the hard work. Just gotta clear them roads out. Ole'Johnny Reb ain't got no chance, no way in hell." Billie was in good spirits and ready for a fight but my gut twisted and turned inside. Something wasn't right, it all seemed too easy this time.

"I suppose." I said unconvincingly. Reaching down placing my right hand on my pistol I rubbed my fingers around the grip tracing my fingers along the wood grain, scratches and cracks trying to calm my nerves.

"C'mon boy. Let's git a move on. Them girls in town are just waitin' for some handsome Union heroes to come in and save them." Billie cracked his crooked smile wide.

"Ain't gonna be no smiling ladies today Billie. They're gonna be runnin' and crying." Billie ran his fingers through his greasy hair.

"No better time to ride up on a horse and rescue a damsel in distress. That's what them stories say anyway." I lightheartedly threw a kick at Billie's leg and he ran off towards his horse. I walked back on over to Abigail who seemed to be waiting impatiently for me to saddle up and get riding but the battle loomed heavy on my heart and mind like a storm brewing inside my head.

"Alright girl, it's alright. Reaching up I grasped the front end of my saddle and threw my foot into the stirrup. "Up we go." I swung my other leg over and into the other stirrup. Abigail bounced in place a little and I pulled back gently on the reins. "Easy girl, easy. Were gonna go find some trouble now, don't you worry about that." I kicked her sides gently and off she went riding straight into the double column formation. The bugle boy sounded the march and we went forward on a dusty trail into an early morning ride. The air was cool and sweet; the birds began to chirp as they rose early for morning hunts of grubs. I turned back to see our supply train and behind that several other Company's from the Eighth followed along. Sergeant Loyod wasted no time in sending a few scouts up ahead to ensure the path was clear. We had been hesitant to send scouts as of late as some of our riders did not return either deserting or more than likely killed and relieved of their earthly belongings; but this time we were sticking to the trails with a long line of sight in front of us. The forests and creek beds were not nearly as forgiving as they were before the war and we lost a handful of boys to Rebs hiding out in these ditches. Oh, they did their job all right, finding the enemy and all, but it was never their messages that pointed them out to us, it was the sound of gunfire. The last sounds those poor souls would ever hear. The scouts rode off quickly kicking their horses hard and slapping the reins. They wouldn't ride any more than a quarter mile ahead. We needed those boys in ear shot just in case there was trouble. Of course, there was always trouble...

\* \* \*

Only two hours or so had past and the blast of cannons could be heard clear as day not too far off in the distance. The scouts were stopped up ahead with what looked like a few Federal sentries and an Officer waiting patiently on foot. Captain Masengill raised his fist in the air. "Halt!" Sergeant Loyod commanded as the Captain continued riding forward accompanied by Lieutenant Campbell. The Captain and Lieutenant greeted the other Officer with a salute and jumped down from their horses to exchange a handshake. I couldn't make out what they were saying but best I could figure it was the Artillery Officer pointing out the location of the guns and the direction of fire. After several minutes of talk and what looked like an exchange of pipe tobacco Captain Masengill jumped back on top of his horse, saluted the Officer and rode back towards us in a slow gallop.

"Circle formation!" he ordered swinging his arm around in the air.

"Circle formation!" Sergeant Loyod enthusiastically repeated. Reins were slapped and the horses tore at the dirt all around spawning a cloud of dust from the ground that rose high in the air. We formed up quickly and calmed the horses as best we could to hear the Captain. Abigail kept pulling her head up and down; I rubbed her mane just to get her to relax for a moment.

"Listen up men and listen well cause I'm only going to say this once. Atop this hill lies a cemetery or cemetery hill if you will. Twelve and six pounders and releasing hell on the town of Blountville the likes of which they have never seen. Despite three hours of bombardment the enemy is dug in deep and determined not to leave. We are to ride around this hill and make our way to the road leading into town, clear out the road and the outlying structures. When we reach the outside of the town the Captain up there will order the cannons to cease firing. That's our signal to ride hard into town and kill or capture what remains of Johnny Reb and drive him out for good. Any questions?" I looked about the faces of Fox Company to witness a reassuring sea of calm. Not one man seemed to question their place in all this. The Captain grinned and slapped his reins. "Let's ride!" The bugle boy trumpeted loud and we broke back into the double column riding toward the sound of fire. With each step the cannons grew louder and louder where even the sounds of hundreds of horses were drowned out in the great roar of cannon shot and smoke. The ground shook violently and I swore to God the mud would open with hell-fire and swallow us whole. Soon passing the flank of artillery I could see the row of cannons; black as night they spit fire and cleared out all the brush in front of them. A small cemetery lay just a few yards beyond the barrels and it seemed that some of the gravestones had been knocked over. It was a shame to disturb the sleep of the dead while we were trying to put more men in their grave, but the high ground is the high ground and we aimed to keep it.

"Stay in formation!" Sergeant Loyod commanded. "Weapons at the ready!" I pulled my repeating rifle and held it upright. Our path led us to two rolling hills and once we cleared the last one the town of Blountville was laid out before us. In the pause between cannon fire I could hear muskets, screaming and yelling from men and women alike. A dark black smoke rose high into the air as several buildings burned wildly ablaze. Between us and the main part of town stood many houses, farms, and barns. I had no doubt in my mind that Johnny Reb would be watching us, waiting for us to make a move before they shot down on us. Captain Masengill lifted his left arm and broke off from the formation taking a column with him to the left while Sergeant Loyod did the same breaking off to the right. We sped up to get behind the Sergeant and now rode side by side at a good pace but not too fast. Sergeant Loyod took us to a farm that had a house, barn, and some other stables that appeared abandoned.

"Clear it out boys! Check every building, every room. If we can't get'em out with guns, we'll just have to burn'em out." he blared. We sped up and rode at the farm clear up to the front of the house. I expected them Johnny Reb to open fire on us but it looked like nobody was there. "Dismount! Check everything and keep yur guns up." Sergeant Loyod ran down to the farm house with his pistol at the ready.

"Anderson! C'mon!" Billie was just behind me with rifle in hand and called me over to help clear out the barn. I ran with him and a few other boys moving as fast as our legs would carry. For a moment, I cracked a brief smile feeling like I was back on the farm running through my own fields; but I wasn't. This wasn't my home, this wasn't my farm, and if anyone was here they sure as hell wouldn't be friendly. The barn door was shut tight with a large piece of lumber wedged between two metal hooks to keep it that way.

"C'mon out!" Billie ordered anyone inside the barn. "Come on out with your hands up and ain't nobody gotta get killed today!" We waited but heard nothing, not even any livestock.

"Let's get the door open." I suggested. Three of us got under the rotten timber and pushed it out letting it fall down to the ground with a dull thud. We pulled the doors wide open as they creaked loudly and let the morning light come clean on through. With guns drawn we cautiously stepped inside ready for anything. Empty stables and large bales of hay lay everywhere strewn about the barn floor carelessly. A small ladder led up top where I saw more hay being stored. We took a good look around walking slowly through the barn, my heart pounding hard with each step; it was all that I could hear in my ears. I went around each corner sharply with my rifle but stable after stable the barn was empty. "They must've gone before we got here." I said.

"Yeah, those cowards knew I was comin' for them." Billie boasted. I lowered my rifle and began walking out with the others.

"Don't be so cock sure of yourself Billie. Were gonna see them boys one way or another and then we gonna see what's what." Billie threw me a devious smile and raised his rifle to his chest.

"Well that's why I got old Tabitha here. She gonna show them, what's what." We laughed and walked outside the barn.

"You see anything?" Sergeant Loyod called from across the field.

"No Sergeant, ain't nobody here." I replied. A loud crack silenced the mood and shocked faces looked around for the source of the shot. "Anderson…" I turned to look at Billie whose eyes were wide with fear as he gazed down at a wet spot on his chest that ran downward. It was blood; Billie had been shot in the back clean through to his chest.

"Billie!" I ran to his aide and caught him as he fell down heavy as a boulder. Just behind his ear I caught the sight of three grey coats covered in hay running out the backside of the barn. Violent explosions erupted behind me and I closed my eyes as the air rushed past my head. Crack, crack, crack, they resonated all around with fierce repetition. My ears rang something awful. I opened my eyes to see Sergeant Loyod running past firing his last shots while the other boys opened up with their rifles. I couldn't hear a thing, not the gunfire, nor the cannons, or even Billie's screams. The bells of hell were the only thing I perceived and they consumed me and everything around me. I closed my eyes tight again until I felt Billie's head crash forward into mine. Opening my eyes again I pulled his head back to get a good look at his face. "Billie?" I couldn't even hear my own voice but I could feel the words move in my mouth like nails across my tongue. "Billie! No, no, no! No!" A firm hand grasped my shoulder and I turned to see Sergeant Loyod looking down at me fiercely, his jaw clenching tight with each spoken word, his eyes full of rage.

"Anderson!" I could faintly hear him now, the bells in my head were subsiding to a dull roar. "Anderson! He's gone Anderson. Leave him be!" I wouldn't, I couldn't let go of my friend. I just needed to get him to Ms. Jenny, she could help him. She could save his life I was sure of it.

"He needs a Surgeon!" I cried out. Sergeant Loyod placed a hand on my cheek, the rage I saw had faded and turned to concern.

"Anderson, let him go." He urged.

"No! I won't leave him. He needs a Surgeon!" Sergeant Loyod placed his hands on each side of my face and shook my head.

"Anderson! Listen to me!" His voice rang hard in my head like the blast of the cannons. Everything was a blur and only the collar of Billie's uniform seemed to come in clear. "Private Roach! Look at him.

Look at Billie!" He turned my head with his hands and I gazed down at my good friend, my dear friend. Blood was everywhere now, Billie's body was still warm but his eyes had rolled to the back of his head, his chest stopped moving up and down, and his breath had subsided. His once warm face and goofy smile had washed away replaced by an ashen grey veil. The bangs of his brown hair danced softly against his forehead as the wind gently caressed them, and I hoped beyond hope that it was the very breath of God coming down to bring him back to us. "He's been shot in the heart Private. He ain't comin' back." I looked over Sergeant Loyod's shoulder and through the barn to the other side I saw three bodies laid out in the grass. "It's alight Private. Set him down. He's in God's hands now. Nothin else we can do for him." I lowered Billie slowly to the ground and gently placed his arms at his sides. Lifting my arm to wipe the tears I felt something wet on my hands, they were covered in blood, Billie's blood. My heart pounded faster, my sadness all but left from me, pushed away like a forceful wind and was replaced with a rage that came over me like a flooding river. I stood quickly and stumbled in my grief but caught myself with my hand before I hit the ground. Walking awkwardly forward quickly ran through the barn and towards the bodies on the other side.

"Private Roach! What the hell are you doing?" The Sergeant asked. I pulled my pistol and drew it on the corpses, squeezing the trigger slowly. One by one I put a bullet in their skulls watering the grass with their blood. Footsteps rushed up behind me,

"You didn't check the hay, did you?" It was Sergeant Loyod. My heart sank and I slowly turned around. It was my fault; it was all my fault. I let Billie die, all because I was careless. "Private, you gotta check the hay. Every time. The Rebs will hide out anywhere they can. Today; today you get to learn from this. Don't let your friend's death be for nothing. C'mon, git back on your horse. We got more work to do."

"Yes Sergeant." I didn't look at him. No weakness, no tears. I walked past Billie's dead body only giving him a glance before I jumped up on Abigail and rode away ahead of my comrades.

"Private! Wait!" I could hear Sergeant Loyod calling to me but I ignored his calls riding fast and hard for the next house. As soon as I came up on the window of a small cottage a shot rang out. I pulled Abigail around to the back side and saw a rifle barrel poking out around the corner. I aimed my rifle at the side of the wall and took a shot. A man's body fell heavy against the railing on the porch and hit hard against the ground. I jumped down from Abigail and ran around the bend.

"Get him...", another Reb came running out the back door and tried to pull his pistol up but I put a shot through his chest before he could draw down on me. His body flew back through the door and down on the ground, motionless.

"Come on out!" I taunted to anyone still hiding out in the cottage. Horse hooves beat heavy on the other side, no doubt the Sergeant had caught up with me by now. Gunfire broke out and I ran through the door to see a surprised soldier with his back to me with a ram rod down his musket. I ran straight for him and smashed through the window with him taking part of the frame out on the way down. I dropped my rifle and we wrestled for a minute back and forth along the porch until we rolled down the steps and into the dirt below. He pulled an Arkansas toothpick on me from his waist and I grabbed his hand.

"Die you sum bitch!" he cursed at me through yellowing teeth. I punched him in the head a few times with my free hand until he dropped the blade but still he fought back trying to choke the life out of me. I reached back, pulled my revolver and put the barrel to the side of his head. He quickly released his grip. "Please, I give up. Don't shoot me Yank." I pulled the hammer back on the pistol, I had one bullet left in the cylinder with his name on it. "Oh please sweet Jesus don't kill me."

"Private Roach, put down the pistol. He's surrendered, we take him as a prisoner of war." I pressed harder into the man's head. "God damnit Roach that's an order!" The man smiled and winked at me.

"You best listen to yur Sergeant boy or yur in for a world of hurt." I squeezed the trigger. The back side of his head opened up like a pumpkin and sent his brains all over the dirt path. I spat on his face and stood up holstering my pistol. A hand gripped me from behind and swung me round when I caught a glimpse of a fist just before everything went dark. Falling hard to the ground I opened up my eyes to see Sergeant Loyod straddled atop of me whaling down on me with his fists.

"Sergeant!" I pleaded with him but he kept hittin' me. "Sergeant please!" He stopped and breathed heavy.

"You do that again and I'll shoot you myself. You got that?" He pointed his finger rigidly at me with his gun still at the ready in the other. He slapped me with his hand and pulled me to my feet. "Look at me boy." His voice lowered now, deep and authoritative. "Look at me boy. Do it again and I'll put a bullet through the back of your head. Do I make myself clear?" My rage faded and the sound of cannon fire brought me back to the present.

"Yes Sergeant. I understand." He slapped my face again.

"I said do you understand?" He shouted.

"Yes Sergeant, I understand!" I shouted back.

"That's a good boy. Now get back on your horse and back in line. We have more fighting to do. Don't make me regret not shootin' you." As I walked back to Abigail a few rounds landed in the gaps between us, stray bullets that came flying out of town. Back on the road we merged up with our half of the company that had cleared out a few ranches on the other side and then rode forward in a single formation. Small groups of Rebels could be seen fleeing from other buildings running straight up the main road. Just outside of town were several work buildings that remained to be cleaned out. A lumber yard, blacksmith, stables, and a granary.

"Halt!" Sergeant Loyod commanded as he swung his horse around. "You men take the blacksmith, you men the stables, you men the granary, the rest of you come with me. Were gonna clear out the lumberyard. When you're done, everyone meet up here before we ride into town. Go!" We were split up into groups of about ten or so and rode like the wind to each building. I followed Sergeant Loyod to the lumberyard and stayed behind him so not to incur his wrath any further.

At the front of the lumberyard lay a small building probably to make payment for goods but behind the building lay a maze of cut and uncut timber that stretched for a few hundred yards.

"Where to Sergeant?" a Private called out. Loyod looked about the yard that had at least three or four long rows of timber.

"Split up. If you find the Rebs shoot'em. If they surrender take them as prisoner. The Captain might want to have a word with them." We dismounted from the horses and made our way inside walking side by side until reaching the rows of timber.

"Roach."

"Yes Sergeant?"

"You come with me. I ain't ready to let you loose yet." He didn't trust me anymore and with good reason. I wouldn't trust me neither.

"Yes Sergeant." We had one other Private with us, an older man with spots of grey spread throughout his neatly trimmed beard.

"What's your name Private?" The Sergeant asked.

"Chesterfield Sergeant. Private Chesterfield." He said with a slight Irish accent as he dipped his cap and then reached back down for the stock of his rifle.

"Alright Chesterfield, take the right side. Roach and I will take the left. You see somthin' then you start shootin'."

"Happy to oblige Sergeant." Chesterfield cocked his rifle and scrambled to the other side that was no more than fifteen yards or so from us. As soon as he reached the other side shots rang out and struck the timber near his head sending splinters of wood flying in all directions. Chesterfield laid down behind the lumber taking cover and then returned fire emptying his lever action as fast as possible. Sergeant Loyod and I crept forward slowly until we reached the end of a pile of uncut trees. We waited patiently for our chance and then another shot rang out spewing sparks and smoke. Those bastards were just around the corner. Loyod looked back at me and lifted three fingers beginning to count down. One, two, three; we ran into the gap and found two Rebs loading their muskets. Without mercy Loyod and I opened up on'em and put at least two rounds into each man. They fell quickly to the ground bleeding out in a puddle of mud. One man landed face down in water and his dying breaths could be seen in the bubbles that came upward from the muck until the last one popped and then the bubbles stopped.

"You alright?" I yelled over to Chesterfield. He stood up from his fighting position and waved enthusiastically.

"Ain't no Johnny Reb gonna keep me down Sergeant. Just worry bout yurself!" Chesterfield ran over and took a good look at the carnage on the ground. He removed his hat and wiped the sweat from his brow. "You boys licked'em good. They never saw it coming."

"C'mon, there's more to clear out. I don't think that was the last of them." Sergeant remarked. We left the gap and continued back down the row. A few shots cracked from several rows over but they silenced pretty quickly. "We need to move faster. If that was our boys getting ambushed their gonna swing around behind and kill us to." We started moving forward at a slow run pointing our barrels at anything that looked like a hiding place. Reaching the end of the row four shots cracked all around us.

"Shit! I'm hit!" Sergeant Loyod cried out in pain. He gripped his shoulder where the shot had struck him. Chesterfield scrambled to the other side and took up another fighting position. I grabbed Loyod and pulled him behind a timber on the ground but there wasn't enough room for both of us, my left leg and arm were still exposed. I peeked around the corner and saw a makeshift bunker where a hole had been made for them to shoot from. Shot snapped against the timber next to me and I got some dust in my eye that blinded my vision. I quickly wiped it away and pulled the larger pieces from my lashes.

"Sergeant! You alright?" He breathed heavy and pressed hard against his wound clenching his fingers tightly.

"Them sons of bitches winged me is all. Just keep shootin'! Don't give those bastards and inch!" I turned away and left my concern for his welfare behind. The shots just kept coming one after another straight down the row of timber. There was no damn way for me to stick my head out without getting hit. I looked across the way to see

Chesterfield pinned down too. I decided to take the time to reload and then flagged him down.

"Chesterfield!" He glanced over at me and I pointed at myself and then up the stack of logs next to me and then back down to the bunker. "Cover!" I called out. Chesterfield nodded and lifted his hand counting down from three. As soon as he stopped he peaked around the corner of the log like a turkey and unloaded hell on those boys. I got up as quick as I could and scurried up the timber. The shots shifted from Chesterfield towards me and I could hear them striking the lumber just behind but I didn't look back, I just kept running as fast as my legs would carry me. I reached the opposite end and got behind the logs to catch my breath. Chesterfield's rifle got quiet after he shot off all fifteen rounds and then I heard the crack of a pistol. Sergeant Loyod must have rolled over and started popping off a few shots. I scrambled down the wood pile and started making my way forward. Reaching the end of the row I peeked around and could see the side of the bunker with muskets peeking out. The entrance must have been on the back side so I ran across the gap a pressed my back against the wood wall. Slowly I crept with each step and the gunfire cracked all around until I reached the edge and peaked around to see the entrance to the bunker.

My heart felt as if it had sunk into my belly; how many men were in that room? I put my rifle down on the ground and opted for my pistol; worried that if I ran in with a large barrel I might get stopped up on something or somebody may grab it and shoot me. As I was about to go in I stopped myself and grabbed my bayonet out of its sheath holding the blade in my left hand. If I ran out of shot or something went wrong I could always rely on a blade. Three slow deep breaths and I ran around the corner, hand extended with pistol at the ready and my blade at my side. Smoke permeated out of the entrance and I could hear voices hootin' and hollerin' some damn thing about killing bastard yanks. My vision narrowed and the smoke was so thick all I saw were three dark figures. I lifted my pistol and fired the first shot straight at the back of a man's head splattering my face and the faces of his comrades with blood. The one to the right turned quickly with his rifle and bared down on me so fast that I swung my blade out at the barrel and hit it. The musket went off and a shot went into his partner's leg on the opposite side of me. He screamed aloud in pain and I lifted my pistol shooting his partner in the chest. He fell like a rock against the wall and slid down. When I turned to the man with the wounded leg I noticed the sheer sight of panic in his eyes. He seemed to realize that his wound was not that important and scrambled to cock his musket back but in his panic his hands slipped.

I lifted the pistol to his head and pulled the trigger. The hammer dropped heavy and clicked loudly but the shot failed to fire. The man's panic turned to anger as he lunged towards me pressing the side of his barrel into my chest. I fell back to the wall and he lifted the barrel to my neck pressing with all his weight behind him depriving me of air. I could feel my limbs start to go numb and my head felt like it was going to explode. Swinging my left arm, I sunk the bayonet in his arm pit, the blade sliding smoothly. The man faltered and screamed loudly. I pushed him off and swung my pistol at his head striking him dead center. Blood squirted out from his brow and he fell back. In a mad dash, I pressed forward and stuck the bayonet in his throat. The blade slipped in like cutting into warm butter. His eyes grew wide as he gripped my hand. Coughing the man spit out steams of blood until his hands and arms went limp falling to his side. I stepped back pulling the blade from his throat; a rush of crimson liquid flowed outward and down his chest. His eyes rolled to the back of his head and he fell to the ground. In my extreme exhaustion, I sat down heavy resting my arms on my knees. My hands covered in blood I wiped them on my pants and rubbed the brow of my forehead removing the sweat with my sleeve. Before me lay three men dead as dead can be with their bloodied uniforms, hats and weapons strewn about the thrashed wooden bunker. Although I was victorious in this moment I did not feel the way I had anticipated, I did not feel as if I had achieved anything great or that I was a hero. Quite simply I was tired in this effort and exhaustion was all that I could feel in the moment.

"Roach!" a panicked voice called out from outside the bunker. "Roach! You in there son?"

"Yeah!" I swallowed hard and corrected myself. "Yes Sergeant!" I could hear the shuffling of feet and the running of bodies towards me. Private Chesterfield and Sergeant Loyod burst into the bunker with weapons drawn but upon inspecting their surroundings they looked at me and lowered their firearms appearing somewhat shocked at the carnage that presented itself.

"Well I'll be damned." Chesterfield said scratching his forehead. "You sure made quick work of them, didn't you? What the hell did you do?" I breathed deeply and nodded pointing my pistol at one of the bodies.

"They put up a pretty good fight." Loyod stepped towards me and extended his arm.

"Git up son. We need to torch this bunker so no one else decides to hole up in here." I gripped his hand and he helped me up quickly. Every muscle in my body ached terribly and I wondered how much longer I could keep this up. Loyod placed his arm over his mouth and nose and breathed in deeply. "Jesus Christ Private, you sure do know how to make a mess of things." Chesterfield walked around the Sergeant to a crate where an oil lamp conveniently stood.

"I got it Sergeant." He cracked the side of the lamp on the crate shattering the glass and proceeded pouring the oil over everything inside. "Go on, git out." Chesterfield urged. Sergeant Loyod and I stepped outside and gazed down each row of timber spotting the other soldiers that had cleared out the lumber yard with us.

"We good?" Sergeant Loyod asked.

"Yes Sergeant!" one soldier replied.

"Yes Sergeant!" another replied. Sergeant Loyod smiled seeming quite pleased at the work of his boys. He reached into his leather ammunition pouch and produced his pipe, tobacco, and a long wooden match. He pulled a pinch of tobacco out of the pouch and stuffed it tight in the pipe then ran the match along the wall of the bunker. The match popped loudly and set to fire; he put the flame to the pipe without delay. Puffing away his pipe was amply lit and he held the match carefully upside down letting the flame run up the wooden stick.

"Alright boys, it's time to go to town." He knelt down and touched the flame to the thin trail of oil left behind by Private Chesterfield. The oil lit quickly and the flame danced mesmerizingly down the trail until it grew and ran up the inside walls of the bunker. The blackest of smoke billowed against bubbling pine tar and flew quickly outside the entrance. In a sort of daze I watched without remorse or emotion the bodies of the boys in that bunker catch to the flame. "Ashes to ashes." Sergeant Loyod uttered. "Dust to dust."

"What now Sergeant?" Chesterfield asked with the butt of his rifle on the ground. Loyod pulled the red-hot pipe from his lips and pointed it towards the main road.

"We gotta flush those rats outta Blountville." The cannons still roared loudly overhead tearing Blountville apart from all directions. Half the town already seemed like it was ablaze with smoke rising high into the air creating a black cloud that hung over it like death. We walked out of the lumberyard and hopped back on our horses ready to ride out again. Despite his injuries, Sergeant Loyod made no complaints nor attempts to receive any treatment for his wound. "Make for that red building and secure the horses on the backside. We're gonna take position at the berm and survey the town from there!" We rode fast and hard, the horses hammering the soft ground with their shoed hooves. I could hear cracks and snaps in the air as we rode ahead and then a scream from one of our boys. A round hit him and he fell hard from his horse. I looked back and saw him motionless on the ground. "Ride! Ride!" Loyod urged. A horse screamed aloud and buckled under its front legs taking its rider with him in a swift violent tumbling flash of chaos. I had no doubt in my mind the rider had died and as we charged forward more men and more horses fell to their deaths. It seemed an inglorious thing, dying without getting a chance to fight or even see the men that killed you. At long last we reached the backside of the red building that looked like a general store or some damn thing. We dismounted our horses and grabbed our rifles from their holsters.

"Load up! Get ready for a fight!" One by one I loaded bullets into the magazine at the top of the rifle and cocked the lever putting one in the chamber. I reached into my ammo pouch and just swapped out the cylinder for my pistol instead of reloading the one I had. If I needed it again I'd have to find cover and reload quickly.

"Ready Sergeant!" I called out. Others followed in my call and Loyod looked about the worn faces around him and nodded.

"Take the berm!" he ordered. Before turning around I gazed at the field behind us one last time seeing it dotted with dark colored spots in the thick tall grass like hogs hiding from the hunter. Horses and men laid strewn about and I wondered how the bullets had picked them and not me. I turned away from the carnage and ran around the worn corner of the building; as I followed my brothers I was immediately greeted by a hail of gunfire.

"Shit!" I blurted out and flung my body hard against the dirt. The impact with the dirt hit me hard and knocked the wind out of my lungs. I crawled up and got a look at the other side. A row of buildings ran far down the road. Those that weren't ablaze were dotted with Johnny Rebs taking up fighting positions at the windows and on the roof tops scurrying like black ants put to fire against the wooden planks. Troops ran back and forth between the buildings taking refuge behind the makeshift cover of wagons that had been pushed over on their side.

"Fire at will! Drive 'em back!" I started with the rooftops and proceeded putting down fire slow and steady. As my shots rang off I could see puffs of smoke and debris explode on the impacts. The silhouettes of soldiers dropped quickly and scattered with each shot taking up new positions and returning fire. Every time their shots hit the ground near me dirt would jump up and get in my eye. I rolled back down the berm to wipe it away and then crawled back up to put down more fire.

"Sergeant!" Chesterfield called out. "Sergeant!" his calls were drowned out by the sounds of the cannons and the gunfire bouncing off the berm.

"Sergeant!" I yelled relaying Chesterfields call.

"What?" he called back seeming frustrated. I pointed at Chesterfield down the line and Loyod turned his head.

"Sergeant! Why have the cannons not stopped?" Loyod took a look back and then looked up and down the battle line. The other companies had taken position around the town as well. The artillery should have stopped by now so we could move in but they just kept hammering the town.

"I don't know! Just keep fighting!" Sergeant looked worried and I had never heard him say that he doesn't know something. "Hold the line, shoot any of those Rebs that are dumb enough to stick their heads outta their holes. Fire at will!" Despite the merciless besiegement of the town Johnny Reb was everywhere thick as thieves running from building to building, window to window and roof top to roof top. Suddenly from behind a bugle bellowed loudly and repeated a sound over and over again that I did not anticipate to hear this day.

"Retreat! Retreat! Pull back behind the artillery! Pull back!" Captain Masengill commanded holding his pistol in the air. My heart sank in my chest and the faces of the men seemed to echo the feeling I had inside. Why would we retreat when we had them on the run? We were nearly assured victory and Blountville was within our grasp. One by one companies began pulling back firing their rifles and pistols as they stepped backward towards their horses. A few men went down taking bullets for their friends as they jumped on their horses and rode out quickly.

"Alright boys! All at once were gonna jump up and fire and git the hell outta here." I quickly checked my ammunition and rapidly loaded a few rounds in to my rifle. "Ready! Go! Retreat, retreat!" I stood from the berm and fired my rifle in all directions stepping backwards as I did so. Once I ran out of rounds I turned and fled following the other men in their mad dash for survival. I heard a scream erupt behind me and looked back as I ran to see a boy fall down dead. That bullet was meant for me had he not been there. Sergeant Loyod pushed me forward and I turned my head back around. I found Abigail waiting just on the other side of the general store and quickly mounted her kicking hard. She took off like the wind and I had to catch myself from falling. Faster and faster we went with hundreds of Cavalrymen through the open fields and down the road. So many horses were there that the sounds of their hooves made the ground shake and tremble drowning out even the sound of cannon fire. It wasn't long before our Company reached the backside of the hill behind the safety of the artillery and the infantry that held solid picket lines. I jumped down from Abigail and joined the other men of my Company who were now in a feverous rage surrounding the Officers and Sergeant Loyod.

"Why did we retreat?" a man called out.

"We had those bastards on the run! What the hell are we doing here Sergeant?" Even I could no longer hold my tongue. It seemed a matter of import to get some answers and get them quick.

"We left men behind! Good men! Why are we going to fight if we're not going to commit!" The yelling and anger had become uncontrollable coming to a pitch. Sergeant Loyod stepped forward removing his pistol and aiming it straight in the air, he squeezed the trigger firing a round overhead.

"That is enough! You will maintain discipline! Is that understood?" The men fell silent but the anger and frustration was still very much painted on our faces hanging in the air like a thick fog. All around I saw only clenched fists and tense shoulders; men that looked like they wanted to throw a punch. "The Captain is speaking with the Colonel. When he gets back we will receive new orders. Until then I want you back on your horses and ready to ride out. Is that understood?" No response was uttered from our mouths and I could see the vane in Sergeant Loyod's forehead become enlarged, his eyes turning bloodshot red. "Is that understood?" he shouted with spit flying angrily from his mouth.

"Yes Sergeant..." said a few meekly through the tension in the air. I didn't reply at all. I had half a mind to hop back on Abigail and get back to the fight and I know many men who would certainly follow me but mutiny and treason was not at the top of my list. We unwillingly mounted our horses, drank water from our canteens and reloaded our weapons ready to head back out into the fight. Captain Masengill rode down from the top of the hill with Lieutenant Campbell at his side and stopped quickly in front of us; his horse sending a plume of dust all around.

"Men! Men gather round! Gather round!" We pulled our horses in closely to a semi-circle as Captain Masengill pulled off his gloves and threw his commanders cap to the ground. "I will tell you gentleman that I am pissed beyond a reasonable doubt. Vexed, terribly vexed!"

"What's goin' on Captain?" a man shouted from the line. Captain Masengill wiped the sweat from his brow and jumped down from his horse looking up at us while he retrieved his now dirty cover.

"We had those boys on the run did we not?" he said pointing back at Blountville.

"Yes Sir!" I shouted with several other men.

"We had them licked good and we were gonna run them sons of bitches straight outta town this day, were we not?"

"Yes Sir!" we shouted enthusiastically in unison.

"Boys if it were up to me we'd be in that town right now stomping the hell out of every last Reb holed up in there. But it's not, it's not up to me. We got word that the Confederates are amassing a large army to move across river and take control of several key bridges. Blountville was just a delaying tactic on the part of the Confederates. We are moving out immediately to reinforce infantry units already engaged some distance away. I don't say this often but I'll say it today, I'm sorry. I never want to rob you of a victory when it is so close but this is war and we have orders. We are soldiers, servicemen, not raiders. Sergeant Loyod, prepare the company to move out. We leave shortly." Captain Masengill placed his cover on his head once more and walked away with his head down in shame.

# Eight
# Siege of Knoxville – November 17$^{th}$ – December 5$^{th}$ 1863

No matter where we went it seemed like the Holston River was never very far away and acted as a constant in an unpredictable world. We arrived just outside of Knoxville atop a small hilly area without having engaged the enemy. A large number of forces numbering in the thousands of Union soldiers had arrived just several days before the Eighth at Fort Sanders. We were in good company and as I could see and smell by the looks of things supplies were no longer short. For the first time in a long time I could smell freshly cooked eggs, bacon, and even sausage. My stomach rumbled furiously and I longed to hop down off my horse and rummage up some of that breakfast but camp had to be set up before we did anything. Winter was here and instead of just me and Chesterfield in the tent it would be nearly four or five men just to stay warm and dry.

"Halt!" Sergeant Loyod commanded. "We set up camp here. Once you're done getting your tent upright grab some chow and stick close to camp. We don't have orders yet and I need you all here if we have to move out at a moment's notice."

"Yes Sergeant." Yes Sergeant, yes Sergeant. Always yes Sergeant. It was rare for Sergeant Loyod to give us good news or just tell us what we wanted to hear but I'd imagine being the constant bearer of poor tidings was not an easy outfit to wear day in and day out. Loyod quickly tied off his horse and marched towards the Officers tent that was swiftly erected by some greener Privates.

"Hey Roach." Chesterfield walked up behind me holding a tent bundle in his hands. "You have your half?" I nodded.

"I certainly do. I unfastened my white tent roll from the back of my saddle and threw it down with Chesterfield's half. We found what looked like a clean plot, kicked out the rocks and stomped the ground to make it just a little more even. Chesterfield didn't waste any time setting the first tent stick in place while I buttoned the two halves of the tent together. My hands were cold and numb and the small buttons of the tent made it hard to button them up quickly but sure enough, one by one I got them done. I stood upright with my hands on my hips and overlooked the landscape surrounding Fort Sanders. The land around Knoxville appeared a barron wasteland. All the trees had been cut to stumps leaving only stripped bark or sporadic saplings behind. Everywhere you stepped the ground was a torn up muck; a most unforgiving place that had seen more suffering than most. What buildings remained here were badly damaged and poorly maintained.

"You suppose they'll have some more of that breakfast ready for us when we get done?" I laughed quietly under my breath.

"If you quit flappin yur gums and help me git this tent up a little faster we might get some of that breakfast." We each grabbed a tent poll and propped up each side and then lashed the small rope to the poles from the tent that had been pulled through the grommets. "Here, you get that side. I'll do this one." I threw the tent stakes to Chesterfield and we set them in the dirt. I was happy to be setting the stakes because it gave me an excuse to pull out my tomahawk and hammer them down with the backside.

"Why do you carry that thing around? You know you're never going to get a chance to use it." I pointed the tomahawk at the old man and bounced it in my hand a few times.

"Have you used your knife or bayonet to kill a man?" Chesterfield nodded and smiled.

"Well yeah but I don't see what yur getting at?"

"If you can get close enough to kill a man with a knife or bayonet you can certainly get close enough to kill him with an axe."

"Alright, well when you kill someone with an axe you come find me and tell me all about it. I heard all them injun stories and Cherokee runnin' a muck throwing tomahawks from a ways away and then scalping. That's a rough sort of business them injuns are into. You suppose that tomahawk belonged to a injun Chieftain or some damn thing?" I looked over the handle and saw cuts in the wood grain.

"Well, it's got tick marks so if it was an injun he killed a lot of white men."

"I bet that Reb corpse you pulled it off was the one puttin on the tick marks. He just put a notch in every time he shot someone."

"I dunno Chesterfield. There's a lot of dried blood on the head. I think this axe has sunk into a few skulls in its lifetime. Maybe even scalped several of us Union Soldiers." I said jokingly. We chuckled at the thought and got back to securing the tent in place. Breakfast was calling and I was not about to ignore its sweet scent. Once the tent was up we grabbed our mess kit and ran up the fortifications of Fort Sanders making our way to the cook. Down into a wide and deep ditch there were men as far as the eye could see digging the trench deeper and placing the dirt in wheel barrels to be hauled off and placed atop other berms.

"I'll race you to the top!" Chesterfield taunted and push me over on my side. I got up quickly and ran up after him. The dirt wall was steep, cold and wet. As I ran up the hill as fast as I could I hit a patch of ice and slipped back down the hill. I got behind Chesterfield who had dug his feet in but even he had difficulty reaching the top. On our hands and feet we climbed digging our hands into the dirt where we could actually penetrate our fingers into the sheets of frozen water beneath the earth. At long last we reached the top; Chesterfield reached down with his hand and I grasped it to take the last step or two.

"You're pretty fast for an old man." I remarked.

"And you're pretty slow for a spring chicken." Chesterfield crossed his arms and looked outward from Fort Sanders in awe.

"Would you look at that. What a shame." I shook my head.

"Doesn't look like much to fight over does it?"

"No young man, it doesn't. Either way, when the Rebs get here were still gonna fight'em." Chesterfield slapped my back. "Come on A.J., let's git some breakfast." The top of the fortification filled with a flurry of activity as cannons were placed into position, cannon balls stacked carefully and gunpowder readied for the fight to come.

"Hey you!" a loud voice barked from my left side. I turned my head to see a grizzled looking Sergeant with long sideburns bearing down on me.

"Me Sergeant?" I asked unsure if I had done something wrong.

"What are you doing up here?"

"Were with the Eighth Cavalry Sergeant. We just got in and came in to grab some chow."

"Well get the hell off my rampart. If you're not digging or piling shot you don't belong up here. Stick to the main road, you understand?"

"Yes Sergeant." The man shook his head in disapproval and stomped away quickly barking away at another solider after taking no more than three steps.

"The hospitality of Fort Sanders is probably not its best quality. C'mon lad. Let's go." We walked down steep wooden steps to reach the chow line. There were several lines where men and women were handing out heaps of food the likes of which we had not seen in months. After waiting half an hour or so we reached the cooks that quickly piled on eggs, bacon, sausage and even filled up our cups with steaming hot coffee!

"Thank you kindly." I said to the older woman that filled my plate. She reminded me of my mother being out here in the cold taking care of her boys.

"Bless you son. You stay safe out there ya'hear."

"Yes mam." Everyone had someone that was fighting this damn war and she was probably no different. We made our way back to the tents and sat down eagerly. I went after the bacon first and put pieces under my lip so I could soak in the juices while I shoveled in big heaping servings of egg. The warmth of the food hit my belly fast and when I topped it off with the fresh coffee I felt the need for sleep creeping in.

\* \* \*

Bugles blared loudly in the early morning hours after I had slept for what felt like a fortnight. The men in my tent rose just as startled as I and we rushed outside our tents grabbing our weapons and running to formation. "Let's go! Let's go! Form up!" Corporal O'Brian yelled. Sergeant Loyod came out of the shadows and pushed Corporal O'Brian out of the way.

"Atten-hut!" We snapped to attention in the freezing cold air. Sergeant Loyod turned about and saluted Captain Masengill and Lieutenant Campbell. "Fox Company is formed Sir!" Captain Masengill returned the salute.

"Very well, Sergeant. Company, at ease!" We relaxed our stance and stared at the Captain who wore a heavy wool coat to keep out the cold. "Men, the Rebs are on their way here to this Fort as we speak! Our orders are quite simple, pack up your supplies and horses, bring everything into Fort Sanders and assist in preparation of the fortifications until the Rebel forces arrive. Is that understood?"

"Yes Sir." We replied.

"You have fifteen minutes to gather your belongings. Afterwards ride your horses into the center of the fort where men are waiting to take them from your care. You will eat breakfast quickly and begin work immediately. We have no time for idleness today gentlemen. The very fate of Fort Sanders and what remains of Knoxville is in our hands. The Ohio Forty Fourth will man the ramparts while we work. Sergeant Loyod."

"Yes Sir?"

"Dismiss the troops and carry out the plan of the day." Sergeant Loyod rendered another salute.

"Yes Sir." Masengill returned the salute and then turned about to walk back to the Officers quarters of the Fort. "Alright men, you heard him. Git your belongings together and ride into the fort. Do not leave your weapons or ammunition behind with the horses. Understood?"

"Yes Sergeant."

"Company, Atten-hut!" We snapped to attention. "Dismissed." Leaving formation, I walked straight back for the tent. Between the four of us the inside of the tent was cleared out quickly and swiftly disassembled and packed away on the horses. I pulled the wool blanket from Abigail and patted her on the side of her front legs. Leaving her outside all night seemed like a cruelty but the horses seemed to be well built for the cold. Even on the evenings filled with snow they kept their distance from the fires. I looked her straight in those big brown eyes and nodded my head.

"Looks like yur gonna sit this one out girl." She snorted and shook her head. "I know, I know. I'll come back for you when all this is over. I promise. C'mon, let's go." I grabbed the saddle ridge and swiftly mounted Abigail. "Git!" I slapped the reins and she marched forward, the cold air rushing by my face. Near the center of the fort the horses were gathering and being pushed into a stable that was completely boarded up. I was comforted knowing that Abigail would have some cover from the musket fire but worried that a mortar or cannon round may find its way to the stables. She may have been a big dumb beast but I cared not to lose her, she had become family to me.

"Git to the ditch." Corporal Uankey ordered. "Breakfast will be brought to you. Once you're fed start digging and don't stop until you're told." Uankey wasn't much of a slave driver so his presence sat well with the other Privates, unlike Corporal O'Brian. O'Brian had been absent as of late and I wondered if he had become ill. With so many soldiers around day in and day out I seemed to come across new faces each day. Chesterfield and I reached the ditch and took a seat leaning against the dirt fortification. A cook and several men came around and quickly handed out bread, salted pork, and even muckets of hot coffee.

"Well this ain't so bad." Chesterfield leaned over the mucket and waved his hand over the steam of the mucket pushing the smell up his nose. "Now that's some proper coffee right there. At least our bellies will stay warm."

"Hey old man." Chesterfield lifted his head and shot me a wide gaze.
"Yes?"

"You believe in ghosts? I mean like spirits?" Chesterfield squinted his eye and leaned forward with interest. I thought for sure he'd laugh at me but he seemed genuinely interested in what I was about to say. "I mean, you've been around a long time. You've seen things right?"

"Why do you ask youngster?"

"I just wonder if Billie is out there somewhere, you know, watching over us." Chesterfield placed his hands on his knees and leaned back comfortably against the dirt.

"Son, listen here. I can tell you I seen many things that make me question life, god, and why we are here. I ain't gonna lie to you, there were many a times I saw strange lights on in the dark; things that look like they floated about. I try not to think too hard bout stuff like that. As for Billie, I'd like to think he ain't stuck here no more but that he resides in the home of the All Mighty. Billie deserves better than this, better than what we got." I nodded and looked down at my boots that were covered in muck. "Hey, don't you fret over Billie. He's in a better place now." I smiled and took a sip of my coffee.

"Thanks Chesterfield."

"Don't mention it. Now git on with your breakfast. We got dirt to dig. This hole ain't gonna make itself."

* * *

The hours passed quickly and despite the constant warnings of a pending Confederate attack, they did not show. We had our lunch rations and shortly after noon I was ready for a nap, but as I dozed off in the dirt a stranger approached.

"You two." I turned my head to see a well-dressed Captain wearing spectacles. Chesterfield and I popped upright and rendered a salute.

"Good afternoon Sir." I greeted.

"Good afternoon Privates. My name is Captain Poe. Are you with the Eighth by chance?" We nodded.

"We are indeed Sir." Chesterfield proudly replied.

"Very good. The ditch is well dug. You boys have done a fine job. I want you to assist my engineers further in the field. I will notify your Sergeant of your assignment."

"What can we help you with Sir?"

"I need you boys to help run telegraph wire between the stumps." I didn't fully understand the Captains meaning. Who were we looking to speak with?

"Happy to help Sir. Where are we running the wires to?"

"You're not." He said with a devilish grin.

"Sir?" Why would we run telegraph wires if they were not going to another company or regiment?

"You boys are gonna run this wire at one hundred and thirty yards from the fort and tangle it between every tree stump you can find. We need to find more ways of slowing down their infantry and I think this just may do the trick. Do you understand?" I'd never heard anything like it in my entire life but was not about to mince words with a Captain.

"I believe I do Sir."

"Good. Head out to the field. Corporal Smith will give you your supplies and directions. He has one eye so it won't be hard for you to find him. Dismissed Privates." We saluted and waited for Captain Poe to return it in kind.

"Yes Sir." We turned away and walked out of the ditch away from the fort. The Corporal that Captain Poe spoke of was already in the distance laying out wire from several bundles on wooden spools.

"Corporal Smith?" I asked. The back of his hair was cut ragged like a mangy blond dog. He turned and looked at us with his one good blue eye.

"Did Captain Poe send you?"

"He did indeed Corporal. Here to help you with that telegraph wire."
Corporal Smith pointed at his home-made spider web with pride.

"Well, there it is. Just do like I'm doing and make sure it's good and
tight. We don't want them knocking it down after one step. We gotta
tangle them sons of bitches up good. Slow'em down as much as we
can. You got that?"

"Yes Corporal." I replied.

"Well, go on then, git to work. We haven't much time left!"

"Yes Corporal." I grabbed a spool and handed the other one to
Chesterfield. One by one we wrapped the telegraph wire tightly
around stumps wrapping the wire around several times before moving
on to the next.

"This is stupid." I exclaimed. "They're just gonna see this and step
right over it."

"I wouldn't be so quick to judgement Anderson. If they come up on
us in the dead of night or early in the mornin' this'll be a fine trap
indeed. Even during the day when they're running down in formation they'll trip over the wire, slow their march, and start falling all
over each other. With the six pounders and the Henry's coming down
on them it'll take them forever to get passed these wires if we make
enough of a tangled mess." I still didn't like it but maybe Chesterfield
was right.

"Fine, let's just get this done. We weaved and weaved the wire
for hours clean around the entire fort. Some of the men pointed and
laughed watching us from the ramparts. As sunset approached we ran
out of wire but it didn't matter. The tangled black web was set and
ready for its unsuspecting victims. I only hoped to god that when
Johnny Reb showed up that they would work a terrible misfortune
on them.

\* \* \*

Bugles and drums sounded in the early morning hours. "To your stations! To your stations!" A bell rang heavy from the Officers' quarters

and a flood of soldiers sprang forth from every crevice of Fort Sanders. Chesterfield and I scrambled to our feet running up the earthwork berms next to so many other soldiers with rifles in hand.

"Fix Bayonets!" an Officer called over the stampede of footsteps and the flurry of rushing war fighters. Laying at the top of the berm I pulled my bayonet from its sheath and fixed it in position. The metal of my barrel was ice cold and unforgiving to the touch. I dare say that if I held my hand atop it long enough my hand would freeze in place. I reached down to my waist to check that the tomahawk was secure in my belt and ready; it to was ice cold.

"Lookie there!" Chesterfield pointed to a spot against the tree line. The early morning mist made for terrible scouting but there was no mistaking the movement of the massive shadows in the background. Like a monster crawling out of its hole the Confederate Infantry positioned themselves just outside of the trees. I felt a tap on my foot and looked back to see Sergeant Loyod placing boxes behind me.

"Forty dead men each. Make'em count. Don't fire until given the order. You got it?"

"Yes Sergeant." We replied.

"I'll be back to check on you before the real fighting starts. Just sit pretty and keep yur heads low."

"How many you suppose are out there Anderson?" Chesterfield asked. I shook my head and squinted my eyes trying to focus in on the moving blobs.

"Two, maybe three thousand. Can't be any more than four." The old man turned to me and shuddered.

"Four thousand? Sounds like they got the whole damn Confederate Army out there."

"Load!" an artillery Officer ordered. The mortars behind us were being prepped. They'd start shelling those bastards before they sent the rifled shot from the six pounders. Once everyone was in position and the cannons loaded and readied to fire; it seemed the whole darn fort had gone silent as the grave. Even the Confederates in the distance had ceased to move. My ears began to ring in the deafening silence and I could feel my already cold limbs growing icier in the frightening quiet. I turned my head to Chesterfield who spat in the dirt in front of him.

"You got chew?" I asked. Chesterfield did not pull his eyes away from the battle line but rather reached back into his pocket and pulled out a rope of tobacco; breaking off a piece he handed it to me and I gladly stuff it under my lip getting the kick I needed to wake myself up right. "Thank you Sir."

"Don't mention it. You just keep your eyes ahead young lad. If we're lucky we'll make short work of 'em."

"I hope your right. If they make it over this berm we ain't got nowhere to run to."

"Well lad, you could always surrender but then it's a one way trip to Belle Isle. I hear those Reb prison camps are worse than fightin' in the fields. Treat you worse than dogs they will."

"No!" I said in protest. "No way in hell am I surrendering. I came this far, I ain't gonna give in now." I ran my thumb against the stock of my rifle where my notches for kills had been placed. Chesterfield's eyes gazed over at me seeming cold and dark. "What?"

"Something tells me you're still tryin' to save Billie?"

"Billie already got saved. He's in heaven now with the All-Mighty." Chesterfield smiled and patted me on the back.

"That he is lad, that he is." A wail of thousands of voices came screeching across the frigid fields as the Johnny Rebs let out their vicious war cry. It sounded like wild Indian savages of every nation were about to descend upon us.

"Alright boys, let's send 'em a message. Fire!" The artillery Officer ordered. The ground shook with great fury as dirt leapt up from beneath our bodies as the mortars were fired over our heads. The shot streak across the sky like a shooting star dousing our heads with sparks and powder. I watched with great anticipation as the round arced and then made its descent until landing right on top of the Confederate formation. The impact thundered and roared spewing dirt, rock, and limbs in all directions. Screams erupted out of the distance but were quickly silenced by the next volley of mortar shot that raged forward. Steel rained down on the Confederates whose masses began to show their numbers under the approaching light of the morning sun. Formations of infantrymen charged forward at a steady run with more regiments forming up just behind them ready to charge into the fray.

"They're comin! Get ready!" Sergeant Loyod exclaimed. I cocked my rifle and put their masses in my sights. My heart pounded heavy in my chest, its fast-paced race interrupted only by the quake of mortar shot. The moments passed slowly as my finger hovered heavy over the trigger ready to squeeze and let the first-round fly down the field to take its first victim. The lead formation of Rebs came up on the entanglement of telegraph wire we had set out just the previous day and I waited for them to stop to notice the obstacle, but they kept running forward, faster and faster they came with all the Souths fury until suddenly the first rank tripped and fell followed by the second and even the third. Bodies tumbled over one another and one by one the entanglements seemed to nearly reach up and pull men to the dirt.

"Let them sons of bitches have it! Open fire! Fire, fire, fire!" Captain Masengill ordered. I pulled the trigger and felt the release of anticipation as the first round flew ahead finding a victim in the pile of bodies. A line of nearly three hundred men along the earthwork opened fire relentlessly as the tangled mass that struggled so helplessly to free themselves; then suddenly the line ceased to move as their scuffle was ended by a barrage of bullets.

"It's like fish in a barrel!" Chesterfield remarked happily. The Artillery continued to pound and beat its deadly drum. Formations of men attempted to maneuver around their stuck comrades but they to found themselves tripping over the wire and finding the same fate as their fallen brothers. I picked my targets no longer firing into the masses but finding those clever enough to avoid the entanglements. Drums beat loudly as the next wave of grey coats rushed forward this time stepping atop their fallen to escape the wire. The corpses began to pile up high creating a morbid fence line that their still living comrades had to surmount.

"Fire!" The artillery Officer called to the six pounders. The guns blared and ripped gaps into the Confederate lines. Barely a shot could be heard coming in our direction. How could their Generals be so careless to order this attack? Victory for Johnny Reb seemed hopeless and yet they kept coming. A loud cry that cut the sky itself erupted and massive regiments came running forward under the cover of Confederate cannon fire.

"Here they come!" a Private cried out. I had never seen so many soldiers charging forward at once. It was a terrifying sight that sent chills down my spine. My hands grew weak, cold, and I clenched my fists tightly to force the emotion away.

"There's too many of'em. How the hell are we gonna hold?" Chesterfield asked. I paid no mind to his question and just kept firing. The entanglements continued to slow down their pace but the bridge of corpses provided some reprieve for the living to move onward. The first of the Rebs reached the edge of the trench and without knowing it was there, fell and rolled down to the bottom. Captain Masengill and other Officers stood in the open with Pistols in hand firing down at them. I caught a glimpse of one boy attempting to stand and look up just to catch a shot to the face. His body dropped hard and slid down to the bottom of the trench that now resembled a mass grave as the bodies piled in.

"The hell?" I pulled the trigger but my rifle did not fire. I cocked the lever and kicked out the round loading a new one. Sighting in on a target I squeezed the trigger and again the round did not fire. I ejected the round and looked down my chamber finding a small rock logged inside. Turning the rifle over I knocked the rock out and cocked the rifle again loading it once more. Dirt flew up in my face as musket fire began to impact the berm directly in front of me. Snaps and cracks could be heard where the Confederates were shooting over us. I scooted back and dug further into the dirt for additional cover until I found a comfortable spot and went through my rounds.

"Get on your feet!" Captain Masengill ordered. "They're coming up the wall! Push'em back!" Standing up quickly from my firing position I felt naked out in the open but my concern was swiftly refocused to the swarm of soldiers down below attempting to scale the dirt wall. Overnight the engineers had ordered water be poured on the wall and it appeared to do the job. The water had frozen! Nearly a solid sheet of ice and not one Reb could get up the wall. As they helplessly slid about we rained shot down mercilessly. Their clothing and flesh was torn from their bodies and still they climbed with great bravery and desperation. Their faces mutilated and hands ripped apart and still they climbed. Wave after wave came and as the bodies piled the living came closer to surmounting the berm. Drums and bugles sounded and another rush of men came forward with flag bearers running behind the first three lines.

"Keep it up! They ain't done yet!" I pulled back from the line and reloaded. My ammo carton was now empty and I turned back to fire my remaining fifteen rounds when I was met with a man's face near my feet. He swung his bayonet at me and I leapt back barely missing the blade. He climbed higher and I stepped forward sinking my toma-hawk in his shoulder. He screamed gripping the wound attempting to lift his musket one last time on me. Kicking him in the chest the man fell back rolling down the hill. The Confederates were everywhere and our line was beginning to pull back from the edges of the walls as the full force of the South came after us. Johnny Reb reached the top but each of their victories were quickly wiped away as bayonet and bullet found its mark each time sending bloodied boys back down the wall.

"The flag bearers!" Sergeant Loyod pointed down the line as one, two, and then three of the Confederate battle flags made it to the top of the berm waving erratically back and forth. "Shoot'em down! Don't let them rally!" I aimed at the flag bearer closest to me and fired strik-ing him in the hip. The boy faltered falling to one knee but the flag remained standing. He held firm appearing resolved to keep their col-ors flying overhead. Bayonets pierced his chest straight into his heart and his head dropped. The flag fell back but continued to stand upright with the pole propped up against his body. Sergeant Loyod ran over to the boy kicking him over by his shoulder then grabbing the flag and throwing it back down into the trench like a spear hitting a few men on the way down. My rifle ran empty and I reached down for my pistol to work the six shots. I walked the line as bodies climbed upward and one at a time I pointed my barrel straight at the top of their heads, squeezing the trigger and sending them back down into the hole. The flag bearers of the Confederates had fallen and their colors were now nowhere to be seen. Soldiers were beginning to fall back still under the relentless hail of gun and cannon fire. With ammunition running low we worked the wall with our bayonets stabbing anything close to the top.

"Get that wall cleared!" Sergeant Loyod ordered feverously. A man reached the top and charged at me. A shot rang out next to my ear causing instant deafness and a terrible ring. Chesterfield shot the boy clean through the ribs. He fell at my feet, his blood flowing out into a small pool on the ground. I nodded at the old man who quickly returned his eyes front. Stepping forward a hand gripped the tip of my boot. Staring downward I saw a boy with bloodshot brown eyes looking up at me. He had no weapon in hand, no knife to speak of. His lips moved quivering in the chaos gripping a wound with his other hand. I reached towards my waist gripping my tomahawk and thrust my arm forward planting my blade in the side of his neck. The boy's lips stopped moving, his eyes full of desperation and pain now emptied and glazed over as the blood trickled out of his body. One last time he stared at me before his eyes rolled to the back of his head. I pulled the blade from his body and let him slide backwards into the carnage below. His face continued to stare upward at me from the pile of corpses that lined the trench below and a cold twinge entered my heart that pulled at my ribs and stomach. I didn't know why I killed that boy; I didn't have to. He was already injured; he didn't have any weapons to speak of. The image of his lips moving in the disorder haunted me. What was he saying? Was he asking for help? For mercy? Now I would never know.

"We did it!" Chesterfield exclaimed. "God damn it all, we got'em on the run!" Cheers and shouts of celebration erupted through Fort Sanders. I stood upright removing my cap and watching as what remained of the Rebel forces fled in utter terror. Those with shot left continued to fire at their backs and even the artillery Officers kept on with their barrage of the larger formations until they to chose to flee from sight. Looking down the line I saw few if any casualties, an absolute victory for us and a crushing defeat for Johnny Reb. No sooner did the Confederates flee and the shooting stop did the crows descend upon the hundreds of Rebel dead. The smell of gunpowder was now overshadowed by the overwhelming aroma of death and decay. A Private standing next to me coughed loudly and then bent over throwing up what food he had in his belly. I lifted my arm over my nose to mask the terrible smells but the sights before my eyes could never be concealed and they could never be forgotten.

"It's not over boys." Captain Masengill remarked.

"How's that Captain? They're on the run ain't they?" I asked.

"Longstreet is indeed on the run Private Roach. It's time to go hunting gentlemen."

# Nine
# Bulls Gap, The Hunt for General Longstreet – December 1863

"Do you suppose they left?" Chesterfield asked me.

"Left? You mean did they leave Tennessee?" He nodded and I shook my head.

"I'd imagine not. Those Generals and Confederate Officers always like to talk about their honor and acting like gentlemen. I reckon him and his boys are hiding out right now; probably skulking from town to town trying to keep warm." It was midmorning and the sun was nowhere to be seen. The clouds hung low but snow had yet to fall on our heads. Abigail seemed to be in good spirits and I had to keep pulling back on the reins to restrain her from running ahead of the column.

"Well I hope we find those boys soon. Captain ain't gonna be happy until we survey the entire damn state. Haven't seen a soul out here for days. Nothing but rocks and trees, rocks and trees while Longstreet and his boys are probably curled up in some cabins somewhere laying next to a fire place."

"Are you going to whine like this all day?" I asked with a crooked grin. Chesterfield laughed and tugged on his beard.

"Whine? Me? Never. I'm just stating a point of fact. While we're out here trudging through snow and ice on bellies filled with crackers and salted pork. I even had a warm cup of water this morning and pretended it was coffee."

"Coffee! Please Chesterfield, no more. It seems like ages since I've had a good cup of black coffee straight off the fire."

"Have you ever had that fancy coffee them New York boys are making out of those muckets?"

"Muckets?"

"Those fancy metal cups with the cloth. Those boys pound those beans fine as sand and strain them. I got one off one of those boys just last night, said he got a new one and didn't need it no more."

"So you've been holding out on me? Where's the coffee?"

"I said I had the mucket, not the beans. C'mon A.J., would I hold out on you?" We reached a small ice strewn stream and the Captain halted the column. Ahead of the stream it looked like mostly flat and forested terrain in a long and wide valley. Captain Masengill raised his sabre high in the air and swung his horse around.

"Alright men, gather round, gather round." Seventy-five horses in all. A few men short of what we started with in Kentucky and my heart weighed heavy thinking on Billie who was buried six feet deep in the frozen earth. "Listen up. We have a large valley ahead and I need to split us up into at least two groups. Sergeant Loyod and I will take the left side of the valley accompanied by the first thirty-five horses in line. The rest of you will accompany Lieutenant Campbell. If you find the enemy perched up like vultures on the hillsides keep your distance, do not engage under any circumstance. Our task is to locate the position of Lieutenant General Longstreet and report this back to the Ohio Forty Fourth so that they can close and engage. Are there any questions?"

"How will we recognize the General Sir?" A Private called out.

"That is an excellent question Private. I am told that the General has large commanding brown beard. More than likely he will be wearing the standard Grey Officers attire with gold piping. He will be riding a horse and is supported by mainly infantry. There will be a supply wagon with a limited number of artillery pieces. If you spot him and his men do not yell or alert them to our presence. It is my intention to keep them in their place until the Forty Fourth comes to pay them a most unwelcomed visit. Any other questions?" The men were quiet and only the sound of a howling wind pierced the spaces between our silence. "Very well. Eyes forward, move out!"

"Here we go." Chesterfield had a smile on his face but it seemed more like a false motivation.

"Why the excitement?"

"The sooner we find this Reb General the sooner we can get back to camp. My mucket is just waiting to get used and I hear some of the boys are gonna scavenge for some wild pig while were out."

"Wild pig? That sounds just fine! Give me a fired pork chop any day." I slapped Abigail's reins and she took off after the horses in front of us. "Yah! Yah!" We rode to the left with the Captain and the Sergeant which was fine by me. I didn't want to get stuck out in a fight with the Lieutenants. Lord knows they've seen a battle or two but to us enlisted men they were still green as frogs. They usually held back letting us do most of the fighting but I was told that was common for most Officer men. Not Captain Masengill though; he kept close to the Sergeant who had been serving since the Captain was a baby. If anyone was going to make it out of this war alive it was going to be that tough son of a bitch Sergeant Loyod.

We kept to the trail that was well marked by cut timber but the fresh powder had covered most of it up. It was going to be a slow ride through the snow to keep from injuring the horses who were nearly knee deep and it made me wonder how the Ohio Forty Fourth and its men would ever get through this terrain. The trail began rise on a steady incline through a thick forest of frost covered trees. At long last a shimmering light came bursting through the clouds and a ray of sunshine pressed against my cheek warming my numb skin. I closed my eyes for a moment and breathed in deeply trying to keep the warmth for as long as I could.

"It's a sign." Chesterfield said. "Yes Sir, that's a sign all right; there from the good Lord himself if I ever saw one. We are in good company today."

"How do you figure?"

"Of all the places of snow covered Tennessee the sun shone on us. If that don't tell you that there is in fact a divine purpose at play, then I don't know what will." I chuckled a bit breathing slower to keep the cold out of my chest.

"Lord knows I am a God-fearing man but I was never one to believe in signs as it were." Chesterfield lifted his arms high in the air.

"You just have to open your eyes Roach. Look at all the beauty around us. You think that just happened by accident?" He shook his head. "Nothing in this world happens by accident. Everything is as the All-Mighty intends it to be."

"And what about Billie? Was that in God's plans?" Chesterfield's grin faded as the creases around his beard settled in deeply into his bright red face.

"Now I don't pretend to understand the Lord's will. I just accept it as it is. Makes life a whole lot easier if you know what I mean." He leaned towards me from his horse and gripped my shoulder like a father would his son.

"I am sorry for your loss my friend. I truly am. Billie was one hell of a fighter. Yes Sir, one hell of a fighter. It was a damn shame what happened to him outside that barn but you need to let go of that shame young man. That's just gonna weigh you down your whole life and I don't think that's how Billie would have wanted you to live."

"But it was my fault." I lamented.

"Nonsense young man. Is it your fault when the wind blows or when the dog barks? Heck no. Just like it wasn't your fault when that Reb jumped out of the hay, pointed his gun at Billie's back and pulled the trigger. Ain't no way in hell that could be your fault. It was just Billie's time is all. We all have a time A.J.; you best believe that. When the good Lord comes for you, ain't no runnin' from that."

"Are you a preacher Chesterfield?"

"No Sir, I'm a sinner through and through but the good Lord has seen to it that if I believe and love in him entirely then I shall be excused of my past misgivings. Besides, I like to drink and gamble. When was the last time you saw a preacher man doing those things while drinking some Tennessee Brown?"

"I don't know too much bout preachers. We had one back in town sure enough but I always snuck off to do this and that. You know, kid stuff."

"Oh I know what you're talking about. Shoot, I think you and I would have gotten along just fine as kids. Long as you don't mind a good fist fight now and then?" I shook my head and smiled thinking of all the times the town boys and I would get into a tussle, wrestling one another down to the ground then throwing a punch or two.

"No Chesterfield, I don't mind a good fist fight now and then. So why are you here?"

"Cause' this is where the Captain told us to go." I laughed aloud.

"No stupid, why are you here in the Army. What made you join?"

"Well, my wife died years ago, my son god bless him died two years ago at the start of the war and my daughter married some man from Maine. I haven't seen her in years. So one day I was sitting in the saloon with whiskey in my belly and a whore on my knee when I saw it; three Union men walking in looking shiny and new. They had smiles ear to ear and pockets full of money and I figured, if they can do it so can I."

"So you joined for money?"

"Among other things but mostly just to get away from the life I didn't have. There was nothing holding me back at home and I needed something better than climbing to the bottom of a bottle every night. Hell, I even got into a few quarrels over my gambling debts. If I stayed much longer they probably would have come to collect. Do you know what they take form you when you don't have any money son?" I shook my head.

"No Chesterfield. Maw always said that gambling was trouble and I should never bother with it."

"Well, your Maw didn't steer you wrong. You see, if I stayed they would have started collecting little bits of me. They would have started with bits of my fingers and then worked their way to my toes, my tongue, my ears, and then after all that they'd show me a kindness by putting a hot poker down my throat."

"That's terrible." I remarked.

"Yeah, I suppose it is. You probably thought you saw the worst of it here fightin' in the fields but you know what I've seen."

"What's that?"

"Most of the boys were fighting out here and fighting with are good boys. They're not cutthroats or pirates. Most of them are patriots with good intentions, some of us just got a different idea of what's right and wrong. Doesn't make either of us evil, just makes us different. Most of the bad folk stayed clear of the army as much as they could. They high tailed it out west where they could steal and plunder to their little heart's desire."

"So it's greed then."

"What's that?" Chesterfield asked.

"Greed is the worst of it?"

"Yes indeed and a sin to boot. Greed will make men do absolutely horrid things. Even when I was deep in that bottle I could see what greed did to men. Didn't make no difference if someone had a lot of nice things or not. Sometimes it was the ones who had a lot who were the greediest people I have seen. Take, take, take."

"Halt." Sergeant Loyod called out softly. Captain Masengill and Sergeant Loyod were taking a long look at a map and pointing out different markers on the hillsides. "Roach, Chesterfield, get up here." Sergeant Loyod ordered. The path was too narrow to ride so we climbed down from our horses and reported front and center saluting the Captain while he looked at the horizon with a field glass.

"You see anything Sir?" I asked curiously. He pulled the field glass away from his eye and pressed it shut tucking it away neatly into a leather pouch on his waist.

"Not a damn thing Private. Longstreet is out there, I know it. I can feel it in my bones. He may have made off after Gettysburg but he's not going to get away this time. No Sir. He's out there somewhere, resting, recruiting, gathering supplies during the winter before they can continue their campaign in the spring. We must find him; we must deprive them of that opportunity if we are to finally put an end to this war." He lifted his arm and pointed outward down a steep ridge that sloped into an adjacent valley. "We cannot traverse this land with even half of our regiment, the terrain is far too steep and crowded, however I suspect that Longstreet and some of his forces may be holed up in that valley. There is a way in it appears, on the opposite side, but it would take us a day's ride or longer to reach it. I need the two of you to go on foot, make your descent and head into the valley below to scout the terrain. If the enemy is indeed in there then they have but one way in and one way out. You will go silently and be back here before sunset while we scout out the rest of this valley. If you happen to spot the General get word to us as quickly as you can. It will be up to the Ohio Forty Fourth to set up a perimeter around their camp and make ready for an assault. Is that understood?"

"Clear as a bell Sir." A look of worry came over Captain Masengill's face; his brow came down and he seemed to purse his lips. "What is it Captain?"

"I would be lying to the two of you if I told you that you would return unharmed. You won't just be dealing with camped out Rebs if you venture down there alone. There are savages roaming these wilds and they do not all take kindly to Federal Troops roaming their lands. They may decide to kill you; or they may decide to help you, so tread lightly. If you find yourself being chased down put a single shot in the air and we'll come for you. God be with you."

"Yes Sir. Thank you Sir." replied Chesterfield. We retrieved our rifles, rations, water, and blankets from the horses. I draped the wool blanket over my shoulders and around my neck in order to find some respite from the cold. My beard had yet to be fully grown and so I pulled some of the blanket over my face to keep the frost from biting at it any further. Chesterfield on the other hand had a magnificent display of facial hair that covered his neck, cheeks, and lips fully. I found it a laugh to watch him talk from time to time as his mustache moved around like a giant caterpillar. We climbed down a steep rocky pass carefully and I shot the Captain one last look before we disappeared into the wood entirely. He waved and threw a smile back. He knew full well what he was asking Chesterfield and I to do.

"C'mon lad." Chesterfield called out. I made my way down the rocky face and soon caught up to him. It was a slow walk down stepping from stone to stone. Our horses never would have made it this way. We proceeded down the rock face and I looked back up the hill to see the silhouettes of the Eighth. They waited for a moment and then turned away riding out slow.

"He should have sent more men with us." I was nervous about this endeavor. There was a lot of land to get lost in and with Rebs running wild who knew if we'd even get a chance to fire a signaling shot.

"What's wrong lad?"

"We've never ventured this far out on our own before."

"Aye, but the good Captain wouldn't have sent us if he didn't trust us. There's a lot that can go wrong out here."

"Do you think we'll find them?" Chesterfield stopped, pulling his rifle lever halfway back looking in the chamber for some brass.

"I couldn't say. Best keep yur wits about you though. Check your rifle, check your pistol and for god's sakes don't stand behind me. I don't need you tripping on a rock and shooting me in the back of the head."

"I might be doing you a favor."

"Aye, you might but right now we got more important things to tend to." The forest floor was eerily still, quiet as the grave and only the sound of snow crunching beneath the soles of our boots filled the space between the trees. After walking a ways the bushes started to play tricks on me. Every once in a while the wind would blow like a whistle and a dark colored bush would shake and tremble. My finger started twitching near the trigger but when I realized they were just shrubs I placed my finger higher up on the rifle. "You look nervous." Chesterfield smiled. "You know this is the closest thing to freedom we've had in a long time."

"What do you mean? We're not free. We're out here doing a job."

"Yes we are, but no one is watching us, are they?" Chesterfield reached into his jacket and pulled out a small glass bottle of whiskey. Half empty, he shook it back and forth with a mischievous smile. "Can I tempt you with a drink?" I reached out and eagerly snatched the bottle from his hand taking a quick drink and handing it back. The whiskey burned going down and warmed my cold belly.

"So this is what you had in mind. Go for a walk and have a drink in the middle of the frozen woods?" Chesterfield shook his head and his eyes opened wide. I turned in the direction of his gaze but saw nothing. "What is it?"

"Quiet boy. Stay quiet." Chesterfield crouched down and I did the same fearing the enemy may be near. I listened and stretched my ears as far as I could but I heard nothing. The old man pointed ahead at a gathering of bushes and in the distance were three white hares all nestled under the brush with their backs towards us. He pushed me to the side and pointed out to the left. "You go over there and keep their attention."

"You're not gonna fire a shot are you?" Chesterfield cocked his head down and gave me a ridiculous look; like the gaze of a man staring down a foolish child.

"Hell no. You think I'm stupid. I just need you to go over yonder and keep them preoccupied while I smash one of them with my rifle. You want a fresh lunch don't you?" I pointed at his rifle.

"Fine, but you get that bullet outta your chamber before you have an accident. I'm not draggin' your corpse all the way back up that hill. Chesterfield nodded and cocked the lever back several times ejecting all seven rounds. He picked them up out of the snow one by one and wiped them clean before sticking them in his pockets.

"Go on then." I took my time and made a wide track around the hares until their heads cocked up and their beady eyes watched me. Crouching down I placed the butt of my rifle on my thigh and my barrel on the opposite shoulder. I pulled at the snow in front of me trying to make a little noise to keep their attention. The old man made his move darting forward and leapt swinging the butt of his rifle downward. The hares on opposite ends turned and ran while the one in the center took a blow straight to the head. A dull thudding sound and he lifted his rifle again taking another swipe at the varmint. Chesterfield walked on all fours towards his kill and lifted it up in the sky for me to see. A white fur coat now turned pink by a splash of blood that dripped, dripped, dripped down to the snow below.

"I can't believe you got him? You smashed him good!" Chesterfield smiled from ear to ear.

"Well like my old man used to say, if you hit'em hard enough they will die."

"Why would he say that?"

"Cause' it's the truth.", he chuckled.

"It ain't very clever."

"Yeah, well who's the one holding lunch? Hmm?" He made a good point and now my stomach started to growl thinking about getting some fresh meat in my belly. "You ever skin one of these?" I shook my head.

"No. I've skinned coons, I skinned a cat once and a few catfish but I ain't never skinned a rabbit." He nodded.

"Alirght, well you go get some wood and start a fire. Make sure it's under a thick tree. We don't need to be sending any smoke signals to Lieutenant General Longstreet." I took off a way and started gathering kindling from under the big trees where it was still a little dry. The bark was wet so I pulled out my tomahawk and one by one I cut it back peeling the skin back until I got down to what was dry. Chesterfield was already done skinning the hare taking the meat and hanging it over a tree branch just behind me. I placed the dry wood atop a rock and started digging in the snow until I reach dirt and then I dug deeper and deeper until I made a hole as wide as my foot and deep enough to catch me up to my ankles. Slowly I broke up the sticks and placed them in the hole being careful not to get snow inside.

"You got matches?"

"Do I have matches? Shoot! Don't you see me smoking like a chimney each and every night?"

"Yeah but that don't mean you didn't run out." He reached into his leather pouch and produced an entire board of matches. "Where'd you get all those?"

"Did you know that the Quartermaster is a gambling man?"

"No, I did not."

"Neither did I until last night. Only problem is he ain't a good one!" Chesterfield laughed aloud slapping his knee enthusiastically. "I got a new pair of socks and a new pair of trousers back at camp." He handed me a match and I struck it hard against the backside of the board. It popped and cracked when it lit and I slowly put it down the hole running the little flame up and down my pieces of kindling. Soon the fire grew and I added more pieces that became progressively larger. Very shortly we had a full-fledged campfire roaring from off the ground. Chesterfield stuck that hare on a stick and held him over the flame turning him every so often. The meat was bright pink and clean. My mouth watered just thinking about the first bite. The air around us wafted with the smell of good old fashioned camp roast and I was getting impatient.

"How much longer?"

"How much longer he asks? Pfft, how much longer? It will take as long as it's gonna take unless you wanna get sick?"

"No, not particularly. I'm just so damn sick of that salted pork. They keep tellin us it's fresh, no more than a week or two old but I think their lying to us. Each day I gotta take a shit in the woods that would offend even a bear."

"Sound to me like you've got a weak constitution. You best get a stronger stomach. It's only December and we've got a lot of land to cover between now and spring." The once bright pink flesh of the hare was turning to a golden brown and it wouldn't be much longer until it was ready to be eaten.

"Drop your weapons!" a voice shouted out from nearby. I stood quickly with my rifle at the ready and looked about my surroundings but I didn't see anything.

"Where they coming from?" Chesterfield asked.

"I dunno, I can't see'em."

"I said put'em down Yankee boy scum unless you want me to fill your bellies full of lead."

"Show yourselves!" I demanded.

"Boy I got about three guns on you and at least two on that old man. Now we'd love to kill yall right here and now but our superiors, god bless'em, might have a more divine plan for you. Now this is the last time, drop them guns nice and slow like on the ground and then step away." I could feel my heart pounding and my palms getting sweaty then I heard the clicks of hammers being pulled back on rifles. "Now!" I dropped my rifle and Chesterfield followed suit.

"Show yourselves!"

"The pistol too and the bayonets. C'mon now, get'em on the ground. Don't forget that little heathen axe you got tucked in yur belt." I removed my bayonet and tomahawk throwing them next to my rifle. I reached down for my pistol and then a dark figure popped up in the distance next to a tree. "Slowly now, wouldn't want us to think you were gonna draw on us or anything like that." Wrapping my hand around the pistol grip I pulled it out slowly from my holster and dropped it barrel first in the snow. "That's it Yank, now both of you, back up and git on your knees." Chesterfield and I looked at each other with worry. I could see doubt in the old man's eyes, the same doubt I had in my heart about what was going to transpire here. As soon as they had those guns they were going to kill us. I knelt on both knees when two other dark silhouettes came out of the shadows. All three approached quickly and the ghostly figures soon looked very familiar. Three Johnny Rebs, all a little older than me. They had furs on and by the looks of the dirt on their faces had been out here for some time.

"You dumb sons of bitches." The first man said as he ran up to the weapons and threw them back to the other two. "What the hell are a pair of fine upstanding gentleman such as yourselves doing in a place like this?"

"We got lost from our Regiment.", replied Chesterfield. "We've been out here for two days starving and nearly freezing to death."

"Starving, well looks like you got a fresh meal here just waiting to be eaten." Another man approached and knelt next to the hare pulling it from the fire.

"This is fresh boss. Good eatin to." He took a knife and ripped a piece off handing it to the man in the center. Another man to our right with a long brown beard came on over to Chesterfield keeping his rifle pointed right at his head.

"Who you Yanks with?" We kept our lips shut tight. If we gave him any information he'd know exactly where Captain Masengill and the other half of the Company was patrolling. We had to protect them at all costs.

"We ain't got a Regiment."

"You ain't got a Regiment. You just told me you been lost. Where the hell is your Regiment boy?"

"We lied." The man behind Chesterfield came in closer pressing his rifle barrel right up against the back of his head. "Were deserters."

"I think their lying boss. They look like Cavalry to me but they ain't got no horses."

"Where's your horses?" Boss asked.

"The frost killed them. We ate what we could but had to leave cause our Captain was out looking for us. That was about two days ride north, north west of here." A dark flash ran across my face.

"Hey boy." Something was pressing against my head and the more I thought about it the more pain it caused me. I squinted my eyes tightly and turned my neck to the left. I felt cold all over my belly and chest when I realized I was laying on the ground. I opened my right eye and felt something running down my left. There was red all over the ground, damn Reb had hit me over the head with something. "Hey boy! You alive down there?" I moaned and turned to my back slowly. "You see that boys, the Yank didn't go to hell after all." He crouched down above me waving a large knife back and forth. "Alirght yank, this here is how it's gonna go. You're gonna tell me where in the hell your Regiment is, or, or, I'm gonna make a knife rack out of your old friend. He pointed across my chest and I turned to see what it was. My eyes were still blurry but I could see something move up against a tree. They focused in and sure enough it was Chesterfield tied up to the base, standing on his feet.

"Chest..." I said weakly. "Chesterfield." He mumbled and moaned loudly a few times. His mouth was gagged with a dirty old rag.

"I think your friend is tryin' to say sumthin'." Boss stood up and walked over me to Chesterfield and pulled the rag from his mouth. "You got something to say to me boy? You better make it quick, I got a game of knife throwing waiting on me." Chesterfield moved his lips but I couldn't hear a thing he was saying. "I thought you had something to say boy, c'mon now. Speak up so we can all hear ya."

"Go to hell!" he yelled in boss's ear. Boss pulled back squinting his eyes and then swung a mean hook at Chesterfields face. I saw blood and a tooth come flying out of his mouth. The old man spit the blood out of his mouth and gave Boss a mean look.

"Got anything to say now Yank?"

"I said, go to hell!" Boss swung again striking Chesterfield on the opposite side and then punched him in the gut.

"You got a mouth on you Yank." Boss pulled out his big knife and put the blade next to his neck. "But that's alright, were about to rectify the situation right here and now. Carter!"

"Yeah Boss?"

"Get his tongue and hold it out so I can cut it outta his mouth."

"No!" I yelled. "Leave him alone. He didn't mean nothin' by it!" Boss turned and pointed the knife at me.

"You shut ur filthy mouth Yank! I'm comin for you next." Carter rushed up to Chesterfield and gripped his cheeks with both hands cramming his fingers into his mouth.

"No!" Chesterfield protested and put up a fight biting down on Carter's hand. Carter yelled and punched the old man.

"You stupid sum'bitch. I'm gonna show you! Bitin' my damn hand." The old man looked weak now from all the knocks to the head. Carter reached his hand into Chesterfields mouth gripping his tongue tight and pulling out hard. "I got'em Boss. Cut it, cut it!" Boss moved his blade between Carters hand and Chesterfield's nose and came down swift on his tongue. With one clean swipe the old man's tongue came clean out. Carter pulled it out quick and waved it in the air while Chesterfield screamed in pain. "Lookie here boys! I got his tongue!"

"Stick it in the fire. We'll watch it dance for a bit." Boss ordered. Carter happily skipped to the fire and placed the tongue on a rock next to the flames. I watched in horror as Chesterfield writhed in pain, the blood running down his beard and the front of his shirt. The three Rebs just stood around the fire pointing and laughing at the piece of flesh that began to blister and bubble.

"Look at it jump! Bet you ain't feelin' so smart now are ya?" Boss took out his bloody knife and held the blade over the flame. He turned back to me with a wicked look.

"You're next boy." I spit at him and gritted my teeth.

"Fuck you!"

"You hear that boys. He said fuck you. Why don't you go on over and soften him up a bit before I work on him." Carter and the unnamed Reb walked towards me and began punching my face, stomach, and ribs. I wheezed and spat blood on the white ground beneath me. They stopped for a moment laughing and snickering at my misery. My ears rang, my head pounded and as I gasped for air I caught a glimpse between my attackers of Boss's blade. It was bright orange, red hot. He wouldn't even need to use the bladed side. He could just run that seething hot metal down my tongue and burn it clean off. Don't even think I would bleed much when he did it either. Boss stood holding the knife at a downward angle and away from his body as smoke rose from it.

"You ready boy?" Carter asked. "I'm not gonna lie to you Yank, I don't envy you. Not one damn bit. This is gonna hurt a hell of a lot." Just then Chesterfield let out a wail and tried to form words out of his mouth. It sounded like an animal trying to speak and the noise rang deafening in my ears. Boss stopped in his tracks and pointed his blade at the old man.

"You know what? I don't think I'm done with him yet. No Sir! I think I'm gonna have to cut off just a bit more. How bout you just sit there and watch pup. It's gonna get a whole hell of a lot worse before it gets better. Work him over some more boys. I want him limp as a drunk when I carve up that pretty face of his. Fists came from all directions and I was pummeled mercilessly doing all I could to take the blows. Boss made his way quickly to Chesterfield and I couldn't make out a word he said until I heard a deafening scream but it was not the old man who cried out. It was Boss! Chesterfield got a hand lose from his ties and pulled Boss in sinking his teeth into his neck and ripping a chunk of flesh out spitting it to the ground. Boss bled out quick and fell to the ground. Before the two Rebs realized what had happened to their friend, Chesterfield grabbed bosses pistol and started firing. They took off like wild hare's in the brush running as fast as they could. The old man grabbed Boss's red hot blade that smoldered in the snow and cut free of his bindings. I started scooting towards him until he reached me and cut me loose.

"Let's go!" I yelled. A shot cracked through the air and a round hit the old man in the back of the leg. He fell hard. "Chesterfield!" I reached down and put his arm around my shoulder. "C'mon, we gotta go." He screamed in my ear but kept pumping his other leg moving as fast as he could. More shots cracked out and I took the pistol from Chesterfield sending one shot back. I saw heads duck behind some trees.

"You can't run forever boy!" Carter called out. "Were gonna shoot you dead for what you done to boss!" We kept running and running and running. Reaching a gentle slope Chesterfield slipped and fell to the ground rolling all the way down. His feet caught mine tripping me up and I fell to.

"Where you at boy? Come on out!" I got Chesterfield back up on his feet and got him moving forward.

"C'mon old man. They're coming." Another shot rang out striking a tree just to the right of me. I pulled Chesterfield harder as sweat fell into my eyes narrowing my vision. I stopped and pressed him against the back side of the tree where he could get some cover. Another shot rang out but it went high above our heads cutting down some twigs and peppering us with snow from the tree leaves. A dark object popped out from behind a tree no more than fifty yards or so. I lifted the pistol quick and fired. The shot missed and went low into the dirt.

"You outta rounds yet?" Carter harassed. "I count at least five. Can't have more than one shot left. I can do this all the live long day!" I ducked behind the tree with Chesterfield; his head hung low with his chin resting against his chest.

"Hey." I said quietly to the old man. "Chesterfield, you still with me?" He grunted and nodded his head. "Look at me buddy." He turned his head, face half covered in gore he opened his bright blue eyes that were absolutely bloodshot. "I got one shot left Chesterfield. Only one. We can't stay here or their gonna surround us." Chesterfield stated to fade away as if falling asleep. His eyes rolled to the back of his head and his body began to lurch forward. I gripped his shoulder tightly and shook him. "Chesterfield, stay with me old man. We're gonna have to make a run for it. I'm gonna wait until they poke their head out and draw some fire. After they shoot were runnin'. You got me?" He grunted and nodded again. "Alight now. Stay with me." Chesterfield had lost a lot of blood. I didn't know how much longer he was going to stand upright but I wasn't about to leave him behind.

"You still there boy? Were comin for ya!" The Rebs began hollering like savages and I could hear their feet tearing at the ground as they ran from tree to tree. "C'mon boy, why don't we do this like honorable men. Just step on out from behind that tree and we can have an old-fashioned shoot out. Just you and me." I scoffed at the thought.

"Ain't no honor left in a man that would cut out the tongue of a tied up solider." I kept hearing footsteps creeping in closer and closer.

"You might be right about that boy but that wasn't me. That was Boss. Boss got his own way about dealing with things. C'mon boy, just step on out and we can settle this like men." Carter and his friend were getting closer. It was now or never.

"Go to hell Johnny Reb!" I shouted as I left the cover of my tree. Two shots rang out both narrowly missing me. I grabbed Chesterfield and we made a run for it.

"C'mon, they gotta reload!" I pulled him from the tree and he hobbled forward with me. The trees ahead were thinning providing almost no cover for us or the Rebs. I could hear them loading their muskets behind us as the ram rods banged against their barrels. As soon as I heard feet scrambling forward I turned and took a shot straight at them. They dropped to the ground escaping my last shot. With my pistol now useless I threw it to the ground to drop some more weight. Chesterfield was wheezing heavy coughing up blood. They started yelling behind us again screaming and hollering.

"We got'em now. Ain't nowhere to run boys!" They were catching up; with each step we took they took at least three. We couldn't get ahead and we couldn't fight back. "Get ready to die boy!" Carter was going to harass us until the last. "I'm gonna gut you like a catfish!"

"Private!" a forceful voice called out from in front of us. I lifted my head and saw a row of cavalrymen atop their horses with guns drawn. "Private get down!" I let my weak body drop and pulled Chesterfield with me. We fell hard and I dug my face into the dirt and snow. A volley of fire rang out and shot filled air above us. When the noise ceased, I twisted my body around and looked behind us. Two pairs of feet pointed straight up into the air. Our pursuers were dead and would no longer torment us. A hand grasped my shoulder and I lunged back. To my surprise it was Sergeant Loyod down on one knee.

"Are you alright Private?" I nodded.

"We heard the gun shot and came riding hard and as fast we could." Loyod then looked down upon Private Chesterfield who barely moved. "What in the hell happened to him?" I opened my mouth but the words would not come out.

"Roach? It's alright son. What happened to Chesterfield?" Tears began to fall down my eyes and I could feel my throat swelling up. It was difficult to talk but I forced the words out as best I could.

"They...they cut his tongue out Sergeant. Those damned devils." Loyod put his hand behind Chesterfields head and lifted him up gently off the ground.

"Get this man to surgeon! Now God damnit!" Several cavalrymen jumped down from their mounts and lifted Chesterfield up on top of another man's horse laying him down on his belly in front of the rider. As I watched Chesterfield ride away I placed my hands on my face and sobbed.

"If...if Chesterfield hadn't of gotten free and took their pistol we'd both be dead. He got shot in the leg as we ran away." Sergeant Loyod placed his hand on my shoulder providing some reassurance.

"It's gonna be alright son. Pick yourself up and get a ride back to your horse. See to it that Private Chesterfield's horse makes it back as well. Can you do that?" I nodded.

"Sergeant!" a booming voice called. Loyod stood and walked toward Captain Masengill who was searching the bodies of the deceased Rebs.

"These are Longstreet's men alright. He can't be far. Send a large group of Scouts forward to get an exact location. The rest of us will ride back and alert the Ohio Forty Fourth. They'll need to get their packs together and move out."

"Yes Sir!" Loyod started pointing and shouting at several men. Riders ran ahead beyond the corpses back toward the fire Chesterfield and I had made.

"If I'm right Longstreet looks to cut off our retreat and starve us out in the cold. I will not allow that to happen. Do you understand Sergeant?"

"Yes Sir."

"By God I will not let that happen. We stomped him and his boys at Gettysburg and we shall do it again." Captain Masengill remarked.

"Just say the word Sir."

"Mount up. To the rear! To the rear! Ride!" Captain Masengill ordered. I hitched a ride with another solider and held on for dear life. A battle with Longstreet's men was coming and more than tongues would be lost because of it. Chesterfield was only the beginning.

# Ten
# Return To Kingsport – December 13<sup>th</sup> 1864

Growing up on the farm we think we are used to boredom. There are just so many moments in which we are waiting on someone or something even with all the manual labor required there's always something that must be waited on. Waiting for the crops to grow, waiting for the hay to be delivered, waiting on the rains to come. As a soldier, boredom has brought a very new and painful meaning. Boredom becomes a punishment in its own right.

You see, there are no crops to harvest as a solider, no weeds to pull or livestock to care for except your own horse. You are constantly waiting, staring out into the open wilds, and waiting. We gather together each morning in formation and we wait. We get in line for chow and in that long sometimes never ending line, we wait. We go out on patrol and are posted out in some field or next to a patch of trees and then, we wait. Try as we might to fight off this excruciating boredom our superiors appointed over us take the utmost effort to keep us from doing so. We cannot play cards when on duty, we cannot sing songs or play the harmonica.

Anything other than staring out into the fields will distract us from the task at hand. Despite the warning from our Non-Commissioned

Officers boredom takes over at every turn. Men fall asleep on post and then they are beaten with canes to teach them to never do it again. Just yesterday I saw a boy get beat within an inch of his life for falling asleep outside a Captains tent. Although I understand their intentions at keeping us in a constant and never ending state of vigilance I cannot help but feel compelled at how hopeless it all is.

With the Confederate Army beat down so bad at Gettysburg we thought for sure that we would be home by now with our loved ones, but we were terribly wrong. Johnny Reb decided to slow things down a bit and prolong the war by carrying out what the Captain called Indian Warfare by ambushing supply trains, destroying communication lines sacking towns with no soldiers in them. It seemed like a coward's game to go on punishing the whole of the United States for their ideals but it was what it was.

We were here at Bulls gap watching the line no matter what we thought about it. The fighting had slowed to a crawl for us. No more riding out far beyond the line or doing reconnaissance for Infantry Company's. Each morning we would wake early, do inspections of our rifles and uniforms and then ride out along the long lines of Bulls Gap making rides of twenty miles each day. The patrols were not all that bad but standing watch at camp was by far the very worst duty a man could have. At one point, I fell asleep on Abigail and fell off nearly breaking my damn arm. Sure enough there were small gun-fights here and there that got everyone at camp excited and set them running in the direction of gunfire. The quiet of the evenings on watch brought me no measure of peace. Instead it brought with it the sounds and voices of the dead. Those I cared for that have passed in what seemed to me like a never-ending war. I could not remove Billie from my thoughts, nor could I come to forgive myself for his death. Chester-field was at a field hospital somewhere and in all likelihood, would not return. I felt I had failed him in some respects but back in those woods we had saved each other from a terrible fate. I wished him well and hoped that even in his present circumstance he could find the happiness he so desired.

Each night I tried to think a sweet thought of Jenny and recall the gentle features of her face and the curves of her body. Day dreams came often out on patrol and I would surrender to them as if they were completely real. I'd see a farm we'd own, the many children we would have and their bright smiles as they ran along white picket fences chasing the dogs through bright fields. Kingsport was not far and I was as determined as the devil himself to make that woman my wife before some other man swept her off her feet.

\* \* \*

After being relieved from Bulls Gap we returned to a familiar camp just outside of London. It had been so long that I barely recognized the place. The camp had grown with established outposts, buildings, and a storehouse for supplies. I spotted a Corporal on guard duty and quickly jumped down from my horse to find my loved one.

"Have you seen Ms. Jenny around?"

"Who?" The Corporal questioned me.

"Ms. Jenny, the Physician? Is she here?" The Corporal looked confused and held his finger up to me.

"Just wait here a moment Private." He walked away from me towards several other soldiers and it seemed that an argument broke out amongst them as I heard some shouting back and forth. I couldn't make out what they were saying but something just wasn't right. The Corporal seemed to shrug off the words of the other men and marched towards me.

"Well Corporal?" I asked impatiently. He seemed upset and perhaps overcome with a sudden illness.

"Come with me." He said meekly. I followed the man deep into the pine woods until we reached a cemetery covered in freshly dug graves.

"Is she here?" I demanded. "Is this where she is treating the wounded?" The Corporal stopped in front of a wooden cross and slowly lifting his arm he pointed at the solitary grave.

"This is it Private." I was confused and looked all around for Ms. Jenny.

"I don't understand Corporal. Where is she?" The Corporal pointed at the grave once more with a voice that shook and trembled.

"Ms. Jenny…" he said quietly.

"Yes?" I asked.

"She's right here Private. This is where they buried her." I stepped forward quickly and looked blankly at the solitary hastily built wooden cross. Light shined down between the cracks of the tree tops and I held my hand up to extinguish its brightness against the snows. With shaded eyes I focused in on words cut deep into the pine planks.

"Jenny Jenkins…" My throat swelled up and my eyes filled with tears. "No?" I questioned. "This can't be right." My heart broke into a million pieces; shattered as if cannon shot had ripped straight through me and I dropped violently to my knees. "No, no, no, no! This cannot be!" The Corporal took a step backward and placed his hand heavily on my trembling shoulder.

"I'm so sorry Private. She caught a fever of some sort just a week ago while tending to the men for Cholera. We tried to knock it down but she was just too weak. I helped bury her myself. She was a treasure of the camp." Every bone in my body ached and my muscles tensed furiously. I threw myself atop Jenny's grave and cried out wildly digging my hands at the dirt and slowly pulling it back.

"No! God damn you! God damn you! Why? Why would you take such a creature? You god damn sorry son of a bitch! Why?" I pounded my fists at the dirt hoping beyond hope that she would rise from the grave, hoping that the impossible would happen for once in this god forsaken war. The Corporal left me and walked back to his station as I stood surrounded by grave posts, surrounded by the long shadow of death. "I hate you!" I cried out to God. "I hate every inch of your being! You don't make any sense! You don't do nothin' good! Why? Why of anyone would you let her die? She was sweet and good inside. She was the best of us. Why would you let her die? Have you no decency?"

I listened intently to the nothingness as a cool breeze passed across my face and waited for a response, a whisper, a sign from above. There was nothing, nothing that God could offer me this day. He remained silent as he always did throughout the war. Nearly everyone and everything I loved had been torn from me and no ounce of mercy was bestowed upon me. I was grief stricken and in my mind determined that God himself was either a lie or simply did not care about the suffrage of man. "Why? God damn you answer me! I have sent soul after soul to you, why will you not answer me? Am I not good enough? Have not enough boys died? Are you not pleased? God damn you! God damn you! What kind of a god would let such a thing happen? What kind of god would let such a pure soul die the way she did?"

Trembling I stood on two feet and pulled the only thing to offer off my chest that I could. I ripped the cross of Jesus Christ from my neck and threw it into the woods; then I threw my fist into the air. "You are no god of mine!" I screamed in righteous fury and stepped atop Jenny's grave falling to the ground and leaning against her grave post. "I'm so sorry Jenny." I said as I wept profusely. "I'm sorry I was not here for you in your final moments. I'm sorry that this war took me from you. I have so many regrets now; sorrows beyond counting." I stared upward through the cracks between the trees up to the great blue sky above. I wanted to die, I wanted to be with her and escape this place. The world meant nothing to me now. We fought for land, for dirt, for the freedom of men who would not rise against their masters. I wanted to be in heaven with Jenny where she would surely be but the more I thought about it the more I realized that even in death I may never see her again. I was going to hell, the home of Satan himself. I had killed, murdered, and slain my way across Tennessee and when the time came for judgement not even the most forgiving Angel would find a way to let me through the gates of heaven for the things I had done. I was cursed to be without my love in this life and the next. I was removed for an eternity and felt as if I would walk this earth for a very long time to continue witnessing and participating in the carnage that had for so long covered my world. "Damn you!" I cried out again. "God damn you!"

There was no sign, no signal that God was listening to my cries of infinite sorrow. I placed my hand on my pistol and wrapped my hand around the handgrip tightly. Only anger filled my now empty husk, only rage gave me any respite from the terrible dark that poisoned my heart and mind. This day I would meet death personally and one of two things would occur. Either death would take me in his ice-cold embrace or I would stick my bayonet straight in that fucker's throat, rip out his insides and take his place on the field of battle. I cared not for my life anymore. I only wanted it to end. Somehow, someway.

\* \* \*

As the days passed my sorrow turned to exhaustion and numbness. I contemplated lifting the barrel of my pistol to my head and ending it all. It had become a daily thought in my mind, wondering when, where, and how I would do it. Eventually even this became tiresome and soon I put it out of my mind. The snows ran deep in what now seemed like a frigid wasteland. No matter how many layers of clothing we put on we could not keep the cold at bay but I found the cold to be a comfort, a constant in an un-constant world. The ice felt as if it ran through my veins and muscles almost setting still my broken heart. Back to Kingsport we came, a town we had nearly conquered if it weren't for the movement of the main Rebel Army that forced us to retreat and reinforce our forces elsewhere. Now we stood near the bank of the Holston River ready to take on what remained of the Confederate Forces, ready to slaughter them down to the last man. It was no secret amongst our ranks that the Johnny Rebs were sorely outnumbered, out gunned, and out supplied. Rumor had it that no more than three hundred soldiers were holding the town and what remained of its inhabitants. From atop a rolling hill I saw a town, or what remained of it; rubble, fires, and ash. I had no illusions of what today would be. Today would be an easy day. Today we would cut men down with the barrel of our guns as if they were cattle running in the field. A messenger rode to Captain Masengill throwing a quick salute before handing him a piece of parchment. He gracefully unfolded the paper and read the contents then crumpled it and threw it to the ground. Turning his horse around he faced us and raised his hands.

"Fox Company! The bridge to Kingsport is in disrepair and we cannot cross here. Our orders are to ride north to Clouds Ford and cross at a federal controlled bridge, then ride back south like the wind to drive Johnny Reb out of his home. Mount up!"

"Mount up!" Sergeant Loyod repeated the order. We turned away from our vantage point of the town and headed north on the road as ordered. Infantry units remained and a few of those boys eyeballed me as I rode past. I could see black in some of their fingers, frostbite for the ones that didn't take well enough care of themselves. They'd lose those fingers sooner or later. The surgeon wouldn't even need to saw them off, they'd just fall right there in the snow. Their feet must have been frozen standing in the snow like that. Every few miles or so I'd find a frozen corpse sitting upright in the ice usually up against a tree or laying flat on the ground. I saw what the cold could do to men, sometimes they'd shiver and shake for hours and then the shaking would stop and they'd say they were tired or sleepy. They'd lay down thinking they were just going to take a quick nap, problem was they never woke up. Those men died, every time they died. Frozen stiff as a log out on the side a god forsaken road. It wasn't the frozen corpses that bothered me so much, it was the expressions on some of their faces. Some of them had a devilish sort of smile as their lips and gums were pulled back on their faces and their eyes froze wide open with a kind of crazed look. It was the nearest thing to death staring back at you. Shoot, I even once caught a solider having a conversation with one of those corpses. It wasn't until he offered him a puff of some pipe tobacco that he realized the man's eyes were frozen over.

What I worried about most was Abigail and her legs. I tried as best I could to keep her to the well beaten paths so her legs would stay dry. It was when the Captain led us into the open fields or forests that I worried the most. Sometimes the snows would harden on top like ice and Abigail had a tough time of it breaking through but then without warning her front leg might slip and get cut up on a stick or a rock deep in the snow. I snatched a black blanket that I found while we were clearing out some farmhouses and used it for Abigail to keep her warm. She did pretty good in the cold weather, better than me anyway.

Halfway to Clouds Ford there was a small house that had been seized by Union Forces. On the tree outside hung the bodies of three men in Confederate uniforms. Their corpses and even the ropes were frozen stiff and hardly moved in the wind. On the porch of the home various Non-Commissioned Officers appeared to stand watch while drinking what smelled like fresh coffee. The chimney stack blew hard fanning the smell of burning oak all around. No doubt there were Officers in that building keeping warm and regaling themselves of their stories of great battles and glory's won. After over a year serving in the Cavalry I came to respect very few Officers that served in the ranks of Infantry units. Many stayed behind while the lower ranking Officers or Non-Commissioned Officers led charges but not the Officers of cavalry men, no Sir. Captain Masengill and the Officers of other cavalry units always led form the front charging into the fray just like the rest of us.

The formation began to swing east back towards the river and shortly we approached a heavily guarded bridge. About one hundred yards or so from the bridge were cannons that pointed directly at the bridge itself with men stationed at each one presumably to blow the bridge in the event they were overrun. We rode across the stone bridge quickly and I peeked over the side at the freezing cold water rushing south. I wish I had a fishing pole handy, it looked like there may be some good fishing here but we weren't camped out. In fact, the column picked up the pace and I gave Abigail a little kick to encourage her forward. Almost as soon as we crossed the bridge we turned south back down towards Kingsport. In the distance above the snow-covered trees I could see a black smoke rising. Johnny Reb must have lit a fire and put out blockades to slow us down.

"Sabers and pistols!" Captain Masengill commanded. I pulled my pistol keeping my other hand wrapped tightly in Abigail's reins. "Fan out! We're getting close!" The trail opened up to large farms fields and we took a wide battle line. I pulled Abigail out to the left into a frozen field and had her tear through the fresh powder. Sergeant

Loyod was just to my right and I gave him a nod to let him know I had his back. Captain Masengill lifted his sabre just as we reached the outskirts of town. "Charge!" The bugle sounded loudly and we rushed towards what was left of Kingsport and I waited anxiously for the shooting to start but as we came closer and closer and closer, nothing happened. No more than twenty yards from the main thoroughfare I was startled by an enormous blast. The Rebs opened up on us all at once from windows, doorways, and rooftops. I swear I felt a shot rip past my eyebrow but there was nothing there. Horses fell hard to the ground, soldiers tumbled and flew from their beasts of burden and then suddenly I was airborne being thrown clear of my horse until falling in the snow just shy of hitting the broadside of a building. I pulled my head and face out of the powder and scrambled to find my pistol that luckily sat upright out of the snow and was easy to find. I turned back to see Abigail laying on the ground rolling back and forth. Shots cracked all around and I trudged through the ice to get to her until shot after shot hit her in the belly. She screamed loudly with each hit and blood went everywhere spraying on the clean white ground. She spun around over and over trying to make sense of what was happening. I couldn't get to her; I couldn't pull her behind the building just to keep her from getting hit anymore without getting myself killed.

"Abigail!" I cried out. "Come here girl!" A shot bounced off the edge of the building shooting splinters at my face and landing right in Abigail's chest. She couldn't cry anymore, the shot looked like it hit her lungs and so she just wheezed deeply until the air in her chest started to run out. She became weaker by the second and soon succumb to her wounds. "No..." I muttered.

"Roach, get in the fight!" Michaels took a spot behind some wooden steps laying prone. I wiped off my pistol to keep the powder from getting wet and got right up next to him standing against the wall. I peeked around and saw a few Rebs out in the open and started shooting. The first round hit a man in the leg, he fell to the ground then took a sabre to the neck as more Cavalry poured in.

"Forward men!" Sergeant Loyod called out from across the street. I reached down and grabbed Michaels by the back of the collar helping him to his feet. We ran forward down the street chasing down the cavalrymen that still had their horses. Johnny Rebs starting pouring into the streets running as fast as they could out of town. I raised my pistol and shot two more men in the back. One went down and didn't move, the other pushed himself off the ground and started to turn around. I rushed to him and put the barrel to the back of his head pulling the trigger sending him back down to the dirt for the last time. There were stray bullets and random shot everywhere but most of it seemed to be coming from a courthouse just at the end of the road.

"Michaels, come with me! We gotta clean out that courthouse!" We ran for it sprinting up behind a stack of crates that were ablaze. The fire and smoke provided some perfect cover but the puddles of mud in the streets were slowing us down. As we crept closer I could see barrels sticking out the windows and musket fire coming down from the roof. "You get your rifle and when I say go you layout three shots on those windows and then the rest on that rooftop. You got me?" Michaels leaned against a wagon and lined up his rifle.

"I got your back Roach, just make sure you git there."

"You ready?" I asked him.

"Ready."

"Go!" Michaels opened up quick with that lever action. The barrels in the windows pulled back after he hit'em. I looked up to see his shot landing against the edges of the rooftop and heads started ducking. Reaching the courthouse wall I pressed up against the side next to a large broken out window. A rifle poked out and I grabbed it pulling the barrel out and the shooter with it. He lost his footing and I got a shot off in his gut throwing his rifle out to the street. I ran past the windows and went for the door and pulled with all my might. The door wouldn't budge; it was barred from the other side. "Sergeant!" I called out but couldn't see Sergeant Loyod anywhere. A few more Union Cavalrymen came rushing towards me and I waved one down.

"What is it?" he asked pulling up next to me.

"That courthouse is full of Rebs but we need to knock the door down." The soldier smiled.

"I got this. Here!" the rider handed me a rope from his saddle. "Quick, tie it off to the door." I ran back to the door with my end of the rope and tied it to the giant iron door knocker and turned back giving the rider the go ahead to knock it down. "Yah!" He slapped the reins of his black horse and ran in the opposite direction. The rope tightened quickly and ripped the door right out dragging it a way down the road. Dust and debris flew everywhere and I rushed into a cloud of dirt without knowing what was on the other side. The room was open and the walls full of holes with bodies strewn about nearer the windows. It looked like nearly twenty men lay dead in this room making a last stand to keep control of the town. Loud bangs came from above and to my left were steps leading to another floor. Michaels rushed in behind me followed by five or six others that starting checking the bodies making sure they were all dead by putting bayonets in their chests. I started making my way up the steps when Michaels pulled back on my shoulder.

"I got this one. You ran across that street so let me take one for you." I stepped back and let him get in front of me.

"Thanks." I said bereft of breath. We crept slowly up the stairs that wound around a tight corner against the wall just five steps up. A quiet shuffle of feet could be heard on the other side and Michaels stopped me in my tracks and turned back to me.

"Watch this." he whispered. The young veteran took the cover off his head and placed it atop his rifle. He slowly pushed his hat around the bend and one, two, three, shots rang out and then a click; he was out of bullets. Michaels ran up the steps and turned the corner firing his rifle. I ran up close behind him and a Reb fell dead at my feet, his pistol bouncing down the steps beneath us. More shuffling of feet behind a swinging door at the top of the steps but they were leaving. "We got'em on the run." Michaels lifted his rifle up to his eye tucking the butt of the gun tightly into his shoulder and cheek. One step at a time we made our way up until reaching the last step. Once he reached the landing Michaels moved forward quickly and entered the room to the left while I went to the right. It was an office with a large desk and bedding laid out all over the floor. They had been camping out here for a long time and didn't seem to be expecting us otherwise they might have packed their other belongings.

"There!" I pointed at an open window where foot and hand tracks were pressed firmly in the snow. "There all on the roof!" Michaels did his hat trick again outside the window but no shots were fired. I took a look outside and saw a wooden balcony and stairs that led to the roof. Stepping over the window sill I pressed my hand into the cold snow and wiped my trigger hand off on my pants before heading up. The gunfire became louder, they weren't very far off this time. With all the noise I had no reason to keep quiet. I rushed up the steps and only slowed when I reached the top of the building. The roof was clear and I waved Michaels on up.

"Where the hell did they go?" A few shots came our way striking the roof and shredding the air around our bodies.

"Down, down!" I grabbed Michaels by the chest of his shirt.

"Where the hell is it comin' from?"

"The next building over. They must have jumped the gap." We crawled closer to the other building getting tight against the wooden planks for some cover. I waved to Michaels pointing him to the far end. He crawled in the direction and I went to the opposite one. Loud footsteps came up behind us and I rolled over pointing my pistol back at the stairs. It was the other soldiers that cleared the first floor with us, they were in the open!

"Get dow..." My warning was muffled by a volley of gunfire in their direction. The first boy went down hard after a round went clear through his head taking the top of his hair with it. The second took a shot to the leg and started crawling towards us. The third crouched down on the balcony and started shooting over our heads. I rolled back over and peaked like a turkey over the edge and took a shot at the first thing that moved. I missed and dropped back down to cover as more shots started coming my way. Michaels popped up and expended all fifteen rounds of his rifle.

"Your good!" he called out to me. I popped up and saw three bodies lying flat on the roof. Peering down the narrow alley below I spotted several wagons, horses, and Rebs loading up a wagon train. I took a shot at the lead horse putting a round right through its head. The beast dropped hard to the ground and the shot startled the men below.

"Back up the wagons!" a man ordered anxiously. I expended my shots and reloaded. Michaels popped back and let'em have it.

"Their abandoning the wagons!" Another rush of hooves came from the street and more Cavalrymen rushed in surrounding the wagons and running down the men who fled from them. Johnny Reb was on the run again.

* * *

Once the town had been cleared out I made my way back to where my most trusted and loyal friend of the war had fallen. Abigail, my quarter horse, had been slain and lay flat on the ground, motionless, lifeless. I knelt next to her body and placed my hand over her muzzle. Her flesh had already grown cold and not a spark of the creature I knew remained. Reaching around her mouth I removed the headstall she had so diligently worn and freed her body of the reins.

"Rest now girl." I said softly. "Rest now." Faint footsteps strolled up behind me and I turned my head back to see Michaels on foot with his horse and holding the reins of another.

"I brought you one of the Reb horses from the supply wagons." I nodded and turned my eyes back to Abigail. "I think her name is Sarah." He remarked, but I did not reply. The vultures had already taken residence above Abigail's body high in the sky and for a moment I thought to shoot them away, to keep the beasts away from my horse. "Well, I'll just meet you outside of town when you're ready." Michaels walked away and left me to my grief. A gust of wind blew hard from the south and Abigail's elegant mane flowed gently in the breeze. "Thank you…"

# Eleven
## Saltville –
## December 20<sup>th</sup> – 21<sup>st</sup> 1864

Our lives for salt; or at least that's what the Officers were telling us. Damned if I was going to die for a pile salt and especially not in Virginia. We were being pushed further and further away from home trying to hunt down the Confederates while they were still weak. Rumors came from the Army and townspeople alike that soon the war would be over. On the road from Kingsport we rode at a steady pace behind several other companies from the Eighth Cavalry. Word was that Johnny Reb was holed up in a salt mine in a town no less named Saltsville in southern Virginia. Without the salt mine, they could no longer preserve their meats or cure leather. As tired as I was of salted pork and beef I knew that we couldn't manage without it. Saltsville had been contested before and the Rebs were clearly the victor in that. This was their land, old Virginia some people called it and if I knew anything about Johnny Reb, I knew he would fight dearly for it.

"Did you bring it?" Sergeant Loyod rode up behind me and then kept pace next to my horse. He seemed in good spirits this day. Maybe there was something he knew that I didn't.

"I did."

"Well, give it here Private." I reached into my leather pouch careful not to fall over and produced a small wooden carton of cigars.

"As promised." Sergeant Loyod happily removed the box from my grasp and proceeded to smell the outside.

"Ah." He said with a great deal of satisfaction. "There is nothing on this good green earth like Virginia tobacco. Where again did you say you procured these?" I smiled and shook my head.

"I didn't Sergeant." By the expression on his face I felt that he had caught my meaning as I did not want to seem criminal or disrespectful in my activities.

"Understood Private, but tell me, as a friend, where did you get the cigars?"

"If you must know, as a friend, I pulled them the leather case of a gunned down Confederate messenger. He had loads of goods but I felt that this one in particular may pique the interest of you and Captain Masengill."

"Indeed it will. I think perhaps we have been together on this journey for too long. You know me better than most."

"I try to steer clear of getting to know anyone these days Sergeant."

"And whys that?"

"Because the war ain't over yet and we ain't done killin' and ain't done being killed."

"Well, all the same. I thank you for the kind gesture. It shall not be forgotten. When we get to Saltsville I want you to keep your horse on the left flank. That's where the Captain and I will be positioned. I need someone I trust to watch my back."

"You don't need to lie to me Sergeant. You just need me for my gun." Sergeant tipped his hat and his smile faded to stern seriousness.

"Indeed I do. Keep'em loaded. Keep'em ready." Loyod smacked the reins of his horse. "Yah!" and rode off like the wind.

* * *

Evening approached quickly and we settled down into camp no more than five miles from Saltsville. Guns could be heard firing in the distance; sounded like they were using the six pounders. Couldn't be our guns, we almost never deploy the sixes anymore unless were protecting a fortification on open ground. The impacts came shortly after the shot so they couldn't have been firing no more than five hundred yards away. I settled down with some salted pork, crackers, and a half full bottle of whiskey. Sarah started pushing her nuzzle into my face so I gave her a few crackers and shared some water so she'd leave me alone.

"Don't you ever stop?" I complained. "Abigail never ate as much as you. You're gonna get fat and slow." Sarah blew out air loudly in protest. She was a good horse but slower and more temperamental than Abigail was. Guess they don't break them in like they used to. Given everything we've been through these horses probably get little training. The pork tasted a little under preserved this day as the fatty pieces were a bit foul. Perhaps it had sat out for far too long but I ate it just the same. At least the crackers were fresh for once. It was pretty damn rare to find a good crunchy cracker and not them stale chewy ones. As I finished my meal I heard footsteps come behind me and then Sergeant Loyod stepped over my log and sat atop it. A deep aroma of southern tobacco now filled the air around me as he gleefully puffed on his cigar. Loyod removed the cigar from his mouth and appeared to look it over in a sort of awe that most men would reserve for miracles.

"This is a fine, fine cigar indeed. I have smoked three since I relieved you of the burden. Why don't you come over and have a cigar with the Officers and I. Captain Masengill would be more than accommodating to have you in our presence." Without hesitation I stood and began walking towards the Officers mess.

"Roach?" Sergeant Loyod had not gotten up from the log and stared at me seeming puzzled.

"Yes Sergeant?"

"You're not going to protest my invitation? I mean, I have held you against your will several times to stay and socialize but now you get up without reservation and of your own accord to join us. What has changed?"

"I said I don't make friends these days Sergeant, doesn't mean I won't enjoy good company or find some happiness where it may be found in our current predicament. Do you have whiskey?" Loyod placed the cigar in his mouth and laughed hysterically.

"Do we have whiskey? C'mon, let's go!" I walked down gleefully to the fire pit ready to fill my belly with some good Tennessee Brown. Captain Masengill was standing with one foot on a log in his usual fashion.

"Good evening Sir." I said as I saluted the Captain.

"Sit down Mr. Roach. No need for formalities here. Have yourself a seat and get your lips wet." Next to the fire lay an entire wooden crate of whiskey bottles acquired at our last engagement; the spoils of war. There was no need to pass a bottle around this time. I happily retrieved a full glass and wiped the dirt from it. The label was simple, *Whiskey and Rye*, it said, but had no markings of the place where it was made. Must have been a small town distillery. I sat against the log next to Sergeant Loyod and the Captain, quietly drinking my fill letting the fire into my blood.

"This is a fine bottle." I remarked.

"It goes better with a cigar." Sergeant Loyod replied handing me one of the cigars I had given him. I retrieved the smoke stick and gave it a sniff before setting it to the fire.

"I will not argue with a Non-Commissioned Officer." Taking several long draws of the cigar smoke deeply I let it sit in my chest a bit before I slowly let it come out. "That is a fine cigar."

"It was good of you to share them Private. Lord knows we rarely get to enjoy the finer things in life out here. To me a cigar and a bottle of whiskey is not simply a good time but represents the greater aspects of humanity itself." I coughed and laughed through the smoke.

"Begging your pardon Sir but I don't think you have seen enough drunkards in your lifetime. I've seen one to many men crawl into that bottle and never come out."

"You are indeed correct Private but all men are susceptible to lure of the Devil. That's why we have civilization, law and order. What

I was getting at is that whiskey and cigars represent ingenuity and man's best work at making the world a more enjoyable place. Without whiskey and cigars how would we find a way to unwind at the end of a challenging day. I dare to say that I do not think I would have made it through this war without whiskey and cigars."

"Made it through Sir? You talk as if the war is over." Sergeant Loyod remarked.

"Indeed Sergeant, the war is nearly over. Four years of bloodshed, four years on the road and camped out in the wilds of North America. Truthfully I think the world has had enough of our foolishness. I am personally ready to retire and return to a normal life."

"What's normal Captain? What do you plan to do when you return to this life?" I asked.

"Well Private if you must know." Captain Masengill sat down and held his hands together. I think this was the first time I in fact had seen him so relaxed. "I'm going to head west, as far west as west goes, to California. Have you heard of a great city next to the Pacific Ocean called San Francisco?" I shook my head.

"No Sir I can't say that I have."

"I'm told it is becoming the new center of civilization, or at least certainly the center of civilization in the west. Business, culture, art, and manufacturing is springing up out of rolling hills surrounded by vast mountains of trees teaming with wildlife and untouched land. A man, any man, could thrive in and around San Francisco. I thought that perhaps I could become a lawyer and maybe even one day an honorable judge. I will of course need to marry into a family of means and I hear the women of the west are the finest this country has to offer."

"That's a fine dream Sir." Sergeant Loyod replied.

"Well then, what about you Sergeant? What will you do when the war is over?"

"Me Sir?" Sergeant Loyod shook his head. "I was in the Army before the war started and I plan to be in the Army long after it's over. Where else can you be paid to do what we do and not be locked away in a jail cell. I have no ambition for myself to move above the rank of Sergeant but am satisfied to continue serving this country. Even when the war is over it won't quite be over. I've already heard rumors of gangs from left over Confederate units roaming the wilds creating all sorts of chaos. Maybe I'll take a wife if I can find one that suits me."

"And what would suit you Sergeant?" Captain Masengill asked. The Sergeant sighed and breathed deeply. A smile crept up on his face.

"I don't care to marry into a wealthy family if that is what yur askin' Sir. No, I just want a fair lady, beautiful and kind that can take care of the household and keep my interests intact." Captain Masengill pointed at the Sergeant with cigar in hand.

"You see that Private Roach. That right there is a simple and strong man of the Federal Army. So what about you? Where will you go?"

"Well Sir I ain't got any plans for marriage or a new line of work. Personally, I am just ready to head on home and work the farm again with my family."

"I thought you hated the farm Private?" Sergeant replied. I shook my head and smiled.

"I did once. I hated the toil in the mud and constant work. I thought if I joined the Union I might find a profession I liked better but to be honest Sergeant I'm ready to return and grow crops. Corn, wheat, apples, anything I can get my hands on I want to grow."

"So you'll just head out in the fields and forget all this?" Loyod asked. I shook my head and took a deep breath.

"No Sergeant. I think I'll take this war with me everywhere I go."

* * *

We halted the company on a small hill outside of Saltville. Captain Masengill had been at it on his looking glass for nearly half an hour scouting out the terrain, buildings, and disposition of the enemy. He'd hum to himself gently and every so often I'd hear an obscenity come out of his mouth. Suddenly he slammed his looking glass shut and threw it back into his riding pouch.

"I don't understand it!"

"What is it Captain?" Sergeant Loyod asked.

"There was supposed to be three regiments and not one less positioned outside of Saltville. I cannot get an accurate count of the number of soldiers before us." Sergeant Loyod suddenly seemed nervous by this response.

"Are there that many Sir? Did they bring the whole damn Reb army to protect their salt?" Captain Masengill reached back into his leather satchel handing his looking glass to the Sergeant.

"Have a look Sergeant and tell me what you see." Sergeant Loyod grasped the looking glass and surveyed the town and surroundings for several minutes then handed the glass back shaking his head. He seemed confused by what he had seen, even surprised.

"Sir, there doesn't appear to be any more than a few hundred men." Captain Masengill's eyebrows rose high on his forehead as he nodded in acknowledgement.

"There is one of two things going on here Sergeant. Either they are woefully unprepared which for us would bring an almost certain victory or it's a trap and they are hiding their men in the buildings and surrounding woods simply waiting to ambush us."

"What are your orders Sir?" Loyod asked.

"I will not rush into the town without knowing exactly what we are running into. Sergeant, send Scouts wide around each side of town. Have them back here as soon as possible and report directly back to me. I will not move until I have the necessary intelligence to do so." Sergeant Loyod saluted.

"Yes Sir!" Sergeant Loyod rode to the rear of the column and picked out some of the Cavalrymen that had not been with us long. I was nearly certain he would have chosen me but perhaps he felt I had done enough.

"Private Roach!" Captain Masengill called out. I gave Sarah a kick and rode to the Captains side rendering a crisp salute.

"Yes Sir?" The Captain pointed to the valley below where a road led straight into town only a mile of so out.

"I want a line formed down at the road. Stay off the main path if you can and conceal yourselves to keep from being spotted. If any

Rebel scouts come your way I'd prefer you capture them or handle them quietly until I know what we're dealing with. If I hear a shot, I'll assume you are riding back in this direction. Whatever you do, do not press forward with an attack. I cannot have our men going into town just yet. Is that understood?"

"Yes Sir."

"Good, take three riders with you. I'll send someone to get you when we are ready to move."

"Yes Sir." I turned around and pointed at the first three men nearest to me. "Let's go." We rode back down and around the hill with three cavalrymen in tow until we reached a wide point in the trail with a thick covering of oak trees. "Stop here!" I ordered. "You two take that side of the road. You, come with me. Keep quiet and if someone crosses your path take'em prisoner or deal with them quietly. No gun shots." They nodded and rode off while I split to the left with another Private. We stopped behind a tree as thick as a house and set the horses behind it. "What's your name?" I asked the Private.

"Davenport."

"Davenport? That's a fancy name. You got a first name?"

"Christopher." I nodded.

"Alright Chris, here's how it's gonna go. Were gonna hole up in that ditch right there and wait quietly. I'm gonna keep my eye on the front of the road, you keep your eye to the rear. Don't let anyone sneak up on me and I won't let anyone sneak up on you. Ya hear?"

"I got it." We sat down quietly in the ditch and got comfortable throwing our wool blankets over us to stay warm in the cool winter air. We were fortunate this day as there was no snow to speak of and no rain either. Just a clear cold winters day. If luck was on our side we'd be inside before nightfall drinking whiskey and eating fresh food, maybe even steak. Steak…I craved a fresh juicy steak more than anything. Even as I reached into my leather case I still had some old salty pork sitting in there and though I detested it, I still put a piece in my mouth and let it sit under my lip.

"You got some for me?" Chris asked.

"Didn't you bring rations?" I asked. He shook his head no and looked down in embarrassment.

"How long you been with us Chris?"

"Two months today."

"Two months huh? Well, first thing you gotta learn is that you need to always have some rations on you, food and water. You never know how long were gonna be stuck somewhere before the cook can git around to us. Secondly, most soldiers won't just share their rations unless you got something to trade." Chris sat there quietly for a moment and avoided making eye contact.

"Well?"

"Well what?" he asked.

"You said you wanted some of my rations. You got somethin' to trade?" Chris slowly reached over to his leather satchel and dug around. He pulled out a pouch of tobacco chew and handed it over.

"I only smoke tobacco so I guess you can have this." I smiled and happily took it from his hands throwing it into my pouch.

"Here." I handed him half of the salted pork I had in my satchel which he gladly took and began consuming immediately.

"Thank you." He said. I shook my head spitting out the salted pork and replacing it with my chew.

"Don't thank me. It was a trade fair and square. Ain't nothing to thank me for. Just make sure you pack better the next time we ride out."

"I will." Christopher promised.

\* \* \*

Morning came and went quickly with the early afternoon approaching. The sun hung low in the air but gave off just enough light to keep the frost at bay.

"Hey." Chris tapped my shoulder and I turned to him. "Hey, I got something', right over there." I looked down the road and behind us was a woman walking with three little girls. They carried baskets that looked like they had provisions coming out of them. "What do we do? Do we stop'em?" Chris asked.

"I dunno, just wait a minute." I watched the girls walk towards us down the road and crouched lower hoping the horses wouldn't spook and make a noise. As they came right across from where we were I noticed the women's hands seemed almost black like she had been handling coal, or gunpowder? "Git up, were gonna pull em'aside and seach'em." I stood quickly with my rifle pointing down.

"Miss?" she turned quickly and dropped to the ground pulling her three girls down with her.

"Don't hurt us! Don't hurt my girls."

"Just come off the road. We ain't gonna hurt'cha we just wanna look at what you got in those baskets." Her eyes grew wide and she looked around nervously as if trying to find a way to escape. "Don't do it." I warned as I pulled back the hammer on my rifle. "Just come over here and let me look through your belongings. I don't want to harm you but if you scream or move too fast my friends back there might put a bullet through you." She turned her head to see my other two riders wave with guns at the ready. It was at that point her expression turned to disappointment. She stood and carried the basket over to me and placed it at my feet.

"Get over there girls. Stay away from them. We don't know what intentions these Yanks have for us." The older woman said.

"Chris, keep an eye on them would'ya." Chris cocked the hammer of his rifle back and kept a keen eye on the woman and her girls while I knelt down and opened the baskets. "Potatoes?" I asked.

"Yes Sir. People in town gotta eat."

"Where you from?"

"A ranch just over yonder a ways. We come here to sell our crops and pick up provisions."

"You came by yourselves?"

"All our men are out in the fields fightin' yur kind. We gotta do what we gotta do to maintain a life." As I dug through the potatoes I found the glint of something shiny and reached down. Below the potatoes I found my hand grasping the barrel of a pistol and pulled it out.

"And what about this?" The woman gasped and placed her hands over her mouth.

"Well how did that git in there?" she said trying to cover up her misdeed. I dumped all the potatoes out and the ground and pulled eight pistols from one basket. I pulled over the other three baskets and did the same. Two were filled with potatoes and pistols and the last potatoes, gunpowder, and shot.

"Where were you going with these?"

"That's none of yur business Mister." She replied defiantly.

"I'll ask you one more time. Where were you taking these pistols?" One of the little girls stepped forward and spoke up.

"It wasn't her fault, they made us do it." Her shrill little voice was something I had not heard in a long time.

"Who made you do it little girl?"

"The men in the town. We heard you was comin' and they told us to bring these to them when Yanks showed up."

"Sit down." I told the little brown haired girl.

"Look Miss, I git what yur doin' but if I don't take these guns your friends in Saltville are gonna use them to kill me and my friends and I just can't have that."

"What are you gonna do?" I looked over at Chris who had a blank expression.

"If I give you over to my Captain they'll hang you and probably your little girls."

"No! They can't do that. Take me but don't take my girls."

"Look Miss, here's what's gonna happen. I'm gonna take these baskets, guns, potatoes and all, and you're gonna get back on that road and go back to your ranch. I don't want to see or hear from you so long as I'm in town, you get me?" She nodded nervously.

"Now if I even get the slightest feeling that you let one of your friends in town know that were posted up here I'll come find you and then, well, you know what happens next. Ain't nobody gonna spare your little girls from justice. So, what's it gonna be?"

"I can leave with my girls?" she asked with tears streaming from her eyes as I nodded.

"Yes Mam." I replied.

"And you ain't gonna hurt us or shoot us in the back while we walk away." I shook my head.

"No Mam." I reached into the basket pulling out a pistol and pointing it at her. She gasped and pulled back, then I spun it around giving her the handle. "Take it." She reached her hand out but hesitated looking at my eyes. "Go on, take it. It's not a trick. For you and your girls, to protect yourselves on the road and at home. I'll just keep the rest for safe keeping." She nodded and wiped the tears from her cheeks.

"C'mon girls let's git on home." The little girls followed their mother quickly and without hesitation. The woman got no more than twenty paces from me when she turned her head around slowly.

"Hey Yank?"

"Yes Mam?"

"Thank you." I tipped my hat.

"You're welcome Mam." They walked off quickly without uttering a word.

"Why'd you let them go?" I shot Chris a stern look and squinted my eyes tightly.

"Do you want to hang them?" He stuttered and tried to spit out a response but couldn't seem to get it across. I was mad at the man. Damnit; I was angry. "What's that Private Davenport? I can't hear you. Speak up a bit." He shook his head quickly and stepped back from me.

"No. I don't want to hang them." He replied nervously.

"That's what I thought. Cause if we turned them in that's exactly what we'd be doing. We'd be hangin' that woman and her three little girls. Stringin' them up, watchin' them dance the hangman's jig."

"I'm sorry Roach, that's not what I meant. I just meant we should do our job and not get into any trouble." I sighed and rubbed my forehead roughly.

"I know what you meant Chris. I know you were trying to do what you were supposed to do but what you were supposed to do was not the right thing to do. There's a lot of things I've done that I gotta live with. Hanging a couple of girls and their momma ain't gonna be one of them. No Sir. I'm not taking that with me for the rest of my life." Another hour passed by and Private Davenport did not speak a word to me. I glanced over at him a few times and could see my words weighed heavy on him, as it should, but I did not want there to be a rough tie between us.

"Davenport."

"Yeah?"

"Where you from?"

"Knoxville."

"Knoville? You a city boy?" Chris laughed and smiled sending a brief glance my direction breaking some of the tension between us.

"I mean, I didn't live in Knoxville. Me and my family just lived in the outskirts."

"What'd your father do for a living?"

"He was a law man."

"Was?" I asked curiously.

"My father died protecting the townspeople from a Confederate raid. They killed him and strung him up in the middle of town with anyone else that got in their way." Suddenly I felt poorly for how harsh I had been on Chris. He had more reason than most to be here fightin' Johnny Reb.

"Why'd you take so long to join the war"

"Recruiters wouldn't let me until I turned eighteen. Said I'd get into trouble if I joined up too early."

"Didn't stop me. You should have lied."

"Do I look like the lying type?" I looked Davenport over from head to toe.

"No, but you're gonna."

"What do you mean by that?"

"Eventually you'll find yourself stuck in a position where telling the truth may get you jailed or even killed. Or maybe you just find yourself speaking with a friend or someone you care about and you tell them most of the truth but not all of it. You know why, cause sometimes the truth can get you in trouble or hurt the ones you love. Sometimes you gotta protect yourself and sometimes you gotta protect others. Everything out there ain't so black and white."

"You sound like someone whose told a few lies yourself."

"I've done what I had to get by. My honor is still intact. Let me ask you this. You shot someone yet, and I don't mean while on the run or from the other side of a field. I mean, have you shot someone and then got a good look at their face after you done it?" Chris shook his head and suddenly seemed nervous again.

"No." he replied.

"Well, let me put it to you this way. Those boys in Saltville in that town over yonder, they ain't much different than you and me. Sure some of them are bad and I bet the ones that strung up your old man were some of the worst. But most of them, most of them are just kids even younger than you and me. The first one I killed, shot in the back in the dark after him and his friends tried to kill me across a creek. It was my first time and I was excited, even happy that I got to be the one that killed him. When I turned him over he wasn't the evil looking man I thought he'd be. He was just a boy, fresh faced without even a hair on his chin. Not a day goes by that I don't regret havin' ta kill that boy but it was either him or me and that night it was him."

"Rider!" one of the soldiers from the opposite side of the road called out. Two Union cavalrymen rode towards us and I walked out in the road to greet them.

"You Private Roach?" The rider asked.

"I am."

"Captain Masengill wants you and the men with you to return to the hill and fall into formation." I lifted my finger in the air and swung it around in a circle.

"Saddle up boys! We got a job to do!" I mounted Sarah and kicked her hard. She took off like a bolt of lightning kicking a cloud of dirt behind her.

* * *

Gunfire erupted down below as several companies stampeded through the town and ours followed in a double column. Captain Masengill was clear, kill the Rebs, burn the buildings and destroy the salt works at all costs. Without the salt they'd have no chance of mounting long term campaign's and would be unable to quickly resupply. We reached the main road into town and rode beyond burning picket lines and makeshift barriers setup by Johnny Reb. Bodies were spread out throughout the road and gunfire still came down from the rooftops and windows. Union soldiers were already on foot smashing lamplights on porch fronts and lighting the buildings on fire.

"Captain! Captain!" A Sergeant came running down from another Cavalry company.

"What is it Sergeant?"

"The Ohio Forty Fourth, they're pinned down at the salt works. Rebs put up their cannons and are firing canister shot. Their getting cut to shreds Sir!" Captain Masengill turned his horse in circles and waved his sword in the air.

"Rally on me! Rally on me!" I pulled in close to Sergeant Loyod and the Captain just like they told me to.

"What are your orders Captain?" Loyod asked.

"We ride like hell towards those cannons. The Infantry can't get up that incline fast enough to overtake the defenders. Keep the men spread out. That canister shot is going to ring like the devils bells."

"Captain, no disagreeing with you Sir but shouldn't we try to flank the cannon." Captain Masengill shook his head.

"No Sergeant, unfortunately there is no time for caution. The Ohio Forty Fourth need us and I intend to be there. Ride out! Ride out! Stick to your pistols and sabres boys! Yah! Yah!"

"Ride out!" Sergeant Loyod ordered. We charged down the main thoroughfare of the town through fire, rubble, ash and musket shot. On the backside of town was a sloping hill on the other side was a narrow road leading up to the entrance of the salt works. Several layers of pickets and other barriers had been erected to slow our advance. Cannons roared loudly and pieces of shrapnel were reaching all the way back to us. Captain Masengill pulled our formation to the side of the road.

"We have to get through those damn pickets!" The Captain exclaimed.

"Just give us the order Captain and well bring'em down." Sergeant Loyod proclaimed.

"Alirght, I want one column on each side pulling the pickets out of the way. Order the Ohio Forty Fourth to push wagons to the center and set them ablaze, I want a smoke screen as wide as the road. Get it done!"

"Yes Sir!" Let's move, single column!" Sergeant Loyod pointed to one side of the road. "Single column!" he ordered to the other side. The company split in two quick and the Ohio Forty Fourth covered our movements.

"Roach, Davenport! Dismount your horses and head for the center of the line. Gather as many men as you can to push wagon to the bulk of the line and light them on fire. We need a smoke screen before we can move ahead. Is that understood?"

"Yes Sergeant!" we replied in unison.

"Go, quickly!" Loyod urged. We jumped down from our horses leaving them sitting behind several oak trees and ran like the devil for the center line. Shots filled the air and with each cannon burst the sky filled with shrapnel and dirt. I threw myself down on the ground once I reached the picket with Davenport staying close behind.

"Who's in charge here?" I asked a Private sitting behind timber as he reloaded his pistol.

"What?"

"I said who's in charge here?" The Private looked up and down the line and shook his head with a dreadful look.

"Nobody!" he shouted. "Their all dead!" Not too far from where we lay I could spot the stripes of a Sergeant, Corporal, and the bars of a Captain all shot dead and riddled with canister shot.

"We need to move wagons to the center line and light them on fire."

"For what?"

"For a smoke screen so the cavalry can take out those guns. Can you get me some men?" The Private placed two fingers in his mouth and whistled so loud it nearly out matched the cannon fire. Six men ran towards us and crouched down.

"He's with the Cavalry. Says we need to move some wagons to the center line and light'em up so they can take down the cannon. We need a hand." The men nodded some replying with a yes and others just a dead stare in their eyes. We left the minor safety of the pickets behind and ran down the short slope where three wagons had been left unattended.

"C'mon, get behind this one!" I urged as the men fell in line and pushed with their every fiber. The wagon provided some much needed cover as the canister shot landed in the timbers sparing our limbs and lives. "Push! Push!" My thighs and calves burned terribly but I was not in a quitting mood. After several strenuous efforts, the wagon reached the picket and an Ohio Private who happily set it ablaze by laying a line of gun powder on a cloth and shooting it with his musket. The wagons went up quick and some of the boys even threw more timber in the back once it was in place. Black smoke rose quickly and the canister shot slowed it's pace.

"Let's go boys! Two to go!" The Ohio Private cheered his other men on. The second wagon went into place just as well and lit up even faster than the first. We ran back up the hill on last time and grabbed the last wagon pushing it ahead when suddenly a wagon wheel came flying off and rolled down the hill.

"God damnit!" I cried out. "We can't get this wagon up the hill!" Private Davenport lifted a lamp light and broke it in the wagon spreading the oil quickly. "What are you doin?"

"If we can't move it were gonna light it. We need the smoke." Reaching into his leather pouch, Davenport pulled out a set of box matches and lit the wagon on fire.

"Ohio!" I called the Forty Fourth Private over. "You get the rest of your men at the picket line and pull back down the hill and to the right. Make it look like you're retreating. If there's enough smoke they won't know the Cavalry is still there. When you hear gunfire and the cannons stop get your ass back up the hill and help us clear those bastards out!" We parted ways, Davenport and I sprinting back to our horses under a hail of gunfire and Private Ohio returning to the pickets to pull his men back. As we ran I tripped over a man's body and fell hard to the ground nearly face first. Hands grabbed top of the back of my shirt and pulled upward away from the corpse.

"C'mon Roach, we gotta go!" Davenport called. He got me back to my feet and we made it back to the horses huffing and puffing as we attempted to catch our breath. Captain Masengill rode his horse straight up to us.

"Well?" he asked before I could compose myself.

"The…" I swallowed and took a deep breath.

"Come now Private! We don't have time!" The Captain urged.

"The wagons are lit. Ohio lost its Officers and Non-Commissioned Officers Sir! I got a private gathering the Infantry to pull back until the cannons stop!"

"Well done men. Get to your horses. Roach, up front with Sergeant Loyod and I." The Captain rode away raising his sword in the air. "Steady men! Steady yourselves!" I mounted Sarah and gave her a kick to move forward. Swinging my head around I looked at Davenport one last time.

"Good luck kid! Stay alive!"

"You to!" He called back.

"Yah! Yah!" I slapped the reins hard and made my way up the slope where the Captain waited with sword drawn and Sergeant Loyod seemed poised for battle with pistol at the ready.

"Get your pistol out Private." Sergeant Loyod ordered. I shook my head.

"I'm out of bullets Sergeant." I reached down and grabbed my sabre raising it high in the air as the light breaking through the smoke hit it giving off a bright red glow.

"Very well then. To the sword!" Captain Masengill shouted. "Charge men! Charge to victory!" A great and awe inspiring roar erupted from our company as each man let out a vicious war cry that silenced the cannons. As we charged forward I glanced to my right to the see a drummer boy of the Ohio Infantry banging away at his drums; the calls from our company drowned him out and so the drums stopped. There was no order, no commands with which the cavalry or the infantry to move by. Our fury raged up the hill through the smoke, over the pickets, and past the bodies of the fallen. When the smoke cleared a small gap lay in front of us and the mouth of the cannons like great fiery dragons lay ahead. "Charge!" Captain Masengill cried out. I raised my sword higher and repeated his call.

"Charge!" My heart pounded, our voices roared, and the charge of the horses made the ground tremble in fear. Captain Masengill rode in front of Sergeant Loyod kicking his horse harder and harder to out run us all and overrun the cannon. Then suddenly a bright flash of red light. Sarah went down and I went down with her. The cannons had fired straight at us unleashing the canister shot. I was thrown forward over Sarah and landed on several dead Johnny Rebs. My ears rang with the devil's fury and I pushed myself up to see the rest of the Cavalry riding past overrunning the cannon and engaging the soldiers on the other side of the pickets. I couldn't hear anything and as I took a step forward I fell and my body swung around facing me back down the hill. The Ohio Forty Fourth charged forward with flags and even the drummer helping to lead the charge. I could feel the percussion from shot and the snaps of bullets flying in the air. I stared at the drummer boy, his face covered in dirt and blood. He peered at me through blond bangs with bright blue eyes that shined all the brighter through his darkened face. He banged away at his drums hitting them harder and harder as the men marched straight up that hill and yet still I could hear nothing. For me in that moment the drums had stopped, the fighting had stopped, the war itself had stopped. I felt as a ghost floating amongst the dead devoid of fear or feeling.

Then all at once my ears came back to me and the sounds of shouts, screams, and gunfire erupted in my head. I found my sword on the ground and pulled it up. Sarah lay just behind me, breathing heavy and coughing up blood, the canister shot had torn through her chest and legs. I found Captain Masengill next to her, his blue eyes staring up at the sky. His once smart uniform had been riddled, torn to shreds by the cannons that showered him with metal. I stumbled towards him and dropped heavily to one knee. Sarah screamed loudly and I winced at her pain. Masengill still had his pistol holstered so I relieved him of it and walked over to Sarah. She stared at me with those big brown eyes begging me to stop the pain. Without saying a word, I lifted the pistol, pulled the hammer back and squeezed the trigger putting a round right into her head. Her screams and struggles ceased, her head falling hard to the ground. She would feel pain no more.

"Roach!" Sergeant Loyod called from behind. He was injured holding his left arm with a bloodied hand. "He took the shot for us. He took it all. That's why he rode so far ahead of us. He faced the cannon head on so that we could live." I returned to my fallen Captain and took a knee once more closing his eyes. I put my hands together and looked up at the sky for a prayer.

"Dear Lord, see to it that this man is given a place at your table. That you bless him with all the comforts and joys of heaven and that he shall feel pain no more. He was a good man, a leader of men. Take care of him. Amen." Sergeant Loyod removed his cap placing it against his chest.

"Amen." Saltville was ours...

# Twelve
# Salisbury – April 12 1865

Word came to us from messengers far and wide that the leader of the Confederate Army, General Robert E. Lee, had surrendered. Never had I seen morale in such a fervor as it had been during the last day. We were all but certain that the wars end was within reach. I half expected to see all the Confederates lay down their arms and give up the war entirely but their undying loyalty to the South, their homeland was far more entrenched than any of us could have imaged. They were determined, every last man, to fight to the death. It seemed to me that anyone, even a Private such as myself could see that the war was over.

We were at the devil's doorstep now, the deep South. Marching into North Carolina it was a warm April morning and we stood in a formation nearly five or seven thousand deep. I had never seen this many cavalrymen gathered in one place.

"Fire!" Twelve and six pounders roared sending hot cannon shell and missile fire in all directions scattering across the town. Smoke began to rise here and there as timber was set to flame from the artillery shelling that stayed at pace. At the front of our formation a rejuvenated Sergeant Loyod was at the ready with our new Captain, Captain Hoyt. Hoyt was young for a Captain and presumably had just joined the war. I wasn't sure if he had ever seen a battle but today would be a good day for him to start because victory was nearly assured. In the distance screams and cries of panic from the people of Salisbury as a flood of civilians ran in the opposite direction carrying what they could. Just to the south of town a Confederate formation moved from the woods to a creek bed setting up a fighting line. The bugles sounded loud and the left flank charged forward and across us down to the creek bed. Our company bugle sounded this time and once the other companies had cleared we ran ahead straight for the town. The artillery ceased their barrage and we rode forward as fast as our horses could carry.

"Yah!" I called out as I kicked my new quarter horse. I didn't give her name, not like Abigail or Sarah because I figured I'd probably lose this one to. She was just another horse. I opted for my sword instead of my pistol and raised it high in the air with the others as we screamed and hollered at the top of our lungs to put the fear of death into our enemies. There was a small picket ahead and a few defenders that took shots at us, but once they saw we would not be deterred they turned and ran like cowards. I kicked my horse harder and harder and she jumped over the picket and into the towns road. Riding up behind what infantry was still in the town I cut down on one on his right, ripping his face open as he turned back to see me. Blood splashed up on my arm and in my mouth. I spit it out and rode faster ahead. A boy turned around with his bayonet and swung it round but I hit him with the horse and trampled him to death before he could get his blade at the ready. He screamed just a little bit but it sounded like my beast took the breath out of him. A few shots rang out ahead and I stampeded forward. Another Reb turned about and raised his hands in the air screaming.

"Please no! I surrender!" I swung hard and lopped off his head at the neck. Looking backward I was hoping it was a clean cut but pieces of his neck still held firm to his body. Turning down a road to the right I saw a large building that looked like a courthouse with a large fat man standing outside of it with a white flag at its height. He waved it back and forth yelling at the top of his lungs.

"Truce! Truce! We surrender! We surrender!" I rode straight up to the man and stopped my horse in front of him. I pulled the reins back and brought my horse up on her hind legs standing tall above the man as I waved my sword back and forth.

"Who the hell are you?" I demanded.

"Billings Sir. The town Mayor. We surrender. This is a flag of truce now please leave us be. There are no more soldiers in this town. They have fled to the woods. We are nothing but women and children here!" My heart felt numb to the man's requests as I made my beast side step towards him. I leaned down and looked him dead in the eye.

"Come here Reb!" I demanded. The man walked over nervously with flag in hand and stopped no more than an arm's length in front of me. "You know what Johnny Reb. I don't like you much." I spit in the man's eye. He pulled his hands up to wipe it away and I swung my sword cutting his flag pole in half. He dropped to the ground quivering in fear and I pulled back on the reigns again getting her back on her hind legs. "Go to hell Johnny Reb! Ain't nobody here give a damn about your truce." I spit on him again. "Damn your truce!" The man stayed on the ground and I smacked the horses reins hard riding ahead to chase down more Confederates in the outlying buildings.

"Private!" I turned back and saw Loyod running up behind me. He stopped his horse hard next to mine and pointed his sword towards an adjacent field. "More Rebs hiding out in the field. Their taking shots at the men in town. We gotta clear'em out. Ride fast and keep your head down."

"Yes Sergeant! Yah! Yah!" Off the road and through field we went. There seemed to be a Reb soldier hiding behind each piece of straw. There was no fighting back for them this time, no position to hold. They ran for their lives for a wooded area in the distance and we rode like reapers turning back and forth in the dirt; as heads popped up we rode them down like dogs and cut them to shreds one by one. I felt a wicked smile creep up on my blood stained face. No matter how many of these boys I cut down I wanted more and more. The closer we road to the trees the more desperate they seemed to get away and the more gratified I was to cut the bastards down in their tracks. I heard a few of them still crying and screaming on the ground and I turned my beast around and rode her right over them extinguishing what life they had left. The gunfire from the trees intensified and the bugles ordered us back to the town. Gazing back at the tree line I saw one more Reb, an old man with silver hair running for the woods. I still had time, I could still cut him down. One less bastard to fight later. I slapped the reins and kicked my horse but no more than three or four gallops Sergeant Loyod called me back.

"Roach!" I pulled back on the reins and stopped my horse in her tracks. "Leave him alone. We got more important stuff to do."

"Just one more Sergeant?" He cocked his head and gave me a look of pure disgust.

"What the hell did you say to me?"

"He ain't at the tree line yet Sergeant. Just let me ride him down so he can't shoot at us later." Loyod looked me up and down and I felt my cruel smile fade to doubt.

"What's in your head boy?"

"Sergeant?"

"I gave you an order Private. That there is an old man running for his life and you want to risk yours just to stick a blade in his back?" My hands grew cold, my throat swelled. I had no way to explain myself, I didn't even understand myself in the moment. All I knew was the sword and killing. It was all that made any sense.

"I,..." I didn't know what to say. A guilt fell over me and I dropped my head.

"Anderson." Sergeant never called me by my first name. Not even once! "I thought you were better than that? Get back to town. We need to keep our men in line and make sure they don't ransack everything. I can't say the same for other companies but they're not my problem. Now ride on back and help clear out the buildings."

"Yes Sergeant." I rode ahead and Sergeant Loyod remained posted up behind me. I could feel the disappointment from his eyes hitting me in the back. It was as if I had betrayed his trust and he was the last man I wanted to question my integrity. I would do better today; I was determined to be better today. Just before entering town I looked down a stretch of road and could see nearly two thousand cavalry still chasing down Rebs in droves but there was no gunfire. Just the screams of men and the galloping of horses. The sounds echoed loud and far despite the clamor in the town. Green grass now painted red, a once pristine town reduced to mostly rubble and ruin. As I rode back into the city I saw Union soldiers making a run for it with valuables of all kind; silver, pocket watches, candles, and food goods.

"Hand it over!" a voice called out from the inside of a saloon.

"No! I can't. This has been in my family for generations."

"You'll hand it over missy or I'll take it off you. It's up to you." Leaping down from my horse I strode forward and kicked in the door walking inside to see a very tall and very muscular union soldier holding a woman and three girls at gunpoint. It was the same woman I had told never to come back and the same three little girls.

"I thought I told you never to come back?" She rapidly shook her head and tears fell quickly.

"Oh thank God it's you! Please, tell him to leave us alone. Tell him. We just want to be left alone and not be harassed by the likes of your kind." The large solider looked me up and down and smiled with a wicked grin and diseased teeth.

"This is none of your business pup. Get yourself outside so I can finish conducting my business." I closed my eyes and without hesitating reached down for my revolver and pointed it at his head.

"Drop the gun." I said softly. His face became enraged and his gun sight moved slightly to the left of the woman and much closer to me.

"What the hell is wrong with you boy? Were on the same side!" I shook my head.

"Not if you're gonna hurt them. No, were not." He pointed at the woman with his ape like hands.

"You're willing to die for them? To kill for them? They probably killed our kin. Probably been feeding and supplying those Johnny Rebs we just run out of town. C'mon boy. It's just some jewelry. What do you care how I take it." He raised his pistol at the woman and I leaned mine closer to him.

"Please..." I urged. "Don't do it. It don't have to be like this. There's been enough killing today. The Rebs are gone. Let them go in peace." He sneered and lowered his pistol.

"Fine. Have it your way. I lowered my pistol, turned and began to walk away.

"Watchout!" The woman yelled. I dropped to the ground as a shot was fired from the soldiers pistol. I rolled over and put two into his chest. The large man stumbled to one knee and began lifting his pistol again. Amidst the screams and terrible noises, I fired once more putting one straight into his head. The round flew out the back of his head and splashed the women with his blood as his large eyes rolled in the back of his skull; he fell like a giant to the ground. When he hit the floor the timber of the saloon shook and the windows vibrated as if artillery fire had just passed by. I picked myself up off the floor and holstered my weapon. The Southern woman looked at me with shock in her eyes.

"What in the hell did you do that for? Now their gonna string you up for sure!"

"That's twice I saved your life today. You and your girls get upstairs and stay put. Don't make me regret what I done here today."

"I'm sorry. I'm so very sorry Yank. You ain't so bad. Not like some of your brothers." I closed my eyes I thought back to all the horrible things I done and looked back at her with guilt in my heart.

"No Mam. I am neither better nor worse. I have done my fair share of cruelty. Even today. You just happen to catch me in a good moment." She walked towards me and wrapped her arms around me. Her red hair smelled like wildflowers.

"Thank you. For me and my girls. I'll never forget you." I walked out of the saloon leaving the woman and her three little girls behind. A worry came over me that I may have to answer for that man's death if she ever opened her mouth but at worst I'd get thrown in a jail cell somewhere for a few months. Ain't nobody gonna fault a man for trying to protect a few women, even if they were Southerners. Back in the streets I found Davenport sitting atop his horse next to a wagon. I grabbed my mare and rode over to him.

"Everyone else seems to be looting and having a good time. What are you doin here all by your lonesome?" I asked.

"If my preacher man asked me what I did this day I'd have to tell him that I stole from these people. I ain't a good liar like some people. What about you?" Preacher? I scoffed. I wasn't gonna talk to no preacher but it was myself I had to live with.

"I don't feel like having to lie over this one. I already cut down a few boys that didn't need to be cut down. I can't take that back now. That's enough for today. I think Sergeant Loyod is mad at me."

"Mad? What'd you do?"

"I was less than I should have been." Davenport didn't ask me anymore questions. Instead we sat back and watched the looting and pilfering of Salisbury. When all was said and done we rode back to camp with a long line of prisoners; the roads completely littered with the belongings of fleeing citizens. As evening approached the camp turned into one giant drunken saloon. Men showed off their loot from Stoneman's raid, ladies of the night walked the roads and jumped from tent to tent trading their services for coin or goods. I did not feel obliged to participate in the celebrations and kept my distance from the men for fear of striking someone who said or did the wrong thing. I was a man on edge trying to find a way to come back. Gazing up through the clouds I spotted a magnificent display of stars and clasped my hands together.

"Dear lord, hear me now. I am a man torn in two. We march and we march to the orders of those appointed over us and in my duties, I have found a wicked joy in the worst of it. Lord, I killed men this day that didn't need to be killed. That sabre just felt so good in my hand, it felt right you know. Then I had to kill one of my own. Lord? Can a man redeem the evil he has done through good actions? I hope so cause I don't know how else I'm goona make up for the things I done. I don't know how I'm gonna face my family if I ever git home. That is, if I make it home." I rubbed my thumbs together raw and stared intently at gods sky above.

"Lord, one last thing. Could you put in a good word with Jenny and Billie for me. Billie was a good man and he shouldn't have died the way he did. I'm told you have a plan for everything, and if that was your plan so be it. Just take good care of my friend. Lastly, watch over Jenny. She was the most beautiful soul I ever seen. My stretch with her was so brief and yet I feel I could have spent a lifetime with her. Please watch over her and if you could Lord let her know that I think about her daily. Amen."

"In the last two years I have never heard you pray like that." Sergeant Loyod came up behind me and sat down against the tree next to me.

"Are you a praying man Sergeant?" He shook his head.

"No. Never been much for prayin'. This war been going on a long time now and I ain't heard or seen anything that would tell me if I prayed it would make a damn bit of difference. What about you? I ain't never seen you pray before. I thought you were about to break out into a full sermon and start quoting the good book."

"I don't usually pray but that look you gave me today. I felt compelled to apologize for the things I done." He nodded and pulled out his corn cob pipe which he proceeded to light. His beard shone brightly under the embers and when it was lit he waved the match until the fire had subsided.

"Want some?" he asked. I placed my hand up refusing his generous offer. "Suit yourself. Look, I know what we done is hard and it don't ever get any easier. Just remember that if you make it through this one day, you're gonna have to live the rest of your life with the things you done." He took a large draw of his pipe and blew the smoke in my face. "Just keep that in mind the next time you act on your emotions and not your head."

# Thirteen
# Hendersonville –
# April 23$^{rd}$ 1865

The Johnny Reb was in full retreat now. No longer were their big armies to contend with on great open plains or heavily fortified fortresses. It seemed like every small group of Confederates were nothing more than a bunch of rag tag criminal's half-dressed and armed with weapons that were in terrible disrepair. We approached the small town of Hendersonville where a handful of Rebs were stationed for a desperate last stand. General John Croxton took command of the Eighth and ordered Captain Hoyt and our company to take this town. As we approach we were challenged by no more than twenty men.

"Captain Sir?" Sergeant Loyod asked.

"Yes Sergeant. What is it?"

"This town is poorly defended. Twenty men don't stand a chance against fifteen-hundred. Can we not persuade them to lower their arms and turn themselves in?" Captain Hoyt appeared to think on it a moment and then nodded his head.

"Very well Sergeant. Keep the line three hundred yards back from the town. I want you, Private Roach and Private Davenport to accompany me. Perhaps we may be successful in talking some sense into them.

"Yes Sir. Roach! Davenport! Front and center! The rest of you. Hold your positions!" Chris and I looked at eachother but did not linger long and quickly rode out to escort the Captain. Galloping ahead we came within twenty yards of the armed group before stopping.

"Good morning gentleman." Captain Hoyt greeted. "Which of you might be the Commanding Officer"

"That would be me." A fat man stood forward and spit chew on the ground. "Williams is the name."

"Do you have rank Sir?" The man look at his compatriots and then gazed forward smiling.

"Were all just Sons of the South here."

"Very well. Mr. Williams, I am Captain Hoyt and I have been ordered to collect you and your men to end the standoff at Hendersonville. I have fifteen-hundred cavalry at my disposal and we would prefer not to shed any blood. If you and your men come peaceably you will not be harmed. You will be clothed, fed, and relocated to begin anew. Do you accept these terms?" The man picked at his teeth and looked down dragging the dirt with his lead foot.

"Ain't nobody gonna leave this town. This is our town. Ya hear?"

"I'm afraid Mr. Williams, you have no choice. Surrender, or die." In the blink of an eye the man raised his rifle and fired striking Chris.

"No! Chris!" I yelled as I jumped down from my horse to help him. What transpired next was a blur and the only thing I recall was holding on to the young boy until his last breath had come and passed.

* * *

"Gather round men. Gather round!" Captain Hoyt ordered. We slowly made our way to a flattened-out piece of grass and sat down crossed legged in front of our now veteran Captain who had proven himself on the battlefield. "Men, first and foremost I want to tell you how damn proud I am to have served with each and every one of you."

"Served Sir?" Sergeant Loyod asked.

"That's right Sergeant. I can't believe I'm about to say this. We're going home. Every last one of you. Hendersonville and Munford will be known as the last battles of the war and you men fought those battles. It is an honor you will be able to carry throughout the rest of your lives. Some of you, few of you have been here for the full two-year stint. I cannot begin to imagine what you have been through nor can I begin to thank you enough for your service. Eat well tonight, celebrate, and tomorrow we will ride back to Tennessee heroes returning to your loved ones. I want Sergeant Loyod to have a few words before I dismiss you. Sergeant?"

"Thank you Sir. As the Captain said he was going to allow me to have a few words. We have faced death, tasted victory, and for some of us even when we won we still had the sour taste of defeat at the loss of our friends. As your Sergeant, I did not make many friends out of professionalism but mostly to help keep you boys alive. However, if we ever cross paths and you find me in some tavern or on a road some-where I want you to come straight to me, shake my hand, and buy me a drink!" The men cheered and hollered for the Sergeant. "Before you start celebrating be sure to pay your respects to the men we lost to-day. There were few this day but, they should not have died on this day above all days. This was our last fight. Well, that's all men. Dismissed." We stood up and left quietly as some men went back to their tents to rest while most of us walked down the sloping hill where our fallen rested. Pale as snow they lay there with eyes and mouths wide open. I found Private Chris Davenports body and gently sat down next to him.

"It's not a bad view you know." I remarked staring out into an open valley of tall green grass that moved like waves pushed by the sweet winds of spring. "I wish you could be here with us. I can only hope you are in a better place." In the distance a wagon pulled up quietly driven by a man all in black up to his neck wearing a wide brim black hat. It was a preacher man. He stepped down from the wagon and retrieved his bible from the cart. As he walked through the blades of grass in his black robe I felt little comfort in his presence. The man was old, bald with heavy creases in his forehead and fancy spectacles on his face that shined brightly in the sunlight. In fact, he seemed like death himself had rode in on a wagon come to take Davenport away from us. He stopped a few paces in front of me and looked down with concern in his weary eyes. Opening his bible, a silver cross came dangling out that he no doubt used as a book mark, and he turned several pages.

"Was he a friend of yours?" I nodded.

"He was." My voice trembled in pain and anger.

"Would you like me to say a few words for him? I have a passage that may bring you some comfort." I looked up with a mean gaze and clenched my teeth. In that moment I pictured myself reaching over and tearing that book right out of the preacher man's hands and throwing it as far I could; but the longer I stared the more I saw the man's intention were good and right. My rage fell to an empty despair and my jaw loosened.

"Ain't nothin' in that book that's gonna comfort me." I stood and gazed down at my friend one last time and closed my eyes to keep the picture in my mind. Just then a tear rolled down my cheek and I dutifully wiped it away. "Just make sure he gets where he's goin'. He done served his time."

# Fourteen
# The Walk Home –
# November 11<sup>th</sup> 1865

"Company! Atten-hut!" Sergeant Loyod ordered. I snapped to attention with rifle at my side and pistol in its holster. Our guide sat proudly atop his steed with a new blue flag and freshly stained staff. The flag was now a deep blue, no longer faded by the long rides in the sun and the sides trimmed with gold strands that wrapped all the way along the edges. The "F" for Fox Company was bright white and seemed bigger than the last flag we had. To the left and right of our company were the other Companies of the Eighth Tennessee Volunteer Cavalry. Hundreds of men stood silently as a Colonel marched to the center of the formation. At the head of each company stood the various Captain's and Lieutenants that had commanded them throughout the war but at the head of our Company was Sergeant Loyod taking the place of our Captain Masengill who had died so bravely while Captain Hoyt was off on assignment.

The Colonel saluted the Eighth with the Company Commanders returning their salutes.

"At ease men." The Colonel ordered. I spread my legs and swung my rifle in front of me leaning on it with both hands. "Soldiers of the Eighth! Good morning!"

"Good morning Sir!" The companies replied.

"It is indeed a fine, fine morning. Today is a day that many of you have waited for, a day that many of you have fought and bled for and that some who are no longer with us today died so that you could be here. It has been just over two years since the Eighth Tennessee Volunteer Cavalry was formed to fight in the bloodiest war these United States has ever seen. After this day, many of you will go back to your homes, back to your lives that you chose to leave behind out of the conviction to do something good in the world. Some of you will go back to being farmers, tradesman, carpenters or you may choose to serve your community working for law enforcement but no matter what you choose to do when you go back to your homes you will never forget what you have done here. You will never forget the bonds that you have built with the men standing at your sides and your will never forget those that we have lost. Go forward to your homes with a sense of pride, with a sense of accomplishment knowing that you have freed men from the bonds of slavery and that you have ushered the United States into a new era of peace and prosperity. I have been honored to command each and every one of you. May god watch over you and may your journeys be filled with happiness." The Colonel took a step backward and stood at attention. "Company, Atten-hut!" Heels snapped back to attention, the field was deathly quiet as a breeze pushed by; the company flag waving proudly in the wind. "Company! Dismissed!" Yells and hollering erupted from all sides. I grabbed my cover and happily threw it in the air with all the others. It was a jubilant time of great celebration. I shook hands with the many men around me and even embraced my brothers for I knew that I may never see them again.

"Private Roach." It was Sergeant Loyod.

"Yes Sergeant?"

"What are your plans after this?" I looked about and then back at a man I admired and respected deeply.

"I have family back in Tennessee. My Maw, Paw, brothers and sisters are probably waiting on me."

"So it's back to farming, is it?" I nodded and smiled.

"Yup, it's back to farming. After everything I've seen here I could use a little farming in my life." The Sergeant nodded.

"The Army isn't going away, it never will. We still need good men like you. Career men who can help us keep the Union together."

"Sergeant, I'm anxious to head home so if you got somethin' to say please spit it out."

"If you stay I can promise you a promotion to the rank of Sergeant. You'll lead a security detail that'll run up and down the Tennessee. The pay is good, much better than what you are used to. I know you've never served in the peace time Army. The food, clothing, and overall treatment will improve significantly. All you gotta do is make your mark on some papers and well make it official. You can still go home, visit your family down at the farm few a few weeks and you'll still have a job waiting for you." I was tempted by his offer. I'd never make near the money farming back in Granger County then I would as a Sergeant in the Army. Then again, I don't think I'd find the peace and solitude I was looking for either.

"Thank you Sergeant, but I must decline." He nodded and extended his arm.

"I understand. It has been a pleasure serving with you A.J." I reached out and returned a hearty handshake.

"Thank you Sergeant. It has been a pleasure serving you as well."

"Good luck son." Those were the final words I heard from Sergeant Loyod. That final walk home was some of the most peaceful stretch of land I had traversed in over two years. Thirty-three miles it was from Knoxville to home. Throughout my walk I passed many small towns where people celebrate and cheered in jubilation of the victory that had been won. Then again, not everyone was celebrating. I was wary of men who were heavily armed and wore one or two pieces of clothing from their units. The war may have been over for us but for the Sons of the South it would be a shame that most of them would carry throughout the rest of their lives unless they gave up their anger. I worried that their hatred or perhaps a feeling they had lost honor would lead them to do terrible things across our land. I guess that's what Sergeant Loyod was trying to get at. I mean, the war was over but it wasn't over.

The United States had a lot of healing to do, a lot of reflection on where we would go with this brave new world. Nightfall came and yet I continued to walk without stopping. Every so often I would get lucky and find a wagon with a few veterans willing to give me a ride for a few miles here and there. Even throughout the night the roads of Tennessee were alive with lamps, torches, and laughter. Newly emancipated colored folk roamed the road with their families seeming fear stricken and hungry in search of new homes, work, and survival. It was the strangest thing to see the roads so busy with people. Perhaps now that the colored were no longer limited to the plantations the scenes around Tennessee would be much busier. I welcomed the thought knowing how lonely the road can sometimes get. Sunrise came and slowly lit the horizon before me with reds and oranges of the most brilliant color. The trees were still turning and had not quite dropped their leaves for winter. At a fork in the road a small colored child, a girl of no more than eight or nine years of age was standing alone shaking like a leaf. I looked around and didn't see anyone on either end of the road or anyone in her company. As I approached her I held my hands open and nodded to show her I was friendly.

"Are you alright Miss?" Her eyes grew wide and she looked down at the mud at her feet.

"Yus Sir." She responded quickly. Fear was painted all over her face and she breathed hard into her cupped hands trying to stay warm.

"Are you here with anyone?" She shook her head.

"No Sir."

"Where are you going?"

"I don't want no trouble Sir." I pulled my hand to the front and the girl flinched dropping to the ground putting her hands up. "Please Sir I beg you. I don't want no trouble no more Sir." I removed my blue service jacket and placed it gently on her back. She swung her head up and stood quickly removing the jacket and handed it back to me. "I can't take no charity Sir." I shook my head.

"It's not charity Miss." She looked confused and cocked her head.

"Then what's it for Sir?"

"What do you mean?"

"Well, what you want from me?" I shook my head.

"Nothing."

"Please Sir I can't take a jacket for nothin'. What do you want?" I grabbed the jacket from her, opened it up and swung it around her resting it gently on her shoulders."

"I have carried that jacket around with me for the last two years and it's gotten me through two winters. I don't need it anymore. Please Miss, take it." She seemed uncomfortable but the warmth of the jacket appeared to set in and she pulled it tighter over her shoulders.

"I don't know what to say Sir. Nobody has ever given me a jacket before."

"Just say thank you and be on your way safely to wherever it is you're going."

"Thank you Sir." I tipped my cap, smiled, and walked away. Getting rid of that jacket was like taking some of the weight of war off my shoulders and the lightness I felt in the crisp November air made me feel alive and free. It was several hours later that I approached a very familiar pair of oak trees; home was just around the bend. I picked up the pace a bit, my heart pumping faster at the thought of rejoining my kin. Once I got around those trees our fields lay out in front of me. The fall harvest had already come and past and now the fields lay dark and barren ready for the frost and snow to take over. Down the path our log cabin had plumes of smoke rising above it seeming warm and inviting. There was no one to speak of outside, nobody tending to the land or the livestock. As I approached the door I heard a clamor of voices from inside. It must have been seven or eight people inside. I hesitated to knock worried they may not recognize me or that someone I loved had passed while I was away. I laid my bag on the trodden ground and hung my head to the ground taking a deep breath and just then the door swung open. Warm air and the smell of food came rushing towards my face and when I glanced upward Maw was standing at the door with tears in her eyes.

"Anderson..."

* * *

"Well Mr. Roach, that was amazing, I'm not really sure what to say. I want to thank you so much for your time today. That concludes the survey. I'll be sure to send this off right away with the others." I nodded and waved from my cane.

"That's fine Miss, that's just fine. I better be on my way home." I lifted myself from the chair and the young woman jumped towards me.

"Here, let me help you Mr. Roach." I caught a familiar smell in my nose, lavender. She helped me to my feet and I straightened out my shirt.

"Well thank you kindly Miss. I don't want to trouble you anymore." She smiled and nodded.

"It's no trouble at all. Safe travels Mr. Roach." I walked several feet before stopping myself, something kept pulling me back like a ghost from old times. I turned back and looked over the girl that stood before me.

"Miss?"

"Yes Mr. Roach?" she replied politely.

"May I have the honor of knowing your Christian name?" She smiled and straightened out her back.

"Jenny, Mr. Roach, my name is Jenny." My heart felt as if it would burst out of my chest, and all at once it came back to me. The chestnut brown eyes, the way she moved her hair behind her ears, the smell of lavender. A tear fell from my eye and I wiped it away quickly. Jenny stared at me with a confused look, one I had seen before from a woman lost to me a very, very long time ago.

"Mr. Roach?" she asked with deep concern in her voice. "I'm sorry Mr. Roach, was there something I said?" I shook my head.

"No Miss. There's nothing for you to be sorry about at all." I looked up at the ceiling and shook my head partially mad that god would choose to play such a trick on me, to bring her back to me at the end of my journey. "Jenny..." I shrugged my shoulders and looked deeply at her eyes that cut back into me, deep within my soul. "That's a beautiful name. One of a kind in fact."

\* \* \*

Anderson J. Roach Died March 9th, 1925 in Lenoir City, Tennessee at the age of eighty-one. His relatives survive to this day continuing his legacy of military service to the United States of America. Several of their names, ranks, service, and dates of service are listed below.

\* \* \*

Airman Bill W. Roach, USAF - 1967
Chief Petty Officer David W. Roach Sr., USCG – 1999 to Current
Lance Corporal David W. Roach Jr. USMC – 2002 to 2008

# About the Author

D.W. Roach is a former U.S. Marine and current Physical Security Professional with experience spanning the globe serving several Fortune 500 Corporations. His personal interests include shooting, fishing, hockey, the outdoors, BBQ's and Military History. He currently resides in the Bay Area with his wife and children.

"I chose to become an Author for several reasons, and in the end, it was for the love of the stories that I could bring to dreamers. As I put words to paper the characters came to life for me. I remember at one point going to bed and all I could dream about was the adventures the main characters were going on. It became exciting and very real.

In many ways, I incorporated much of my own life experiences into the books I write. I wanted to convey what it was like for the warrior, the guy on the ground, fighting against nature with the odds stacked against him. I also wanted to show readers and fans of epic adventures something they haven't seen before. I hope you enjoy the Marauder Series as much as I enjoyed writing it!"

You can find my books and social media at the below links;
Main Web Page https://marauderbooks.com/

Facebook
https://www.facebook.com/marauderbook
https://www.facebook.com/whenthedrumsstop/

Amazon Authors Page
http://www.amazon.com/David-Roach/e/B00QBBZDNQ/

Made in the USA
San Bernardino, CA
09 February 2019